THE STING OF PEPPERCORNS

António Gomes, also known as Anthony Gomes, MD, FACC, FAHA, is a native of Goa. He is a Professor of Medicine and Director of the Cardiac Electrophysiology Consultative Service and Senior Consultant, Cardiac Electrophysiology at The Mount Sinai Medical Center, NYC, The Zena and Michael Wiener Cardiovascular Institute and The Leona M. and Harry B. Helmsley Charitable Trust Center for Cardiac Electrophysiology. He has published extensively in Medicine including a textbook of cardiology, *Signal Averaged Electrocardiography: Basic Concepts Methods and Application* (Kluwer Academic Press, London/ Amsterdam, 1993). He has also published articles in the Humanities in anthologies, books, newspapers, and magazines; two books of poetry entitled *Visions from Grymes Hill* (Turn of River Press, Stanford, Connecticut, USA, 1994) and *Mirrored Reflections* (GOA 1556 and Fundacão Oriente, 2013).

Praise for *The Sting of Peppercorns*

'*The Sting of the Peppercorns* overpowers with a wave of nostalgia, emotion, *saudades* and serendipity. Gomes weaves a fictional story, all too real, about the tiny ex-Portuguese state of Goa on the west coast of India, of a troubled and changing time in its history. For Goans who have been through this era, this book opens up the beauty and the wounds of culture and assimilation. For future generations, this novel will serve as a sort of memoir, related by the main protagonist, Dr Roberto, of a time of innocence, far removed from the Goa of today. A splendid read by a natural writer whose pen churns emotions: high, low, stormy and calm... like the tides of the Arabian Sea lapping on Goa's shores.'

~Wendell Rodricks

Fashion designer, writer, Goan environmental activist

'*The Sting of Peppercorns* is a dazzling first novel by a master storyteller. António Gomes presents the life of a family in Goa, on the west coast of India, against the background of Goa's fall to India in 1961 after centuries of Portuguese rule. Gomes weaves his tale of love and tragedy as it is witnessed by Dr Roberto Albuquerque, a doctor who returns home from a hiatus of years in the United States. This book is original, compelling, and magical: it will draw you in from the opening words.'

~Grace Schulman

Winner of the Frost Medal for Life Time Achievement,
author of six acclaimed books of poetry including,
Days of Wonder, The Broken String and
Without A Claim, and professor of English at
Baruch College of the City University of New York.

THE STING OF PEPPERCORNS

António Gomes

AMARYLLIS

AMARYLLIS

AMARYLLIS

An imprint of Manjul Publishing House Pvt. Ltd.
• 7/32, Ansari Road, Daryaganj, New Delhi 110 002
Website: www.manjulindia.com

Registered Office:
10, Nishat Colony, Bhopal 462 003 - India

Distribution Centres:
Ahmedabad, Bengaluru, Bhopal, Kolkata, Chennai, Hyderabad, Mumbai, New Delhi, Pune

The Sting of Peppercorns by António Gomes

Earlier published by Goa 1556

Cover and Illustration by Pinaki De

ISBN: 978-93-81506-33-2

This edition first published in 2017

Printed and bound in India by Replika Press Private Limited.

Râgena badhyate loko râgenaiva vimucyate.

By passion the world is bound
By passion too it is released

—The Hevajra Tantra

Be it life or death, we crave only reality.

—Henry David Thoreau

Contents

In December of 1961, the Indian armed forces invaded and integrated the Portuguese colony of Goa, on the west coast of India, after four hundred and fifty-one years of Portuguese rule. A few years later, an opinion poll rejected the demand for the merger of Goa into the neighbouring Indian state of Maharashtra. These are historical facts. Otherwise, this is a work of fiction. All names, characters, incidents, and the Albuquerque family are products of the author's imagination. Any resemblance to actual events or persons, dead or alive is entirely coincidental. Certain liberties have been taken regarding the location of streets, bars, et cetera.

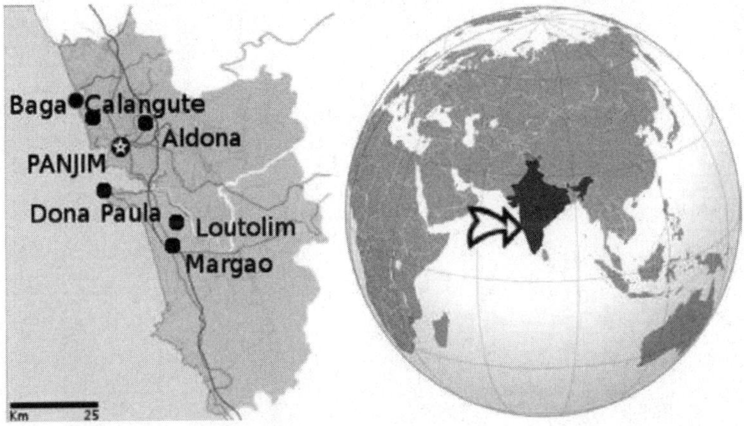

MAP OF GOA AND INDIA

Large dots reflect the villages (Loutolim, Aldona), the town and city (Old Goa, Panjim/Panaji), the end of the peninsula (Dona Paula), and the beaches (Calangute and Baga), where the story mostly unfolds.

I

Prologue

1988

As flight IA-45 approaches Goa, the ocean, dotted by dark barges carrying loads of iron ore, shimmers in the afternoon sun. As the plane circles awaiting landing orders, a lush tropical jungle appears. In the distance, a white church stands starkly perched on the banks of a winding river. Islands of coconut palm trees swirl, lazily scattered among brown and green paddy fields. When the plane swiftly veers to the right, the beaches rise from the south, offering their blonde splendour.

The sight of sandy shores rekindles memories of a catastrophic night twenty-one years ago on the Calangute beach just miles to the north of here. Then, a different grain of sand, silvery moon sand, had blown in the oppressive night air. As the clouds had moved hurriedly on and the moon had appeared, images of my brother and sister that haunt me to this day had come in full view.

Buried deep in my mind all these years, they had recently started playing back more frequently, like spools of a stilled movie. Lost in those memories and gripped by a strange sense of unease, I neglect to notice the warning lights come on, until the stewardess requests that I fasten my seat belt and pull up my seat.

The heat is oppressive at the poorly ventilated airport; the wait for the luggage is long. My wife, Maria, expectantly stretches her neck to spot the family among the receiving crowd. She finally sees them waving and a broad smile crosses her face. 'There they are, Grandma and Grandpa,' she says, pointing them out to our twelve-year-old son, António, who stands tall and handsome with his mother's features. Kisses and tears follow as Maria embraces her parents. I wave and hurriedly approach them.

'Of course you'll be staying with us,' says Manuel, my father-in-law, in his self-assured way. 'Your home in the village is in need of some repair.' I nod rather nonchalantly and take a seat next to him in his blue Maruti 800. He seems overtly delighted in his new possession, the pride of middle-class Indians.

Maria, António and Maria's mother, Dona Claudia, climb into the back seat and begin to chat in rapid-fire Portuguese.

'Great car,' I say, turning towards my father-in-law. 'Smooth drive.'

'Yes… it does… thirty kilometres a litre, on the highway,' he says. 'How was the flight from New York to New Delhi?'

'The flight was good… we travelled business class. But the welcoming stink at the airport was unbearable,' I say.

'Yes, the pollution there is bad,' he says. 'Was the conference in Delhi crowded? Lots of doctors wanting to hear the latest news on AIDS?'

'Yes, indeed! There were doctors, journalists and students anxious to ask questions. I had little chance to rest or to catch up on my sleep.'

'You're the expert, after all.'

His eyes steady on the road, my father-in-law turns his head each time he talks to me. The oncoming traffic barely missing us on the narrow winding road scares me witless.

The ride from Dabolim Airport to Panjim is reassuringly bumpy. The smell of raw and burnt garbage filters into the car as it heads towards Chicalim.

'Dad, this place stinks,' says Antonio.

'The smell will go away soon,' I say.

'Yes, yes,' says my father-in-law. 'The foul smell of burned garbage will disappear soon.'

The scene abruptly changes after a distance of a few miles. The silver sheen of the Zuari River is blinding as its waters, intermingle with the Arabian Sea. Floating canoes, swaying ferryboats and coconut palm trees perilously leaning towards the water, line its banks. I feel rather reassured with the landscape. The Goa of my youth comes alive.

As the car speeds past Agaçaim, the countryside turns a modest brown and dusty green. Tall cotton trees, leafless, but flaunting bright pink flowers, dot the hilly landscape amid cashew trees and mango groves. Christmas decorations hang from churches and verandahs of homes and the mood along the roadside is loud and merry. December in Goa is a pleasant, festive month.

The open window of the car lets in the afternoon breeze; it lulls my senses and puts me to sleep.

The next morning, after a breakfast of my favourite spicy Goan *chouriço,* fried eggs and bajji-puri, my mother-in-law urges me to rest, but I have an important matter that will not wait. A couple of months back, in New York, I had received a call inviting me to deliver a lecture at the South-Asian Symposium on AIDS to be held in New Delhi. While I was deciding whether to accept, a package arrived from Goa, containing stacks of age-yellowed papers tied in red thread and a notebook. When I began to read at about eight in the evening after attending to my patients, I soon realised they were my mother's and my sister's diaries and a few letters from Portugal addressed to my elder brother. I knew my sister kept a diary in which she often wrote poetry, but I was astonished to discover that my mother had kept a diary as well.

The contents of my mother's diary written with a shocking deliberateness took me entirely by surprise. And yet, a large piece of the complex story seemed to be missing. I wondered why ayah Carmina had sent the package now. Did she know some secret that was not obvious in my mother's diary? The lecture at the New Delhi conference gave me a plausible reason to return to Goa to talk with her.

While Maria stays home, bedridden with a jetlag-induced migraine and António is being doted upon by his grandparents, I quickly walk the half mile or so to the taxi stand. The ever-increasing traffic is chaotic with taxis, rickshaws, bicycles, lorries, buses and competing hordes of pedestrians, all dodging each other with reckless precision as they cross the streets. The honking, the ringing, the clatter of metal, the cursing and shouting are maddening. Gone is the serene and stately Panjim of my youth. I feel rather strange under its oppressive roof.

On the roadside, the sights and smells of golden brown cherries and the abundant chiku fruits, the favourite fruits of my childhood, are enticing. I buy some of each.

The hot sun, the glare of vibrant colours with the blend of pungent smells is heady. Facing a long ride ahead, I pick up a local newspaper and then hop into a taxi, telling the driver to take me to my village of Loutolim. Browsing through *The Goa Times*, I'm pleasantly surprised to see my arrival prominently reported: 'Top Goa medico, Roberto Albuquerque, Chairman and Professor of the Department of Infectious Diseases at New York University, returns from USA after brilliant lecture in New Delhi.'

The article is filled with laudatory references to my work. Indeed, my research on T-cells and AIDS had gotten national and international attention. Years of hard, patient work were finally paying off.

Close to an hour goes by before the gaugeless, speedometerless taxi turns into my ancestral village of Loutolim and rolls past the baroque-era church, its façade partly blackened by dry dead moss left over from the monsoon. As I turn to admire the venerable structure, I'm thrown violently forward as the driver slams on the brakes to let a herd of buffalo cross the street. The clatter of clanging teacups and stirring sugar spoons emanates from the roadside teashop. As we approach a downslope, the taxi continues slowly and silently, for the taxi driver has turned the engine off and placed the gear in neutral.

'Is there something wrong?' I ask rather alarmed.

'Must save petrol... very expensive like everything else,' the taxi driver says. 'Goa change *baba*. Tourists... traffics... accidents... *sosegad*—easy days are over.'

I give a confirmatory nod.

The taxi passes the lily pond where my older brother, Paulo and I played as kids: jumping into the shallow pond, harvesting water lilies and hunting frogs. Past the lily pond, a vast paddy field comes into view with square patches of green separated by brown, a large patchwork quilt dotted with peasant women in muddy red, dirty yellow and pale purple saris tucked under and around their loins. Bent over, knee-deep, while planting rice, from a distance their ample bottoms look like the rumps of grazing cattle.

My heart begins to pound as the taxi approaches my old house. My anxiety about the diaries comingles with the shock of returning home after a long absence.

'Stop here,' I say to the taxi driver, who jams hard on the worn-out brakes that creak. I pay him generously and step out, requesting that he return in a couple of hours.

The house that I had left twenty-one years ago had gradually floated away into the distant sea of my memory. And yet here it is, perched atop a small hill, like a ship wrecked on a coral reef. From the outside, the house looks uninhabited. One stone lion has fallen off its pedestal; the other is headless. The iron gate is closed but unlocked. The surrounding wall, once ablaze with purple, red and white bougainvillea, is overrun with weeds and wild peppervine sagging from the weight of peppercorns. Hungry, jet-lagged and dehydrated from the heat and a bit dizzy, I hold on to the wall with one hand; a clump of the vine comes away in my semi-clenched fist as I snatch it from the wall. The strong, pungent smell of the crushed green peppercorns makes me sneeze and the blood pounds in my head.

Indeed, pepper seems to have been at the centre of everything: the love affair, the hate affair, between East and West; and, for a while, it was an integral part of my family's history. Yes, pepper, that enigmatic spice—when crushed and powdered, flavours many a dish and yet when bitten into whole, it stings the tongue like the bite of a scorpion. The great Portuguese explorer, Vasco da Gama, had come in search of it in 1498, followed in 1510 by Afonso de Albuquerque, the 'King of Peppercorns', who wrestled the spice trade from the Arabs. Soon after, the Portuguese—the 'Peppercorn men'—began marauding the Arabian Sea for spice and subsequently for Christ.

It was here, in Goa, on the heels of Afonso de Albuquerque, that spice met bland and East met West in a violent confrontation. Goa became the seat of the Portuguese Eastern Empire, which extended from Mozambique in the Indian Ocean all the way to the Sea of Japan and later crumbled under the onslaught of the Dutch and the English who followed. Ultimately, societies and religions were crushed, powdered like the peppercorns themselves and sprinkled around the world—the universal landscape forever altered.

At one time, in the sixteenth century, my family dealt with peppercorn cultivation and its export to Portugal; however, the peppercorn trade was abandoned in favour of the more lucrative rice, cashew and coconut plantation sometime in the eighteenth century. During my childhood, peppercorn vines grew wild in the garden and were harvested only for our family's consumption.

Overcome and flushed with the smell of fresh peppercorns, I climb up the steps and push open the gate. The outer walls of the house are covered with islands of green and yellow-brown moss in a sea of fluffy white and gray, while mud castles of termites rise like miniature volcanoes on paint-crumbled walls. The garden is overgrown and wild and buzzes with the susurrations of many-legged lives. The branch of a fallen mango tree lies across the path; a pair of monkeys perched on it, oblivious to all, are making love.

I somehow feel responsible for the decay. I did send money to Carmina for living expenses and for the upkeep of the house, but as often happens in an old home, the years and the heavy monsoons had taken their toll. Before I embarked on this trip, I lived with a sense of change, a metamorphosis so to speak and however unsettling, I felt no guilt. But now, the decay hits me hard as I remember the amount of tradition and also a kind of perfection in this grand old house, reverberating with life and hopes that went awry. Time and history had moved on relentlessly; at this moment, however, I am left nakedly exposed to the past.

I walk up the stairs to the unfurnished front balcony of the house. Sitting on the now cracked cement seat, I sink my teeth into the succulent sweetness of the chiku fruit and ponder the decay around me. The monkeys follow, jumping from the mango branch onto the balcony grill and staring, as if to say: 'Stranger, why are you encroaching upon our territory?' I offer them some remaining fruit and approach the door.

The front door is closed but not locked. 'Carmina, Carmina,' I call out several times to my ayah. There is no answer. As I'm about to leave, rather disappointed, a glow of light appears in the foyer through the crack in the door to the oratory. I enter the room. The kerosene lamp's yellow and emerald-green flame undulates, emitting black soot, casting shadows on the wall.

The altar seems timeless. The ivory carved statues of St Thomas, St Anthony, St Francis Xavier, St Jude, the Archangels and baby Jesus in his gem-studded silver crib, Mary and Christ on the Cross, are all there just as I had left them.

I bow in obeisance.

As I continue looking around the room, visions of my long gone ancestors appear, rolling rosary beads with their delicate fingers, some dozing in-between the Hail Marys and Our Fathers. I hear voices: the whispers of my ayah Carmina, the giggle of my sister Amanda, the laughter of my brother Paulo, the trenchant snores of my grandfather—voices of my childhood and adolescent years, ghostly but real.

Like ripples in a shallow lake, the yellow light flickering in the semi-darkness, enlarges and twists their image. I hear my grandmother's faint footsteps and the voice of my father calling: '*Roberto, venha para tua bencão*—come for your blessing, my son.'

Suddenly, the door opens: the rustle of sandals, the sound of approaching footsteps.

'Is that you, Carmina?' I ask.

I feel a hand on my shoulder and a soft voice nearby: 'Baba, Baba... you have returned!' A voice I instantly recognise and then, I begin feeling dizzy and pass out.

I had the fainting illness that started when I was barely twelve. I passed out in school, on the playground, when hurt or stressed. My illness was labelled variously as a seizure, a nervous condition, a possession, for which I was made to drink the brew of the bitter gourd, then purged with castor oil and Epsom salt, rubbed, cupped, massaged, wool-blanketed, blessed and sprinkled with the holy waters of Lourdes. The girls in school had teased me: *Robby-bobby dizzy-gelebi—hah-hah, you make peepee!*

Luckily, by the age of eighteen, the fainting episodes had decreased in frequency. When I was in medical college, a visiting Portuguese professor diagnosed my condition as vasovagal syncope and recommended drinking a lot of water, eating salted biscuits and taking a few precautions like lying down to avoid the fainting spells. Many years later in New York, a well-known cardiologist, also originally from Goa, placed me on a beta-blocker and though it did me a world of good, I had recently stopped the drug for affecting my sexual libido. I will have to start back on the pills, soon—a lower dose perhaps?

I wake up within a few minutes and still a bit dizzy, I find my way to a nearby rocking chair. I had caught a split-second glimpse of her face in the semi-darkness. It was wrinkled like the bark of a dying tree, the eyes sunken in their sockets, almost hidden. The hair was sparse and grayish, with a few silver strands that glowed in the semi-darkness. It was Carmina, my old ayah.

Feeling somewhat stronger, I walk from room to room, looking for her. Sunlight enters through cracks in oyster-shell windowpanes and through broken tiles shattered by falling fruit and wild mating monkeys that abound in the jungle behind the house. I try the door of the hall but find it locked. A ray of sunlight streaking through a broken tile lights the long corridor leading to the kitchen. On the chopping table there is a saucer with condensed curry and a half-eaten chapatti by its side. The curry smells of vintage Carmina. Most certainly she is in the house, sitting somewhere like an old piece of furniture. Retracing my footsteps, I bang into a chair and nearly fall. The soft glow of the lamp once again beckons me. As I'm about to re-enter the oratory, I notice several faded family photographs on an old Chinese chest. One in particular, of my brother, my sister and me, taken when my brother had just returned from Portugal, catches my eyes. I pick it up and take it closer to the light. I choke and once again seek the safety of the rocking chair. As I rock to and fro and stare at the photograph in my hands, cobwebs of sleep spread over me.

A hand on my shoulder, a gentle touch, awakens me. The fragrance of hot steaming chai wafts through the room.

'Baba,' Carmina's voice quivers, 'you have finally returned after so many years. When you fainted, I ran to see if I could find someone to fetch the doctor. My legs wouldn't carry me far.' She stretches her hand and glides her fingers over my face as if it is some familiar sacred ground. Her sunken eyes moisten with tears.

We embrace each other. I sit back on the rocking chair looking at the photograph in my hand. I fondly recollect memories of ayah Carmina, chasing me to drink milk, feeding me morsels of rice and curry and protecting me from scoldings and the stick from my father and mother. Her love for me was like honey in a cup of milky tea.

'Do you remember how excited we all were when Paulo returned from Portugal?' I say.

'Yes, I remember.'

'I read the diaries, Carmina. There are many things I cannot understand,' I say in-between sips of the hot, milky chai. She nods mutely.

'A few days after she died, I found them in your mother's cabinet,' she whispers after a long silence, 'but you had already left.' She went on, 'And since there was no one around I could trust with them, I hid them away. I forgot about them until recently, when I found them while cleaning the drawers. The chaplain helped me mail them to you.'

'You have to tell me everything you know.'

'Yes I will, but later. I must go to the store next door and get you something to eat. You sit right here and rest.'

While I wait for her to return, the photograph stares back at me like some living relic of the past, catapulting me twenty-seven years back in time when my brother Paulo had unexpectedly returned from Portugal and all hell had broken loose.

Our lives would never be the same again.

One

Hustle and Bustle

1961

It was a sultry morning in the village of Loutolim, 10 May, 1961. The jackfruit and the mango trees lay still and sullen in the early morning glow, pregnant with fruit, some ripened, some bursting, ready to deliver their bounty to the crows and the rich landlords—the *batcars*. The scorched red earth, the weed and the knotted grass anxiously awaited the monsoon with its pouring rain and its temperamental winds that drove the storm clouds to play hide-and-seek with the sun.

I was awakened that morning by the shrieking: 'Cock-ro-coo! Cock-ro-coo! Cock-cock-cock-cock... cock-ro-coo!' of the ever-fornicating red rooster, king of the chicken coop. As soon as I jumped off the bed at seven in the morning, I heard my mother, Dona Maria Isabella dos Santos Albuquerque, known as Dona Isabella, hurriedly wake up the servants one by one: Carmina, Mari and Pedru, ordering them with a call to arms with broomsticks, tumblers, basins and mops.

'Hurry, everybody, and get the house clean. Paulo-baba will be here in just a few hours.'

With the recent passing of my grandmother, my mother took control of the household and ruled with an iron hand. My aunt, Tia Rosita, my father's sister, was relegated to second place.

Our house was bustling with activity that day, what with the servants, the cooks and their assistants running around doing their respective tasks. The servants on their calloused hands and knees hurriedly cleaned the Portuguese mosaic-tile floors of the balcony, the verandas along the hall and the hall itself that remained closed except on special occasions. The ebony sofas that were carved like lace and upholstered in maroon velvet and the intricately carved dressers in the hall were polished, until Mari, the youngest servant, barely eighteen, could see her cherubic face and her white teeth mirrored in the flowery and leafy design of the wood. Tulsi, the peasant woman who lived in a hut just below our house, dusted the large and small vases and plates of antique Chinese porcelain, the Cantonese and the Ming that were scattered all over the hall, some elegantly hung on the wall and others placed in the wall cabinet of the dining room.

The coat of arms in colours of purple, red and brown was dusted. It was bestowed by the Portuguese governor to my great-great-grandfather who was honoured with the title: *Fidalgo Cavaleiro da Casa-Real,* for his loyalty to the Portuguese empire in India. Besides, family legend suggested that we had a distant link to Albuquerque, the Portuguese conqueror. According to the story, Afonso de Albuquerque fathered an illegitimate son. The mother was a Muslim woman whose husband, the commander of Adil Shah's army, was killed in 1510, together with the entire Muslim male population, after the re-conquest of Goa by the Portuguese. Albuquerque's son fathered a daughter by marriage to a local woman, apparently of a prominent Hindu family, but while returning to Portugal, he, together with his ship and its cargo of spices, gold ornaments and silk, sank in the Cape of Storms. The mother and the daughter, subsequently, lived in the village in their joint family home. A Hindu ancestor of mine, enamoured by the light-skinned, blue-eyed and beautiful daughter, asked for her hand in marriage.

Perhaps because of her mixed origin, this link, which may well be apocryphal, was kept a family secret.

A branch of my family, Goud Saraswat Brahmins, converted to Catholicism during the latter part of the Inquisition, brought to Goa to persecute the Marranos—the Portuguese Jewish converts. Serendipitously, the family was baptised with the Christian name Albuquerque—probably the surname of the priest responsible for the conversion. However, legend has it that my ancestors took the name Albuquerque to reflect the alleged ties to the Portuguese conqueror. Although the family became strong adherents to the Catholic faith, the new religion was superimposed on ancestral Hindu customs and beliefs and our Brahmin caste.

Visitors marvelled at the grandeur of our house: the semicircular steps of cement painted dull red; the pink and white bougainvillea entwining an imposing garden gate; the royal purple, golden yellow and white colours of the outer walls; the heavenly cherubs and the elaborate flowery design above the huge oyster-shell windows, each with their individual veranda; its east and west wings with their spacious high-ceilinged rooms connected by corridors around an enclosed rectangular garden.

Carmina, our ayah, a thin and slender woman now in her fifties, was running around supervising the cleaning and cooking. She had come to the house as a young woman, as part of my mother's trousseau and fed and bathed all three of us when we were young. We loved her dearly and confided in her during our childhood and adolescent years, just as Mama had. She had had no schooling, but being in our company most of her life had enabled her to understand Portuguese and some English and she could speak a little of each.

Mama personally attended to the flower garden with its patches of red, white and yellow hibiscus; giant hostas and ferns; caladiums, dahlias, begonias and roses. But begonias were her passion. She had them planted in pots, in the shade, around the balcony: pink, yellow and red, with their fleshy zebra leaves. She would stroke them, whispering a flowering mantra and they would bloom in profusion. She habitually arranged flower vases for the dining room and the prayer room with green and yellow leaves, twigs of pepper vine, ferns and dahlias and roses. That day, after breakfast, she made a large one for Paulo's room.

I was a twenty-year-old young man on holiday from my first year at the *Escola Medica,* in Panjim, with not much to do but pass my time cycling up and down the village dirt roads and chatting with village folks. Not surprisingly then, Mama gave me the early morning errand of dragging Tulsi's perpetually drunk husband, Vishnu, to attend to the three heavy chandeliers that had to be washed with soap and water and fitted with candles and placed in the sconces fitted high on each wall. This had to be done early in the morning when Vishnu was more likely to be sober.

After attending to Vishnu, I hopped on my bicycle and sped on winding dusty roads intersecting paddy fields and hills past the Loutolim church, past the village of Ambora to the ice factory, to pick up a slab of ice—a precious commodity in those days. It had to be done early in the morning before the relentless afternoon sun would melt it on the way from the ice factory to our house. After tying up the slab of ice covered with sawdust and inserting it into a large bag of jute, I sped back home. Despite my speed and diligence and the mild early morning sun, one-third of the slab had succumbed to the heat. As soon as I arrived home, Pedru, the butler, carried the ice slab on his head and deposited it in a homemade metal icebox.

At about eleven in the morning, after the cleaning and dusting and polishing were over, Mama and Tia Rosita supervised the final touches to the evening meal. A piglet was killed and roasted. Dishes such as the ink-coloured cabidel of duck, the spicy red pork *sorpotel* and the spicy, dark-red peppercorn-loaded pork vindaloo had been prepared the day before. Only the chicken broth, the mayonnaise fish, the puffed toddy bread and the Portuguese codfish dish, *bacalhau a Gomes Sá*, remained to be cooked. From the enclosed garden came the spinach which, when tossed with red onion and green chilli and dressed with vinaigrette and olive oil, would make a pungent-tangy salad to accompany slivers of the roast piglet, a favourite dish of the family.

In the dining room, Tia Rosita was trimming her dark-brown dessert cake, the bebinca, made of two-dozen egg yolks, coconut milk, clarified butter, white flour, powdered nutmeg and sugar.

'See my bebinca—just look at the golden-brown colour,' said Tia Rosita.

'Yes, Rosita, it looks like a sugar-coated moon,' attested Mama.

Tia Rosita boasted that her bebinca fame stretched from the Goan sandy shores to the local bazaars, to the Goan boarding houses of Bombay, to the banks of the River Tagus in Portugal. She was also known for her fiery mango pickle and the dark and violent Goan *chouriço*—the sausage that would have startled even the bowels of Montezuma, the Aztec emperor.

Amidst all this nervous activity, this hustle and bustle, my father, Senhor Afonso, went to the village square where the village elders discussed and heatedly argued politics—my father's favourite pastime. He was the mayor of Loutolim and subsequently, the administrator of Salcete (taluka of South Goa). Although respectful of the Portuguese rulers, he was well known for his independent streak and his outspoken anti-colonial views. He had trained as a lawyer in Goa and attended a refresher course at the University of Coimbra in Portugal, but hardly practiced law. Much admired for his sincerity, truthfulness and high moral standards, he was a man who could set his mind to a task and despite his independent political inclination, was rewarded by the Portuguese regime with high-level administrative posts. He was dark in colour, good looking and of average height with a slim imposing figure that he carried with an aristocratic air in light-coloured three-piece suits and a bow tie and an ivory-tipped cane with a carved handle in his hand that he liked to dangle. For his rigid poise and demeanour, he was soft spoken, but always declared his opinions with frankness. When he spoke and that wasn't often, everyone listened. However, with us, his children, except to ask after our grades, reading habits and the company we kept, he rarely engaged, leaving that function to Mama, whom he adored from a distance. Now retired at the age of sixty, he looked forward to tending to his vast estate.

It was almost noon when Amanda and I began practising the piano and violin in preparation for the upcoming musical soirée, when suddenly from below came the screams of Tulsi's adopted son, Tucaram. Tulsi had tied him to the tamarind tree as a punishment for stealing an *anna*, a penny, to buy candy. Upset at his screams, Amanda stopped playing the violin and went to her room. Mama and I went out to the balcony and shouted at Tulsi, ordering her to untie the boy immediately. Today, nobody would spoil the day.

The Tulsi and Tucaram matter resolved, Mama walked past the foyer, stroking her hand on the arms of the antique palanquin, once used by my great grandfather as a mode of transportation. When I was ten years old, I often sat in the palanquin and imagined being carried like a prince into far away distant lands, winning battles on the way like Genghis Khan. Finding the palanquin dusty, Mama called out to Mari to attend to it immediately. She entered the pillared space within the house that opened onto an enclosed garden of white and flaming red bougainvillea, an assortment of begonias and vines of spinach, cucumber, pumpkin and beans.

'Roberto, can you please water my begonias, all the servants are busy,' Mama yelled out. She was much admired by all who knew her for her meticulous ways and her attention to detail. She was forty-four years old and a woman of considerable beauty. She was fair in colour, with striking features: a heart-shaped face with high cheek bones and jet black wavy hair that both Amanda and I inherited. She was a society woman entirely involved in household matters, her children, her begonias and her piano playing.

After I rapidly watered Mama's two dozen or so begonias with a handheld watering container, I went back to practising the piano. I called out to Amanda to join me with her violin, but she stayed in her room, down with a headache from the earlier Tucaram episode. That Amanda and her overbearing sensitivities.

After lunch, to confirm its accuracy, Mama and I looked once again at Paulo's telegram, which had arrived from Portugal just two days before. To our utter joy the telegram simply stated that he was coming down to Goa to assume the coveted position of assistant attorney general. His unexpected return came as a total surprise. Mama held the telegram to her heart. Like many of my ancestors who were prominent lawyers, judges and administrators, Paulo, who was studying law in Coimbra, Portugal, was following another treasured family tradition.

'I'm so happy Paulo is returning. I was always afraid he would get married to a European and we would never see him again,' said Mama, addressing Tia Rosita.

'It's the prayers, Isabella, my prayers,' answered Tia Rosita.

I burst out laughing.

'Don't laugh unnecessarily. God will punish you,' Tia Rosita snapped.

Thinking about Paulo's unexpected return, Mama went to her room and lay down for her usual afternoon nap. Later, she would go to the hall to practise on the Bechstein piano. She had announced that tomorrow, after the welcoming dinner, she would play Chopin for her returning son.

The household was in a frenzy over Paulo's imminent return. Since his departure for Portugal, four-and-a-half years ago, we all missed the musical soirées we had at least once a month: Paulo on the guitar, Amanda on the violin and I on the piano. He was the tour-de-force for these musical soirées—the maestro. And the stories and the jokes he told always made us laugh. But, at the same time, I must confess, I was jealous of all the attention and adulation he would receive. For Mama, it was as if her son Paulo was the only jewel in her crown. That was no wonder. Paulo, even before he left to study in Portugal, was already a heartbreaker. Almost six feet tall and of fair complexion, fairer than Mama, he possessed a certain poise, a flamboyant charm rarely seen in Goans of those days, except in those who returned home after their studies in Portugal. His favourite stand was posing in profile, having meticulously studied his own reflection in the mirror: in profile, half-profile and frontal views. Now, twenty-three years of age, I wondered how the years in Portugal had affected his personality and demeanour.

Two

Magic of the Flying God

The lone Mercedes Benz taxi in the village arrived at the gate, all horns blaring, to take us to the airport. Mama came running to the balcony in time to see me and Amanda rush out and hop into the taxi, with Tia Rosita and an exited Carmina some paces behind. The taxi ride from Loutolim to the Dabolim airport was uneventful, until a lorry with Portuguese and African soldiers passed by.

'Look at those strong Portuguese and African soldiers,' said Tia Rosita, laughing. 'They will make mincemeat of the Indian satyagrahis.'

'Well, we'll see about that,' I shot back. 'After all, the satyagrahis were unarmed Indian civilians the Portuguese forces gunned down as they marched across the border.'

'Isn't Satyagraha Mahatma Gandhi's non-violent civil resistance in the Indian independence movement against the British?' asked Amanda.

'That's right,' I said. 'But if the actual Indian Army attacks, the Gurkas, the Sikhs and the Marathas will make mincemeat of the small Portuguese army.'

'*Merda*—the Indian army! Who they think they are going to fight? Our beloved St Francis Xavier?'

'Be realistic, Tia Rosita. It's time we joined Mother India.'

'I agree with you,' Amanda chimed in. 'Goa should be an independent state. Even Papa is all for it.'

'Yes, Papa is for cessation from Portugal and some union with India regarding defense and foreign affairs—almost an independent nation. I would also like Goa to be an independent country, but that won't happen Amanda. Neither Jawaharlal Nehru nor the Portuguese dictator Salazar would consider such an option. Besides, although most Goans are probably for independence, no organisation inside or outside Goa is ready to shed blood for an independent Goa.'

We lapsed into a dispirited silence as the taxi sped by green paddy fields, coconut and mango groves, but broke into unrestrained laughter as we passed a grove of the *matuma* fruit trees and a fetid smell filled the cab. I wondered out loud how a tree with a putrid smelling bark could produce such a sweet-tasting fruit.

'Well, why not?' said Tia Rosita who had an answer for everything. 'Imbeciles produce geniuses and vice-versa—*tatswat-a-titiss*!'

'Do keep quiet, Tia Rosita,' Amanda said crossly. 'We should have kept you home with Mama and Papa.'

'Shh… Amanda, don't talk to Tia Rosita like that,' I said.

Surprisingly, Tia Rosita did shut up but not for long. In her youth, she had been a rather plain yet bright young woman who excelled in cooking and knitting, among other things. Her legs were straight and thin—kids teased her about her bamboo-sticks. While science was her strength (the first woman in Goa to pass her matriculation exam with a gold medal in biology), languages were her weakness. Her spoken English resulted in somewhat disjointed sentences and sometimes, when nervous, she used odd pronunciations like *tatswat-a-titiss*, for 'that is what this is,' which became her leitmotif.

She easily got into Grant Medical College in Bombay, having ranked tenth in her Intermediate Science exam. There, she fell in love with a fellow medical student from South India named Joseph and openly boasted of her love affair to her cousin, a blabbermouth at whose house she was boarding. When her parents learned of the affair and Rosita's plans to marry, they were enraged. The man, being a non-Goan, was declared an unacceptable match. Rosita was called home and forbidden to leave the house; her letters to Bombay were intercepted and her medical studies cut short. Her father had been against the medical college venture right from the outset. But at his wife's coaxing, he eventually agreed that she continue her studies in Goa at the Escola Médica.

The young and stubborn Rosita locked herself up in her room and went on a two-day hunger strike. 'I'm following in the footsteps of Gandhiji,' she proclaimed, perpetually threatening to become a Carmelite nun and refusing to entertain any proposal of suitable boys from eminent Goan Catholic families. She ultimately joined the Escola Médica but dropped out after six months, complaining that she couldn't bear to dissect human cadavers.

When I entered the medical school, she warned me about the awful smell of cadavers and because of my dizzy spells, advised me to carry a bottle of smelling salts at all times. After her father's death, she began corresponding with Dr Joseph who became a ear-nose-and-throat specialist in Bombay. Nobody knew why they never married; perhaps it was just too late or there were no sparks left to fly. She often visited him in Bombay; however, once India imposed a blockade of Portuguese Goa, the visits to Bombay came to a halt.

The Albuquerque elders were personae non gratae in India, for reasons that were not entirely clear. Perhaps it was related to my father's association with the Portuguese government officials, although he was well known in local circles as being against the Salazar regime and for an independent Goa.

During Rosita's last attempted visit to Bombay via a circuitous route over land, river and sea, that took almost three days to cover a distance of barely three hundred miles, Rosita was denied a visa at the Indian border and had to turn back with two heavy trunks, one of which was full of gifts for her beloved: an assortment of Goan mangoes, two large jackfruits, pickles and preserves. This trying and humiliating experience made her rabidly anti-India. Now at fifty-eight, she was a somewhat jaded spinster with a bittergourd tongue. The villagers spoke of her as a *Beatin*—a sort of holy woman wholeheartedly devoted to the church. Fortunately, she was also devoted to cooking. And, our family loved her cooking.

At the airport, we got out of the car and hurriedly entered the waiting area only to learn that the flight had been delayed in Karachi, Pakistan. Portuguese troops carrying machine guns patrolled the airport. There were reports of sightings of genuine Indian troops at the borders. Krishna Menon, the fiery defense minister of India and head of India's UN delegation, hung like the sword of Damocles over Goa. He had stated in no uncertain terms that India had not 'abjured the use of force' in Goa. The nervousness and tension were so palpable that I wanted to question a Portuguese soldier about the troop movements, but Amanda, alarmed, held me back.

TAP 121, a barely visible speck in the sky, was sighted two hours later, arousing much excitement in the waiting crowd and the commotion increased by the minute, erupting in cheers as the plane approached the runway. Carmina, who had never seen a plane land before, stood on a chair and stretched to get a better view. She almost fell over. For her, the plane was magical—a flying god carrying Paulo that came all the way from a far off distant land. Wide-eyed and wide-mouthed, we waited to catch a glimpse of him. Finally, there was a cry from Carmina: 'Baba, Baba!' She had spotted Paulo descending the stairs. As I watched him stride jauntily along the tarmac, in dark glasses and wearing a three-piece brown suit of Cashmere, a cigarette hanging from his lower lip, I wondered how all these years in Portugal had changed him. He seemed fairer than the fair, more European than the Europeans. A whiff of jealousy crossed my mind, but I was overtaken by the excitement of the moment.

'Look at him, what a handsome judge he will make,' said Tia Rosita.

Paulo hugged us all in turn, uttering what we soon discovered was his favourite Portuguese expression: *Opa!* Staring back as if astonished and whistling, he said to Amanda in Portuguese: '*Que bonitinha tu estas! Opa! Que noivinha!*' He gave her a generous hug that squeezed the air out of her lungs, telling her how beautiful she looked, like a bride.

Amanda blushed, '*Basta uumm*—enough,' she said. 'You've only just returned and already are teasing me?' Barely twenty-two, Amanda was a frail beauty with marvelling eyes, wide pouty lips, high cheekbones and wavy black hair—a mirror image of Mama, but for a darker tint to the skin; inwardly, she was highly sensitive, but stubborn with a mind of steel. Today, her brown pleated skirt over a pale yellow blouse highlighted her milky-tea, cinnamon-brown complexion.

'He has definitely changed—more dapper,' I whispered into Amanda's ear, when Paulo anxiously waited for his baggage.

'And jolly as usual,' said Amanda.

Paulo loosened his tie and removed the vest and jacket. Tia Rosita wiped the sweat on his brow, while Amanda fanned him to circulate the stifling May heat trapped in the overcrowded car. He had hardly landed and the fuss had already begun. The taxi sped through the mud roads with their potholes, red dust clouds, muddied buffaloes and dozing dogs, finally arriving at the Albuquerque mansion. At the sight of the Mercedes taxi, a loud cry went out: '*Bab pauló, bab pauló. Baba* is here!' And then firecrackers were lit.

Close to fifty villagers, most of them peasants from our estate, had gathered by the gate at Mama's urging in anticipation of Paulo's return, as if waiting for an important government dignitary to arrive. Paulo stepped out of the car into the arms of Mama and Papa. The peasant-tenants simultaneously clamoured to touch his feet. '*Bab, Bab, amcho Pacló Bab*—our White Baby' they said, marvelling at the fact that he had lost his tan, which gave him an almost European look. Mama was light-skinned as well, whereas Papa was of a much darker complexion. When Paulo was born, his fair complexion was a delight, like vanilla icecream; and so, the peasants had nicknamed him *Pacló Bab*. He would always be their special White Baby.

Mama wanted a girl for a second child and hoped that she, too, would be fair like Paulo. She got a girl all right, but a pretty little brown-skinned *morena* this time. When I was born, my darker complexion was not a very welcome sight; it was as if disaster struck. In my youth, I always felt a colour complex in front of my fairer brother.

'Look how fair, how handsome my Paulo,' Mama would say ruffling his hair and everyone: visitors, villagers, cousins, peasants and servants concurred. Whiteness was equated with handsomeness, like day with light. I resented this attitude. Indeed, I was of a darker complexion, but handsome with Mama's fine features.

When I was born, Papa wanted to give me an Indian name. He had read and admired the Bengali poet Tagore. When Papa suggested the name *Tagore* to Mama, she wouldn't have it.

'A Hindu name for my Catholic child? That's a sacrilege.'

'*Merda*! He is my son and I'll decide what name he gets,' said Papa. He apparently put on his trousers, a bush-shirt and a hunting hat, then took his walking cane from the dresser and walked out furiously in the midday sun. It was rare for Papa to lose his temper with Mama. Perhaps he was mad at himself for contemplating such an unconventional proposition.

Mama had immediately consulted with Father Monteiro, the vicar, who assured her that he would have a chat with my father. He met him at Ferrão's Bar, near the church, when he was having a whisky-soda and struck a compromise. Tagore would be the second name; the first name would be Roberto, my grandfather's name, chosen by Mama to appease Papa.

'She always gets her way, *merda*. I will call him Tagore and my side of the family will call him Tagore,' muttered Papa to Father Monteiro. But the name Tagore never stuck. Only Papa sometimes called me Tagore. He told me all about Tagore when I was twelve and bought me his books to read. I was very proud of the name and wished I were called Tagore.

Paulo waved to the peasants, greeted some by name, patted a few backs and climbed the steps to the house with a swagger of importance. After the photographer specially commissioned for the occasion had taken the ceremonial photographs, with all the family grouped at the top of the steps, Mama ushered Paulo to the oratory where he genuflected, made the sign of the cross and kissed the statues of saints.

When he asked Carmina for a whisky-soda, she insisted that Paulo come to the kitchen first to have the evil eye removed. There, Carmina lit a fire in the chulha and picked up the ingredients she had kept ready for the ritual of *distt*. Holding three large scarlet-coloured peppers and a piece of asafoetida in her right hand and a few grains of *calo girem* and coarse sea salt in the left, she mumbled and mouthed a few words interspersed with silent movements of lips while quickly juggling her hands over Paulo from head to foot, again and again, in rapid successive movements. Then, she touched the concoction to his forehead and in one fierce movement flung it all in the fire, which roared to life as the dry peppers exploded, emitting a red-purple glow with a dizzying leap of flames and loud popping sounds. Carmina smiled, satisfied. The sound of the bursting peppers like the firing of guns signified the smashing of all evil eyes directed at Paulo.

In the meantime, the peasants gathered near the kitchen for a glass of liquor. Mama always made it a point to personally serve the peasants a drink of the local cashew brew on special occasions; today was one such occasion. She was familiar with all the peasant-tenants living on the Albuquerque estate; intricately involved in their births, deaths, weddings and debts. She often advised them, assisted them and rarely scolded them. As always, Vishnu jumped the line for the first glass of liquor that he gulped down with a smack of his lips, a loud cry of good health saying '*Saud*,' and then stretched his hand for another.

After the *distt* ritual, Paulo went to his room and I followed behind. Rather tired, he lay on his canopy bed, looking around the room. Nothing much had changed: the bed itself, the trophies he had received in the lyceum, the Spanish guitar—all were as he had left them. He then sank into a deep introspection as if consumed by a sudden melancholy.

'Come on, tell me about your trip,' I said. But Paulo did not answer; he looked tired and distant as if immersed in his own thoughts.

'Is anything the matter?' I said. He just shook his head. I wondered if Paulo already longed for the life in Portugal he had summarily abandoned. He then suddenly jumped off the bed with his usual gregarious laughter and came and embraced me. '*O pa*, Roberto, you have become a man and are soon to be a doctor,' he said.

'I'm thinking of going to Lisbon or Coimbra to specialise in Tropical Medicine.'

'Coimbra definitely—I will teach you the ropes—set you up in a wonderful boarding house—better and cheaper than Dona Figueira's.'

A feeling of warmth, of familiarity, came over me. I worshiped my brother for his looks and his flamboyance, wishing I were a recipient of such charm.

Carmina entered the room with a whisky-soda and offered to knead and massage his feet. Paulo thanked her, took a sip of the drink and began opening his trunk when Tucaram snuck in, expecting some gift. Carmina yelled at him, threatening to inform Tulsi. I gave him some candy with which he ran out all happy, at once doing his special rotatory spin, which consisted of rapid turnovers, like that of a ballerina.

It was not in Paulo's character to come empty handed; he had presents for everyone. He handed me several silky blue and beige shirts. I immediately ran to my room to try them on and nearly bumped into Mama who was on her way to the kitchen to give orders for dinner to be served.

Tia Rosita announced that the rosary would be dispensed with today, but tomorrow there would be a *ladainha*—a special prayer sung in Portuguese, Konkani and Latin.

The bright, kerosene-fed Petromax lamps, hanging in the dining room, had been pumped up to brighten the glow and their sharp white light, in addition to giving the house a festive mood, highlighted the murals in the dining room: on one side, the river Zuari with a solitary fishing boat and a silvery broken moon in it; on the other, the River Tagus with Lisbon in the background. Fireflies, dazzled by the light, circled the Petromax, crashing into the hot chimney and dying on the ground.

Dinner at the long rectangular table that seated more than twenty had just been served when Pedru, the butler, all dressed up for the occasion with a long cotton shervani coat, made his entry.

'Oh no, he's going to make one of his crazy speeches!' I whispered to Amanda.

'The Honourable Senhor Afonso, the Honourable Senhor Paulo and Dona Isabella,' said Pedru. 'By decree of His Excellency the Governor-General Manuel António Vassalo e Silva and His Excellency, the Archbishop of Goa and Damão, I pronounce the festivity of this day, the tenth of May of the year 1961, Anno Domino, to be a day of celebration of Paulo-baba's return. I hereby announce the appointment of Paulo Isidoro Santana de Albuquerque as judge, by order of Salazar. *Viva, Viva, Viva!*'

'*Viva!*' rang the response as we, the younger members of the Albuquerque household and the servants giggled. Papa and Mama always maintained a serious demeanour during and a forced smile after Pedru's absurd proclamations. Pedru, who was considered half-insane, was allowed these dramatic proclamations on special occasions. We tolerated his eccentric pronunciations as if they were sooth-sayings from the Oracle at Delphi. He could read and write Portuguese and English, which was unusual for a servant and during his speeches at the dinner table, he often quoted from the Bible.

Pedru was no ordinary servant. The second of ten siblings of a poor family, he was chosen by his father to join the seminary at the age of eight. In those times, it was the rule rather than the exception to offer one son to the Church.

It is said that many are called, but the Lord chooses only a few. It is doubtful that Pedru was ever called and consequently ever chosen. He marvelled at the idea during his younger years, but by the age of seventeen, doubts crossed his mind as his interest in the opposite sex kindled his libido.

A year or so later, as he was coming close to being ordained, he would take long walks in the forest behind the seminary, immersed in contemplating the agony of the crucifixion, when one day, during one of his evening walks, having taken a wrong turn and ventured away from his usual path, he heard sounds of splashing water. Knowing there was a stream close by that was fed by rainwater from the mountain behind, he decided to follow the sound of the water. He became apprehensive as if he was about to witness an apparition.

As he approached, he saw a woman dressed in a flimsy sari

bathing in the stream with a tumbler of water that she poured over her body, which was ample and glistened with soap. Pedru instinctively turned his face away, but curiosity consumed him, melting resistance like liquefying ice. He hid behind a banyan tree from where he could watch her. He would come again and again to watch her bathe and every time he would rub his body on the tree, violently, until it spasmodically spouted hot guilty semen. Consumed with remorse, he comforted himself in the night watches by using the whip on his own back, repeatedly.

'*Castigo corpus meum,*' he would say as he raised the lash to punish his body. And yet, desire would gradually seep upwards like liquid mercury in a fevered thermometer. He fought Satan with prayer and penance; but more often, he succumbed and momentarily forgot God, until one day this running battle scrambled what remained of his wits and he finally lost control drifting away from the seminary, delusional and paranoid. Poor Pedru, he was cornered by both: the Holy and the Evil.

Papa apparently found him delirious and dehydrated behind the Albuquerque house. He was tended to by Carmina and, when he came to his senses, he did not know who or what he was for a couple of months. He kept pleading with my father that he be allowed to stay and work. He had a faded scapular in his pocket, a chain of silver with a wooden crucifix around his neck and a tattered missal in his pocket with his name in it. He often sat by himself in one corner of his room, all dishevelled, speaking to himself, telling his story and cursing at the female devil that had seduced him. Not unusually, he wandered off in rags on full moon days. Our family accepted Pedru as an entity with a tragic past and marginal sanity. For almost twenty-eight years, he remained profoundly loyal to us all, performing any and every task without uttering a word of protest—the epitome of true servility. Once, when I was eight years old and being bullied by an older visiting cousin, Pedru had come to my rescue: he snatched the slingshot, ear-twisted the cousin and handed me my toy. Since that day, I always had a soft spot for Pedru.

After Pedru's speech, Mama pressed Paulo to help himself, but the aroma of more than half-a-dozen dishes that wafted over the dining table did not seem to stimulate his appetite. He had a few morsels of the codfish, but seemed more intent with his whisky.

As usual the ritual of serving, insisting, fussing over a dish on such occasions continued at the dinner table. Papa, after finishing his dinner, sat in an armchair with elevated leg rests that placed whoever sat on the chair in a compromising position reserved for elder men. In our youth, Paulo and I, up to our obstreperous ways, imitated Papa when he was not around, calling it the farting chair where Papa expertly blew out his farts: *porrrrrrrr*, like loud honks and looked out at the wide-angle view of the balcony and the steps leading up to the house. Now, Papa dangled his legs in the air, puffed on a cigar and sipped on a glass of Portuguese brandy.

'So, Paulo, what do they think in Portugal of the threat from India? And this Krishna Menon?' he asked.

'The Government in Lisbon doesn't take the threat from India seriously,' Paulo reluctantly answered. 'The argument in Lisbon is that Goa is part of Portugal. Goa is not a colony like India was under the British. So there is no question of ceding Goa to India. And this man you are talking about, I haven't heard or read about him in the newspapers.' Papa looked at Paulo rather surprised at his throwaway answer.

'But how can you rely on newspapers under the Salazar dictatorship?' I asked. Papa concurred, shaking his head.

'*Cala-te*, Roberto, shut up! Let Paulo speak,' Mama said.

There she goes again taking his side as usual, I thought to myself, while refraining from further remarks. Certainly, Mama would always support her favourite son in any argument, above all, a political one. Having studied in Bombay at St Xavier's College, I was well versed in the activities of the Indian National Congress unlike Mama, my aunt and my brother. Besides, Jawaharlal Nehru, the prime minister of neighbouring India, was my political hero. Our diverging political viewpoints were the source of heated debate between Papa and me on one side, Mama and Tia Rosita on the other. For Mama, India was a distant land with strange men in white Nehru caps and the non-violent Gandhijis, the satyagrahis, who came across the frontier to claim her Portuguese-Goa.

'I agree with Roberto. One cannot rely on newspapers here or in Portugal,' Amanda unexpectedly objected, supporting my contention. This was a pleasant surprise. But Mama ignored her.

'I'm tired, I'm going to sleep,' Paulo said. He wished us all goodnight and headed to his room. At that moment, the lame and rather lazy housedog Xanu began barking ferociously, something he rarely did and scratching at the front door. Pedru leashed the dog and dragged him to the doghouse near the kitchen, limping and still barking.

Three

Botched Guerrilla Attack

What with the jet lag and the whisky-sodas Paulo had downed that evening, he seemed befuddled when he left the dining room and stepped into the dark corridor leading to his bedroom. I was startled, but not entirely surprised, when I heard a thud in the corridor and a muffled cry. Before I could reach the door, Paulo reappeared and he was not alone. Three masked men in battle fatigues had him firmly by the arms.

The gunmen ordered me back into the dining room and everybody to stay put. We all sat frozen in our seats. The leader of the guerrillas, a young heavyset man, paced the floor nervously. Papa, who looked ashen, begged them not to harm the family. 'I am pro-India! Please take whatever you want,' he said, somewhat shaken.

'You landlords, you are all pro-Portuguese!' the guerrilla leader shot back. 'Where do you keep the jewellery?'

'The d-d-d-dresser in our bedroom,' stammered Papa.

'Go get the jewellery! *Chalo*! No, not you—your wife.'

It was obvious that they were in a hurry; their unease was written all over their faces. As I edged forward in my seat, about to get up to confront the leader, Amanda and Tia Rosita, who were beside themselves and in tears, held me back. It was then that I began feeling dizzy and slumped in the chair. A high level of excitement—an adrenergic rush—brought on one of my fainting attacks. Tia Rosita and Amanda began fanning me. They were shaking all over. The servant Mari suddenly began to scream and roll on the floor in a hysterical fit. Carmina went to her and held her in her arms. The leader spoke to one of the masked men, who then approached Mari and told her to shut up or else. He lifted the gun butt. That got Mari's attention and she quieted down.

The leader, who seemed apprehensive as he paced the floor, ordered one of the masked men to go with Mama. As the masked man left with Mama and the leader followed far behind, Paulo winked at me and made his move. He caught hold of the man guarding the door and slammed him against the wall and wrestled for the gun. They were both on the floor when the leader, hearing the struggle, ran back and overpowered Paulo. The two gunmen then tied him to a chair.

I should have rushed to help my brother who had obviously signalled me by winking. Although I was too weak and wobbly to offer any assistance, maybe the two of us together would have overpowered the man guarding the door.

Mama returned with a carved sandalwood jewellery box that contained a gold chain, a set of silver bangles, a gold tiepin of Papa's, trinkets from Kashmir and Rajasthan and plenty of cotton. She trembled as she handed the box to the leader. Her set of platinum, diamonds and rubies had been pawned and was in safekeeping and the rest of the precious family jewellery was hidden in the attic. It was almost two years since Mari, while cleaning the attic above the master bedroom, had accidentally reached into a hole in the wall and found a box that contained a variety of gems: old gold coins and other ornaments of gold including rings and bangles studded with rubies and diamonds, probably hidden by an ancestor who had forgotten its whereabouts. It was in this same hiding place that Mama hid the jewellery from robbers and guerrillas, who made occasional sorties at rich homes and police stations in Goa villages since the start of the freedom struggle.

Suddenly, the leader, who now seemed even more apprehensive, possibly on his first guerrilla operation, screamed at the masked man who had returned with Mama. Pointing at Paulo, he shouted, 'Say *Jai-Hind*!'

'No! Never!' answered Paulo.

'Chalo, say *Jai-Hind!*'

'*Viva Portugal!*' responded Paulo.

'Say *Jai-Hind!* Basstarrd!'

'*Viva Portugal!*' insisted Paulo, who began singing the Portuguese national anthem.

The situation was spiralling out of control. Suddenly, the leader exploded: 'I order you shoot the man! Just shoot him in the head,' he ordered the masked man at his side.

'Sir, though he looks like a European, he's not Portuguese—he's Goan,' said the masked man.

'Spare my son, please spare my son. You can kill me instead,' Mama cried, prostrate at the leader's feet. He just pushed her aside. Now Amanda, Tia Rosita, Carmina and Mari knelt down and sobbed and begged him to spare Paulo's life.

'Chalo, just shoot him. I order you,' the leader insisted. There was no reaction from the masked man who seemed stunned as well. The leader then pointed his revolver at the very heart of Paulo. Papa stood up suddenly and positioned himself in-between Paulo and the leader. The leader caught hold of Papa's arm and swung him around. Papa came crashing on the divan.

Paulo remained still, with eyes shut, as if resigned to his fate. To me it all seemed like a dream.

Then Paulo began singing the Portuguese national anthem again and proclaiming that he would die for the fatherland, while Mama's crying became a loud wailing and pandemonium broke loose. Papa again got up to confront the leader when one of the masked men pushed him back. Then Carmina who ran towards Paulo crying, 'Baba, Baba,' was kicked aside by the leader and fell to the ground. I looked at Papa who was slumped in his chair with a blank stare, as if his own life was rapidly ebbing away. Tia Rosita and Amanda sobbed and covered their eyes with their hands.

I mustered all my strength and rushed towards the leader with the gun and toppled him to the ground. I then momentarily passed out right in front of Paulo and in the process, fell on top of the stunned leader. It was then that one of the masked men stepped in front, shielding Paulo.

'Let's go, let's go, no killing!' he said with authority, as the barks of the dog Xanu came closer and louder. Taken by surprise, the leader got up and clutching the jewellery box disappeared with the other men through the main door into the darkness of the moonless night.

Amanda, Mama, Tia Rosita and Carmina rushed towards Paulo. They untied him, hugged and kissed him, stroked his face and cried over him. I managed to pull myself onto the chair with the help of Mari, who brought me a glass of coconut water with which I felt much better.

Pedru, who was in the kitchen, had quietly slipped out through the back door after letting the dog out of the doghouse. He ran to the police station, only to find that there was another attack by a second group of guerrillas that had just been repelled by machine gun fire, causing them to flee in disorder. On his way, he alerted some of the peasants on the Albuquerque estate. They arrived, too late, in full force with bamboo sticks and machetes.

Commandant Videira, originally from Caramulo, Portugal, came with two police officers: one a Goan, the other a Portuguese. He was confident that his troops had subverted an attack on the police station and that could mean a decoration. While he debriefed the Albuquerque household, the other officers searched inside and around the house and interviewed the neighbours. They came up with no clues except for the gun that was left behind, some footprints just below the window of Paulo's room that had been left open, a few broken twigs and a cigarette butt. The presence of the tall, heavily built and well-armed Commandant Videira, as well as the several armed peasants from the estate, provided a sense of security and to some extent, the euphoria that attends a happy outcome of a near-tragic situation.

I wondered at the identity of the masked man who had saved Paulo's life. Could he have known Paulo at one time? Paulo had absolutely no idea who the man was. However, I was certain that the leader was a non-Goan, most likely a Maharashtrian from across the frontier.

'That was very courageous what you did, Paulo, but very risky. You could have been killed,' said Commandant Videira.

Paulo was hailed as a hero—his heroic stand, his singing of the Portuguese national anthem, was recounted all over neighbouring villages and was the subject of conversation at the governor's mansion. The governor personally presented Paulo with a medal of honour and a cash prize of five hundred rupees to both of us.

'I don't think they would have done it,' said Papa. 'I think they were trying to frighten us, indirectly sending a message to the government to expect more violent attacks. Who knows what might have happened if Roberto hadn't rushed at the leader.'

'All's well that ends well,' Amanda faintly uttered.

'My poor Paulo—such a horrible reception—*que ma sorte!*' Mama piped angrily. 'The government has to take strong action against these Indian guerrillas. Afonso, you have to go to Panjim and see the governor general about this mess.'

'I will see the proper authorities tomorrow,' said Papa.

'Your dog must have picked up their scent,' said Commandant Videira. 'Next time, don't ignore his barks. And bring your rifle to the police station. I want to check it out thoroughly and give you some fresh ammunition.'

'Yes, yes, and I will have two peasant-tenants sleeping in the balcony to keep guard from now on.'

'We'll ask for additional reinforcements from Panjim and increase the number of night patrols,' said Commandant Videira. 'The guerrilla warfare is at its peak. We've seen more than one-hundred and fifty such attacks, at least a hundred successful acts of sabotage and more than thirty Portuguese soldiers dead. I'm sure that the terrorists belong to the *Azad Gomantak Dal* (The Free Goa Party) and most come from across the border. They operate from bases inside Indian Territory and under cover of Indian police forces. The damn Indian government gives them financial, logistic and armament support.'

'I entirely agree with you,' said Papa. 'Their tactics will not work here in Goa.'

'Goans are peace-loving. Most will not join these guerrilla fighters from India,' said Mama.

'I entirely agree,' I said. It was the first time I agreed with Mama's political viewpoint.

After Commandant Videira left with the police officers, our anxieties resurfaced. Tia Rosita suggested we pray and the deferred rosary was said in the prayer room. In the middle of the Hail Marys, Tia Rosita broke down, wailing and beating her chest.

A special prayer was offered to the Sacred Heart of Jesus and a novena was started to St Jude for bringing Paulo home safe and for saving his life. Ayah Carmina suggested adding a prayer to St Francis Xavier.

Paulo, exhausted and washed out, sat dozing just outside the oratory. After some time, he retired to bed.

We all, masters and servants alike, huddled together in the oratory. I saw to it that all the outside doors and windows were closed and bolted. Papa paced the floor the entire night with a loaded gun, inspecting and re-inspecting every window and door. That night was a sleepless one for all of us.

Next morning, Papa ordered the carpenters to install double padlocks on all the window frames and to secure all the doors on the inside with iron crossbars. He would check every window and door before he went to sleep and slept with a revolver under his pillow and a shotgun under the bed, to the anguish of Mama who was afraid of an accidental discharge. Needless to say, the unsettling incident lingered in the household for a long time, but we all felt a greater degree of security after reinforcements of Portuguese troops arrived from the Panjim military quarters and with the nightly vigil of two armed peasant-tenants in the veranda.

four

Mama's Diary

The following morning after breakfast, as soon as Papa left for Panjim to report the attack and request additional troops, Mama began playing a Chopin Nocturne on the piano, but soon broke down in tears and retreated to her room. She was upset not just by the guerrilla attack itself, but also by the cancellation of the welcoming dinner she had planned for Paulo, to which several socially prominent families with marriageable daughters had been invited.

Later, that very afternoon, Mama began writing in her diary, the one that I had come upon recently in New York.

11 May, 1961.

Yesterday was an eventful day in our lives. My Paulo returned from Portugal and was almost killed. I am terribly shaken by the events that transpired. More than ever, I feel the fragility of life itself and an urgency to pen my feelings in my dear diary.

It was the music, Chopin's Nocturne that brought back the memories, as always.

I was only twenty-one then, innocent and beautiful, Isabella Rosa Linda I was called, when Captain António Borda de Mar walked in on my piano playing. That moment a story began and as with every story, mine too had its shooting star that flew across the sky and disintegrated, leaving memories that I kept hidden in those crevices of my mind that I rarely disturbed. Only Carmina was privy to my secret.

We met at my cousin's wedding. He asked me for a dance and we waltzed effortlessly, as in a dream. He asked me for another and held me close. I tried to resist under the watchful eyes of my mother and my aging spinster aunt, but he was so young and handsome that I felt helpless. He gazed into my eyes remarking that they were the colour of coal and mesmerising like a leopard's. I wondered whether he had seen in them a hidden passion that was raw and waiting to burn. I glanced up into his blue eyes, having never seen blue eyes before; and, as in his name, Borda de Mar, I saw the blue sea, in them. That night, as I lay in bed awake, I kept seeing his eyes. Ashamed and remorseful for such sinful thoughts, I got out of bed and knelt in prayer and recited aloud the Act of Contrition.

I went for Mass the following Sunday and then to visit my cousin Teresa, whose house was near the police station, where the captain was waiting. I felt awfully shy and lowered my head. He greeted me: 'Good morning, Isabella.' 'Good morning, Capitão,' I responded. That was all. We went our separate ways.

One Sunday after Mass, I stayed back to discuss with the vicar the choir arrangements for the annual feast of St Thomas. I was reluctant to see the vicar alone, but my mother insisted that I sing in the choir. He was notorious for inadvertently touching his crotch when he saw a pretty woman, as if to say, 'this is forbidden territory'. 'Forbidden to whom?' was a matter of female speculation and laughter; and, not surprisingly, he had done it again.

After the meeting, I walked angrily past the ornate biblical murals: a fresco of a dead man ascending to heaven; a dying sinner pulled by the black-tailed devil into Dante's Inferno. I briefly superimposed the image of Father Vicar on the dying sinner and regretted such a malevolent thought. As I walked past the open main door of the church, I genuflected, made the sign of the cross and asked for forgiveness.

I walked down the zigzagging steps with the Mandovi River below and stopped midway onto an overlook to watch a canoe laden with people being ferried across the lazily flowing river. Like a child, I hopped and stepped and hopped on the mud road intersecting a vast paddy field. On an impulse, I decided to take a short cut to my house through a path in the forest. At the entrance to the forested path, the captain was waiting. I stopped, surprised.

'What are you doing here?' I asked.

'I am patrolling the area. There was a robbery at the Correia house. You shouldn't be walking this way by yourself. There are cobras in the forest that camouflage themselves so well that it's hard to make them out.'

'What do you know of cobras?' I laughed.

'Enough to know that the bite can be fatal,' he said.

He insisted on accompanying me. I was embarrassed. I did not protest.

We walked the narrow path, brushing fingers. Now and again, our bodies touched each other as we avoided the thorny spiky vines or the rocks that jutted out in the path. A mongoose scurrying in the undergrowth startled me so much that I grabbed his arm for protection. I remember my heart racing as if it wanted to explode out of my chest. I instinctively embraced him as a viper crossed our path. He held me close, not wanting to let me go. More frightened of him than the dangers in the forest, I broke loose and ran.

I was reluctant to see him again, but when Sunday arrived, it was as if I was mysteriously pulled towards the forested path. He was there, waiting, smoking a cigarette.

'I knew you would come,' he said.

'I was just taking a short-cut,' I replied.

We would meet again and again in the forested path, always on a Sunday. I knew he would be there waiting for me. As always, we walked holding hands. He did not attempt to embrace me again. I felt more relaxed. I began trusting him. He talked to me about the city of Coimbra, its cobblestone streets and its university where he would study law after his tour of duty. 'I have only one year left,' he said. 'I will marry you, my love, minha Rosa Linda, my lovely rose and take you there.' Our secret encounters went on for nearly three months.

And then, one day, he entered the music room that overlooked the garden of white bougainvillea. My mother was away at my cousins in the neighbouring town of Mapuçá. I did not know where my father was—perhaps sleeping off his binge at a friend's house? The captain was in his uniform with khaki shorts that were too short and a khaki short-sleeved shirt with a captain's stripes on both shoulders and sunglasses that gave him a hunter's look. He looked sharp and seductively handsome.

He apologised saying, 'I followed the music like a cobra follows the snake charmer. I'm here to call on your father.' I was wearing a white taffeta dress with a pink and white flowery design. I had no makeup on and my long wavy hair rolled untidily over my shoulders, a few loose strands tickling the corner of my lips. I felt embarrassed to be seen in such a state.

'Keep playing,' he insisted. My fingers trembled. I began missing the notes. He placed his hands on my hands and we began playing the Nocturne together. I felt reassured.

'I thought a military man plays with guns and not with solfeggios,' I said, giggling. Turning around and staring into my eyes, he responded. 'This military man shoots better solfeggios than bullets.'

At that moment I felt a hot wave of desire wash over my body. Having boarded and been schooled in a convent of nuns, I was taught that the body was evil—susceptible to temptation and sin—that it should be shunned and be ignored. When I was fourteen, I had dared to ask Mother Superior about the red stains on my panties. Sitting me on her lap and placing her hand on my shoulder, Mother Superior had said: 'Come child, come, you are a young woman now and these are the monthly stains of sin. If you have pain, pray to the Virgin Mary and all will be well. Come now, child, and go to bed.' I didn't know what to make of this monthly blood-letting and the enlargement of my breasts. I often felt a tingling sensation between my thighs that tempted me to touch, but I had resisted the sins of the flesh.

'My, my, Isabella, you have blossomed like a red hibiscus in the marsh,' my cousin, Angela, had said.

I kept playing the Nocturne. I felt relaxed, but soon, the tempo was lost; the piano keys seemed to be glued. A few half tones like the beat of caged bird wings were let loose and then silence.

Captain Borda de Mar had his arms around me. He kissed me. Ah, the touch of his lips, like burning coals, the accidental meeting of tongues. His hands kept exploring my uncharted body like some unmapped land and although I pushed his hands away, my grip was weakening.

I repeatedly protested: 'No, no, not here, not now, somebody might come,' but he wouldn't relent. Perhaps overwhelmed by his infectious enthusiasm, I closed my eyes as we slipped gradually from the piano stool to the ground of mosaic tile. My limp hand struck a note—a C-sharp on my way down. In the heat of the moment, neither of us had had the presence of mind to bolt the door.

Carmina, who was sweeping the floor of the side room, opened the door and casually walked into the music room with her broom. She saw me half-naked beside a half-naked white man. She had never seen a naked white man. As a matter of fact, she had never seen a naked man before.

'Bai!' she screamed and ran out of the room into the dining room, through the corridor into the kitchen where she sat for a while utterly confused and alarmed, then ran back as fast as she ran out. I closed my eyes in anguish, stunned now by the shame of having been discovered. I could hear the captain scrambling to his feet and his footsteps as he headed for the garden door.

'Merda!' he muttered. 'Merda!' When I opened my eyes, Carmina was by my side.

It all happened so fast. I wondered whether the captain knew that my parents were not at home. The remainder of that day I felt utterly confused and ashamed. Carmina scolded me in no uncertain terms. 'How could you do this, Bai? Shame on you! If your mother comes to know, she will lock you up. Oh my God, Bai, you have to go for confession soon. You have to stop seeing this Pacló—this white man.' I begged of her not to tell my mother. I told her he loved me and that he would marry me soon. I made her swear that she would keep it a secret. That night and on subsequent nights, I cried in Carmina's arms.

I was deeply in love, ready at any moment to run away with the captain. I knew my mother would never permit my marriage to a Portuguese soldier. 'After all, we are Brahmins,' she would have said. 'Who knows what this man is. Besides, very likely he already has a wife.' I wanted to go and see him the next day, but I was confused and overcome with guilt and shame. I cried in Carmina's lap the entire day.

Carmina had consoled me with her own tears. I had gone for confession, but couldn't confess my sin. 'What is it, my child, you can tell me,' the kind chaplain kept asking. I didn't know how or where to begin. I sobbed. The young chaplain became distressed at my crying. He blessed me and let me go in peace. After Mass I stayed back in the chapel and when I was alone, I confessed to Jesus Christ and gave myself penance. I made a vow that I would say two rosaries every day for the rest of my life. Forgive me God for my sin—till this day I have kept my vow.

I waited for him after Mass on Sunday. There was no sign of him. In the evening, he sent a letter through a messenger boy. My mother snatched the letter and read its contents. The letter said that he had to leave for Portugal immediately because of a family emergency. He apologised for not coming over to say goodbye. He asked me, 'Minha Rosa Linda,' that I not stop playing Chopin and to think of him when I did. There was no word that he would return. There was no mention of marriage, or that he would come back for me.

My mother summoned me and showed me the letter. 'What is the meaning of this?' she asked. 'And he has the audacity to call you Minha Rosa Linda? How long has this been going on?' I wasn't listening. I began to cry. I didn't care that my mother had read the letter—I was simply heartbroken that the captain had left. Just like that. Perhaps, I would never see him again. I felt like a wounded heron whose wings had been clipped, left to die.

My mother went on asking me what exactly had happened between us, but I refused to reply. She slapped me. I lost my footing and almost fell. She snatched off her slipper and swung her arm to strike me, but ayah Carmina shielded me and took the blows on her shoulders.

'Nothing happened between Isabel-bai and the captain,' Carmina answered for me. 'I was there. She was playing the piano. They played the piano together. He is a very nice man—please, please, let them marry, Batcani.'

'Shut up!' Mother retorted angrily. 'It is none of your business, Carmina. Your business is in the kitchen.' Then she composed herself, saying with a wave of her hand, 'Besides, this captain, whoever he is, has left for Portugal. I'm sure the man has a wife there. God is great.'

I spent the whole day crying in my room. The red hibiscus wilted.

My mother soon forgot this incident. After all, Captain Borda de Mar had left for Portugal. But it awakened urgency in her to get me married. At my cousin's wedding, Afonso António Albuquerque, the Mayor of Loutolim, a rich man from an elite family well connected with the Portuguese dignitaries, had taken notice of me. My mother made inquiries through a cousin who informed her that Afonso Albuquerque was impressed with my beauty and poise. The dowry was of no concern. Afonso's mother knew that I came from a high-class family that had at one time been very wealthy. My father had no big dowry to offer but I had beauty. The interview was at my cousin Angela's house. I was not interested. Still reeling from recent events, I wore a gaudy purple dress down to my ankles and made my hair into pigtails. I wore no makeup in the hope that I would look like a girl entering a nunnery. My mother made me change into a dark red dress, dabbed my face with rouge and pinned a pinkish-white acacia to my hair.

When I saw Senhor Afonso, I took one look at him and shuddered. At first glance, he looked a bit shorter and of a darker complexion than me and older by sixteen years. I only had eyes for the captain with his boyish face, a fine Roman nose, lips the shape of hearts and blue eyes like ocean water. I came home and cried in Carmina's arms. Carmina consoled me pointing out that it may not be so bad. 'Colour is not everything,' she said. 'He is a good-looking and kindhearted man, intelligent and rich—that's what they say. Besides, that captain left for Portugal without even saying goodbye.'

'No, no, I will not marry this man,' I said. But my mother, who had already arranged a battalion of cousins and friends to convince me to the contrary, had sealed my fate. Gradually, I gave in. Did I have a choice?

'I will marry this man, but I will never love him,' I said.

five

Love and Rejection

Our family spent every summer holiday in a rented cottage on Calangute beach. There, men in suits and women in knee-length cotton dresses strolled the length of the beach in the evenings, as though they were walking on the Champs-Élysées. After sundown, we gathered in groups, made small talk and played all sorts of games, while our mothers and fathers retreated to their rented bungalows. A few old gamblers got together and played rummy or bridge on the veranda of our cottage that overlooked the Arabian Sea.

The men returning from Portugal and Africa on holiday often walked barefoot on the sand in suits, scouting for wives, while marriage-minded mothers and aunts scanned the terrain for prospective bachelors. Tia Rosita spotted a Mozambique-returned doctor, Francisco Lobo, a very suitable man from an eminent family. She knew of his return and had casually mentioned to his mother the beauty and the domestic virtues of Amanda, who of course knew nothing of this, while Mama, who had been informed in advance, discreetly masterminded the show.

Tia Rosita, like a puppet-master, nudged Amanda to go this way, that way, near, but not too near, in profile, but not in full view, like in Indian movies, for Francisco's mother to see her. Francisco's mother, on the other hand, nudged her son to look this way, that way, way over there, at the pretty girl in pink with a white hibiscus in her hair.

'What now, Tia Rosita, do you have someone in mind? I'm not interested, Tia. I will marry the man I fall in love with and elope to Bombay.'

'*Sshhh*, Amanda, don't speak like that.'

After dinner, on starlit or moonlit nights, we would return to the beach with guitars and mandolins, forming a large circle where boys and girls sat back to back. Mama wouldn't allow Amanda to go out at night even in our company. It infuriated Amanda, who spent her time reading novels and writing poetry late into the night.

Paulo was the star on the beach. Dressed in his Portugal-tailored beige suit and a blue half-buttoned shirt, he treated his friends at the Caravella or at the Souza Lobo Bar and Restaurant. 'Bring 'em on,' he would say to the waiter—'your specials and put it on the tab: St Pauli beer, port wine, gin with cordial and sardines or *bajjas* or fried oysters or xamosas.' He sat in the circle and told us open-mouthed boys, with much braggadocio, about his adventures in Paris, of how an Eastern European aristocratic woman had fallen in love with him after hearing him sing the Portuguese Fado at a party on the Left Bank and how they cavorted with caviar and champagne and endless lovemaking until the early morning hours.

Another story that was a blast with us boys was about his relationship with his landlady in Portugal, Dona Figueira. Apparently estranged from her husband, she often went to his room with all sorts of excuses. Once, when Paulo came down with the flu, she took upon herself to nurse him at home rather than take him to the hospital and after checking his temperature and giving him a couple of aspirins, she insisted on giving him a sponge bath to bring the fever down. With a soft towel soaked with luke-warm water and alcohol, she rubbed his forehead, back, his legs and the inside of his thighs. As the rubbing continued, he got bigger and bigger like a sausage-shaped balloon pumped with hot air until he exploded like a cannon into the bathtub. Cleaning him up, gently powdering his body and dressing him in a clean pair of pajamas, she fed him a hot cup of chicken broth and put him to bed. They avoided each other for the next few days. Both seemed embarrassed by the incident.

Hearing these stories from Paulo, we boys dreamt of going to Paris and strolling on the Left Bank. On my way to America, years later, I, too, went to Paris and sauntered on the Left Bank, but to my chagrin, met no European princely types.

The girls would ask Paulo to sing. And Paulo, who liked being lionised, would wait until the requests became supplications. He would then sing Portuguese, Spanish and Brazilian songs: *Igreja de Santa Cruz, Coimbra, Malagueña, Maria Dolores, Cucurrucucu* and *Manhã de Carnaval* among others. He charmed them with his husky tenor voice well suited for the songs and the chords of his Spanish guitar and there were always plenty of encores. Paulo sang the same songs every day and every day he left the crowd gasping for more. I, on the other hand, had recently returned from a visit to Bombay as the puffed-up Elvis acolyte. In my Bombay-tailored jeans and T-shirt, I sang *Jailhouse Rock, Tutti Frutti, Love Me Tender* and *Bye Bye Love*; but it was Paulo's romantic music that turned the girls on.

Among the many girls in the group, there was Maria who was in the last year of lyceum. Barely eighteen and two years younger than I was, she sang with passion the local duets and the Mandos with her brother. On a scale of 1 to 5 for fairness, she was a 3, plus 2 out of 2 for her stunning face, plus 3 out of 3 for her family background, which made her on a scale of 1-10, an 8.0: a very suitable girl. I was attracted to her irrespective of the scoring system in vogue for marriage-minded suitable men.

Maria's specialty was to sing counter melody in her silky voice with her eyes closed and her arms outstretched, as if waiting for some prince to arrive and to rescue her from eternal sleep. When she wasn't singing, she was dancing, laughing and talking with her hands and twirling her dark long hair that fell in braids to her waist. I was delighted when my sister, Amanda, befriended Maria and they sang *Mandos*—the local love songs—together.

That summer, the competition for Maria was intense. Unlike most of the other girls, she wasn't shy at all and had an endless fund of funny stories to tell, that she'd act out with her eyes sparkling, biting her magic lips to stop herself from laughing before the punch line. I had never met a girl who was so adorable, so captivating and so full of life. To some extent, she reminded me of my mother. She was often dressed in pink, her favourite colour. 'Pink rose,' I called her. She would blow a raspberry with those pink lips and shrug the compliment aside, which made me feel like a silly pup. But soon I realised that like so many of the other girls, she too was infatuated with Paulo, who, not surprisingly, flirted with her, complimenting her on her looks and her singing. Unlike myself and the other boys, she had no idea about Paulo's many amorous liaisons in Portugal.

I, the hapless Elvis imitator, sang *Love Me Tender,* intending it for Maria—looking her way, as I sang. She ignored me and focused all her attention on Paulo, who then sang the Spanish song, *Maria Dolores.* At that moment, I felt, and perhaps Maria felt as well, that it was meant for her. Mesmerised with his singing, Maria was unable to take her dreamy eyes off Paulo, while he gave her his tried and tested seducer's look. I left the scene, downcast, with a heavy heart. Alarming images of what went on between Paulo and the Eastern European princess and Dona Figueira would be replayed in my mind at those times. Could my brother take such liberties with Maria? I had to protect her innocence, shield her from this male predator. It was thereafter that the rivalry between us brothers became intense. Jealousy has a peculiar way of affecting humans: men become irrational, while women smoulder and burn.

The more Maria rejected my overtures, the more I fell hopelessly in love with her. One night, a few days before the end of our vacation, Paulo and a few of his friends joined the party after a couple of shots of gin and cordial at the Caravella Bar. Paulo sat beside Maria for a while; subsequently, they slipped out of the circle and disappeared behind the sand dunes. I could do nothing but strum on the guitar and sing: '*There goes my baby, with someone new. She sure looks happy, I sure am blue…*'

Strange thoughts crossed my mind: Was Paulo groping her all over? Was she allowing herself to be seduced or was she resisting? Was this all that went on behind the sand dunes or was there more? I became despondent and left the crowd walking all the way to Baga beach where I contemplated ending my life. I stood at the ocean's edge with the silvery waves nibbling at my feet, hoping that somehow the Arabian Sea would claim me. I envisioned my shark-eaten carcass—the face untouched—lying on the beach and Maria hysterically crying: 'Oh my love, what a fool I have been.' I stood there full of misery until the high tide arrived and then went home.

The last few days of our holiday on the beach, Maria seemed moody, staying in her beach bungalow most of the time. I was taken by surprise by the sudden change in her personality: I had presumed that she wasn't the moody, melancholy type. I wondered if something unpleasant had happened between her and Paulo. Or was her attitude a reflection of guilt? I remained jaded for days and nights and tossed and turned, sleepless until dawn. But I got no answer to my silent questions.

Back in the village, Papa supervised the harvesting of coconuts, setting out early in the mornings accompanied by Vishnu and Mari. Vishnu carried a chair and a table on his head, Mari an umbrella to shield Papa from the sun and Tulsi and Tucaram would later arrive with a pot of rice broth with condensed fish-curry and some pickle. The table was laid out in the patio of the peasant-tenant Kashinath's hut.

Papa sat on the chair reading the newspaper, *O Heraldo.* I sat by his side. Bosteão, the coconut plucker, looped a length of rope around his feet and hopped his way up one coconut tree after another with his sharp sickle strapped to his loincloth. On reaching the crown, he showered an avalanche of ripe and a few tender coconuts, while Mari, Tulsi and Tucaram, after counting them, gathered them in a pile. Both Papa and I jotted the numbers on a pad of paper, first in pencil and then in ink, after the final count. This year, the harvest was plentiful.

As the final count was going on, Tucaram quietly hid a tender coconut under a mound of dirt. He was spotted in the act by Senhor Pissurlencar who leisurely strolled by, dressed in a *pudvem,* a white cloth wrapped around his legs and loins and tucked under the waist; a shirt, a tie, a coat, a hat and a walking cane. That was his signature dress code that demanded a certain cross-cultural respectability. From the waist up, he dressed like a Portuguese gentleman; below the waist, like a Brahmin Goan Hindu, carrying himself elegantly and stylishly, always half-lifting his hat with a slight nod of the head for a passing lady or a gentleman.

'*Arey* Tucaram, I saw you hide the coconut,' said Senhor Pissurlenkar who held the boy, as he was about to run away. Tulsi immediately ran to them and slapped the youngster sharply, dragging him away. Finding a bamboo cane, she was about to beat the boy when I intervened and separated them. Papa gave Tucaram the coconut, scolded him and advised him that it is better to ask than to steal. Tucaram promised not to steal again and ran around with his coconut in his arms while everybody went about their business. We drank fresh coconut water, which Vishnu handed us after skinning the harvested tender nuts and splitting them in half. My father welcomed Senhor Pissurlenkar, who had returned the day before from Bombay, with a generous embrace.

After the coconut harvesting was over, we chatted about village matters and Senhor Pissurlencar told us the latest news about the political climate in India in reference to Portuguese Goa. I could see my father's face light up as he and Pissurlenkar exchanged views; undoubtedly, he was sorely missed by Papa.

'Is there talk of military invasion of Goa?' I asked.

'I haven't heard of any such talk in Bombay. Anyway, if a military invasion is contemplated, it must be top secret,' said Senhor Pissurlenkar.

'Nehru preaches peace and non-violence all over the world. I doubt he will invade,' said Papa.

A close friend and guru of my father, Senhor Pissurlenkar was highly regarded in the village for his Vedic wisdom and an even East-West keel. He was nicknamed by some landlords as *porque-serve*-Pissurlencar, which meant, 'what's-the-use-Pissurlencar' for his constant use of the Portuguese phrase. As we walked home, we discussed my future after medical school.

'I'm considering going to Portugal to specialise in tropical medicine,' I said.

'But you're going to come back to Goa after specialisation?' said Senhor Pissurlencar, tapping me on the back. His own son and daughter had stayed back in Portugal and England, but promised to return in a couple of years.

'Oh yes,' answered Papa for me.

'Don't worry about me—I'll definitely be back,' I said.

Whenever possible, I accompanied my father on these harvesting sessions. Paulo on the other hand, showed no interest whatsoever. There is no doubt that Papa always intended for me to walk in his footsteps and be his heir. Besides, Papa was upset with Paulo whose tabs on the beach had piled up and my father had to pay up for them.

The mango and jackfruit season ended. The monsoon was late; the land was parched and cracked. The mid-day sun with its relentless rays had scorched and darkened the already dark skin of the local

Kundbi tribe who roamed the village idly, with bodies exposed and loins covered by the kaxti—the loin cloth that kept getting muddier every day. The whole village waited in anticipation for rain, raising their eyes to the sky, palms turned upwards in supplication. Then, all of a sudden it happened: a mass of dark clouds gathered and day became dusk. There was lightning and thunder and street boys remarked, 'It's St Peter and St Paul playing football.'

First came a few big drops that sent a steam of dust into the air and the sweet pungent smell of red mud. Then the torrential showers came down that would soon fill the wells to overflowing and create streams and ponds and jobs. And the street boys chanted: 'St Peter has finally turned the keys and opened the heavenly doors.'

The wells, filled to the brim, were dived into by the peasant boys to celebrate the water festival of São João. As this takes place in the month of June, the apocryphal story has it that the water symbolises the leaping of Jesus in the womb of Mary, when she is greeted by her cousin Elizabeth and she flowers into the beauty of the *magnificat*.

On the festival day, in the evening, young men and boys and Vishnu among them, appeared wearing crowns of flowers, while others wore foliage for headgear like Roman senators, all wet and already a bit drunk. Mama gave them several bottles of local liquor: the feni and a carafe of urrak. They set off singing boisterously: '*Viva, Viva, São João*.' Several jumped back into the well, half-drunk.

Paulo, Amanda and I went to the dance at the Clube Vasco da Gama in Panjim. The dance started at ten at night and finished at dawn. Johnson and His Jolly Boys were playing and Goans loved their homegrown band like they loved their rice and fish curry.

The high society girls sat in the veranda around the parquet-floor hall of the club that looked out onto the municipal garden, while the boys roamed around the hall or lined up at the bar for whisky sodas, or St Pauli Girl beer. Johnson usually played a flourish on his violin as a signal that the next dance was about to begin, which always set up a male stampede to ask a girl for a dance. The popular and the beautiful ones like Maria and Amanda, all in tailored dresses, were often booked in advance. Dr Lobo and I waited by the side door of the veranda to ask Amanda and Maria, respectively, for the next dance. For me, Calangute had been a failure; here was a second chance. Maria politely told me that she was booked for the next six. Dr Lobo on the other hand got lucky. He got to dance the first dance with Amanda, but no more.

Paulo, in his three-piece Parisian cashmere suit and Maria, in her long, pink, chiffon gown, danced the tango stunningly while I was relegated to watching them. Her mouth was open as she danced. I wondered if it was inviting Paulo's. Suddenly, she brushed Paulo's lips—I saw a passionate kiss. She was almost stuck to Paulo and he held her close dancing cheek to cheek. What a fool I was, fantasising about her, my pink rose: about kissing her full pink lips the shape of a heart and if lady luck smiled my way, holding onto them like a butterfly on a flower. At that moment, I had to relinquish the fantasy and come to terms with it. On the contrary, consumed with jealousy and terribly let down, I wished my brother had never returned from Portugal. In fact, I wished Mr White-Handsome dead. But after several whisky-sodas, I calmed down and admitted to myself that Paulo would always be the winning competitor. And why not? He was fairer!

Dejected, I waited my turn. I danced with the less attractive and more available girls. When the seventh dance came (I was counting), I approached Maria, but at the same time Arnaldo appeared, saying that she had promised him the dance. An argument ensued and we were about to come to blows, when Paulo came to my rescue. Taking charge of the situation, he told Arnaldo that it was my turn and he could have the dance after that. Paulo would forfeit his turn. Maria, who wanted to dance the next dance with Mr Handsome, was displeased. Reluctantly, she accepted the arrangement. During the dance, Maria did not cling to me like she did to Paulo.

I was stung as if pepper had been rubbed on a freshly opened wound. When the dance ended and Maria sped away without a word, I felt terribly rejected for the second time. I abruptly left the dance hall and walked all the way to the Miramar beach unable to shake away the image of Maria dancing cheek to cheek with Paulo. I stood on the beach at the water's edge and for the second time, contemplated the end. Isn't it our biological make-up to *fall in love* with the most acceptable, most compatible, the most beautiful or whatever other attributes we choose for ourselves and even with the least likely person, or the least compatible one, or even the least beautiful? She was the first girl I had feelings for and obviously, the feeling of pain, anger, jealously, irrationality I had never felt before accompanied the state of *being in love.* Was it her looks, her personality, her melodious voice that blinded me? I wouldn't give her up that easily; it wasn't in my character to cop out. As I was deeply in thought, unexpectedly, Father Ribeiro, a distant cousin, who was strolling on the beach and praying with a missal in his hand, approached and asked me what I was doing there so early in the morning.

'I am contemplating my sad and tragic life,' I said, rather thoughtlessly.

'What nonsense. You must be in love, my son. You have a bright future in front of you. Go now in peace, my son,' he said, putting his arm around me.

Embarrassed, I walked back contemplating what the priest had said. I stopped at Café Real for a potato bajji. Amanda, Paulo, Maria and some other friends were also there, as it was a favourite stop for breakfast after the dance ended at dawn.

'*Ó pá*, where the hell have you been?' said Paulo. 'We have been looking all over for you.'

'I took a walk. I couldn't take the stuffy atmosphere of Club Vasco anymore.'

I ignored Maria, hoping that she would notice.

In the taxi, Paulo asked me why I was sore. I did not answer.

'Is it Maria? Were you upset because I was dancing with her? Come on, Roberto, don't be a sissy. If you want her, go get her. She was coming on to me.'

'*Merda*,' I said. 'Coming on to you, you think you're Mr Handsome, Portugal-returned, Mr Handsome Prosecutor, Mr Handsome Judge? We are still waiting for your appointment.'

Paulo did not respond. I knew I had hurt my elder brother badly. Perhaps it was not Paulo's fault. Mr Handsome could have all the girls, whether he wanted them or not.

For many days and nights and in subsequent years that followed, the memory of that night would sometimes come to me, a memory of pain and wounded ego, as if from a distant dream, of Maria dancing cheek to cheek with Paulo.

Six

Tucaram's Crime and Punishment

When we arrived home late that morning, the house was in an uproar. Tulsi had been acting up, cursing Tucaram. Then, in a mad frenzy, she pulled the sobbing boy and tied him to the tamarind tree that stood by the side of the dirt path almost one hundred feet away from the gate of the house. Sugar water was sprinkled all over his naked body so that ants could crawl all over him to find their meal.

The big red ants had sensed their breakfast and were approaching in a long file. Seeing this red marching army, Tucaram wiggled his arms and legs and cried out loud. His teary snot-dripping, contorted face emitted screams that echoed through the coconut and tamarind trees. Unable to bear the boy's screams, Amanda shut the door of her room. She always took everything to heart—the blood churned in the ventricle. The pain of Tucaram felt like her own pain, knotting it in her gut. She had pleaded many times with Mama to do something about the harsh punishments Tulsi inflicted on the hapless boy, but Tulsi would always agree, only to do it all over again.

'Please, Mama, do something about it,' said Amanda. 'I can't bear to hear Tucaram's screams.'

'Yes, I agree. Let's stop this once and for all,' I said.

'I'm with you,' said Paulo.

Mama stormed out of the veranda and down the steps with

a long bamboo cane in her hand. Startled at seeing my mother charging angrily with cane upheld, Tulsi stepped back, tripped on a stone and fell to the ground. Rather surprised at Mama's sudden outburst, we ran down the steps. Mama brought the cane lashing down on Tulsi's arms. Tulsi begged Mama to stop.

'*Paim pottan, Batcani*—I fall at your feet, landlady,' she cried as her heaving breasts popped out of her choli. I tried restraining Mama and received a few accidental whacks in the bargain.

'This boy stole money from me and bought candy. He should have been dead when he was born,' Tulsi protested.

'Untie him and give him a bath,' Mama said.

'We have already complained to the authorities, Mama. I hope they take him away soon from this crazy woman and find him another home,' I said aloud, pointing at Tulsi.

Tucaram looked up, pleadingly at my mother. It had finally happened: a great and powerful entity, the imperial landlady—Isabella *Batcani* had come to his rescue. Amanda untied the boy and gave him a slice of sugared bread to eat. Tulsi looked at her disapprovingly but said nothing. Tucaram went running around in a circle, kicking in the air, as if at his shifting shadow. It was a ritual he assiduously performed after each beating.

I never felt so proud of my mother than on that day when she finally stood up for the boy. I wondered what kind of scars all this would leave on Tucaram's psyche. What memories would he retain? What passions, what ghosts, whose character would he act out? The ritualised horror of those punishments followed by nightly petting and cuddling haunted me, suffusing a sense of guilt for my own indifference. It was Amanda who had impressed upon us that we go to the authorities.

That night, encouraged by my mother's intervention on behalf of the boy, I went to Tulsi's hut to give her a piece of my mind. When I entered the hut, Tucaram was sucking on Tulsi's dried-up sugar-sprinkled breast, while Tulsi was petting and coconut oil massaging his lean naked body and singing a lullaby. Pushing the boy aside, Tulsi got off the mat and asked me to come in, but I walked away. As I was leaving, Tulsi remarked: 'See, Roberto baba, how much I love this boy of mine? He steals and you want to protect him? Then have him. Feed him. Keep him as your servant. He will end up being a criminal if I don't teach him a lesson.'

Amanda and I were more than ever determined to have him placed in a home for orphaned kids.

The next day, Paulo and I approached the police authorities with Mama's letter. The presence of Paulo carried a lot of weight with the Portuguese police who otherwise refrained from interfering in local family matters. The following week, Tucaram was taken away. Tulsi began screaming and cursing and begging Mama to intervene. But my mother would not come down the steps of the house to meet her. Tulsi would not speak to me and Amanda for some time.

Tucaram was taken to an orphanage in Panjim run by nuns, where he would learn to read and write. Before he left, like a bird let out of captivity, he came running to the house and, in gratitude, fell prostate and kissed Mama's and Amanda's feet.

Seven

Coimbra

The monsoon was well under way with its torrential downpours. The banana trees loudly flapped their wings. The drenched crows sat quietly atop mango trees. The servants slammed all the doors and windows of the house shut. The village turned into a greenhouse: lush, emerald-green grass like a wavy carpet floated on water in paddy fields. The mud roads were overrun with patches of soft red earth like mushy islands surrounded by pools of orange water that splashed on the sidewalks and passersby, as the twice-a-day bus made its rocking and rolling ride, prompting loud Konkani curses at the bus driver: *dukor... morh-re bebdo*—pig, drunkard, may you die!

Naked and half-naked children frantically searched for their glass marbles that had been swallowed by the gushing water in drains by the roadside. Others played football when the sun looked down, exposed by the parting clouds.

Life proclaimed itself in all its glory: shrill cries of mynahs, kingfishers and egrets, the deafening screeches of parrots, incessant mating calls of frogs, the constant *crrrrring* of crickets, bellowing of water buffaloes, the gushing sound of mountain water, the faint footsteps of peasants covered with raincoats made of coconut palm fronds like walking tents, the thuds of wooden clogs on wet paths of the faithful as they made their way to Sunday Mass. The days were boring and easygoing at our house. The night was rich with the steady sounds of the drumming rain on the Mangalore tiles, the thunderous clash of clouds, Czardas on the violin, Chopin and Rachmaninoff from the Bechstein piano and the Rosary said out loud. For the peasants, the days were busy, wet and rain-soggy with ploughing and sowing and weeding and transplanting of paddy in their landlords' paddy fields. In the dark and silent night, their drunken exhausted bodies slept deeply.

I left the village for Panjim to continue my medical studies and came home on weekends. Amanda landed a job in Margão, teaching English composition and history to the pre-matriculation class. It was a little more than three months that Paulo had returned. He was at home, anxiously awaiting his appointment as assistant attorney general. At least this is the impression he gave. At times he seemed nervous, particularly when Commandant Videira came for a visit. He often tried to engage Paulo in conversation, but Paulo was reluctant to be drawn out. His sudden and unexpected return to Goa had come as a surprise to all of us and, after the first excitement had worn off, Paulo seemed ill at ease. Papa was suspicious but unconcerned, while Mama was just happy to have her favourite son back.

Paulo had gradually changed since his arrival. His gregariousness was gradually fading, the spark in his eyes dimming and his swagger faltering. Often bored, he sometimes went to Panjim or to Anjuna beach, staying there for days with friends and cousins. He would be cheerful for a time when he arrived back from these trips, but gradually his nouveau-Portuguese accent and his clothes that were constant reminders of his Portugal-returned status were losing their novelty. He occasionally drank heavily, at which times, he became morose and detached. At other times, he regained his old flamboyance when he sang the praises of Coimbra, Lisbon and Paris and boasted of his four-and-a-half years in Portugal and his amorous conquests. He expressed a sentimental nostalgia for Portugal as though he had left a precious jewel there. The Coimbra Fado lingered on his lips. He often sang: '*Coimbra... tem mais encanto... na hora da despedida'*—Coimbra is more charming at the hour of farewell.

Although his return had been preceded by a telegram stating that he was to assume the position of assistant attorney general in Goa, more recently his story had changed somewhat; now there was a possibility he was going to be conscripted into the Portuguese army and sent to Angola.

Unlike Amanda and I, who had studied primary school in Portuguese, secondary school in English and had both attended college in Bombay, graduating with distinctions, Paulo had been an average student at the Portuguese lyceum, but endowed with the gift of the gab. He got through lyceum with distinctions as well, more so because of the small bribes of fresh snappers and cases of beer that Mama sent to his professors before the examinations. Not that he would have failed if not for the gifts. He was bright enough, but rarely opened the books until a few weeks before examinations. The scores he received, however, seventeen, eighteen, out of twenty, seemed otherwise out of his range.

These high scores would ultimately enable him to get into Coimbra, one of the oldest universities of Europe and the most prestigious of Portugal. There was another helping hand. The ex-governor's wife had a shop of antiques in Portugal and she often scouted the elite homes of Goa for antique Chinese porcelain. Being the governor's wife, she was offered whatever she liked for free in these homes, although she made a token gesture to pay. Mama and Papa were expecting her and Mama was prepared to seek a scholarship in exchange. So when the governor's wife arrived and was simply enchanted with an antique Chinese plate, Mama brought the issue to the surface. The white porcelain Chinese plate was of circular design and decorated with cobalt blue; it dated from the Ming dynasty, the Wanli period in the last quarter of the sixteenth century. Instead of the usual decorative Chinese elements, the plate carried the Coat of Arms of Matias de Albuquerque, Viceroy of

Portuguese India from 1591 to 1597. In the 1960s, our family was entirely ignorant of its worth.

'I will die of disappointment,' Mama said, 'if my son Paulo doesn't get a scholarship to go to Coimbra to study law. He is such an intelligent boy, so fervently enamoured with the fatherland. He wants to be a bastion of Portuguese law in Goa. I am making a novena to *Rainha* Santa Isabel, the patron saint of Coimbra, that my dream may come true.'

'Dona Isabella, I am sure that Santa Isabel will intercede on your son's behalf and your prayers will be answered,' said the governor's wife. And with the right hand and a smile, she accepted the Ming plate. She gestured in an attempt to open her black velvet purse.

'No, no, this is a gift to you from Santa Isabel,' Mama said, satisfied that the connection was made, a commitment given between man and God.

In Coimbra, Paulo had boarded at the residence of Dona Figueira in a neat and clean four-bedroom apartment in an old, somewhat run-down building situated near the university campus on *Rua dos Estudos*—a small, narrow, cobblestone street, midway between the high and the low levels of the university city. It was a colourful place with bookstores, cafés and students sauntering about with black capes with coloured ribbons of red, yellow, purple and orange that indicated their course of studies. Paulo hurriedly had his picture taken with a black cape and a red ribbon indicating that he was a law student. Mama was excited when she received this photograph, carrying it in her purse and proudly showing it to relatives and villagers.

About a year ago, when I was in Portugal as part of a troupe performing at a folklore music festival, I had spent time with Paulo in Coimbra. During my stay there, I got acquainted with Paulo's landlady Dona Figueira, her daughter Ana Sofia and many of his friends there, including Angelino de Tor. I got the impression that Paulo usually goofed around town, spending most of his evenings in coffee bars with an open book and a two-sip Portuguese espresso—a habit of the university students.

Paulo took me out for dinner with friends where he flashed Portuguese escudos like he was a Goan maharaja, telling tall tales about the voluptuous temple dancing girls and his hunting escapades on elephant back near Dudhsagar—the Sea of Milk waterfall in South Goa. It struck me that my brother had developed a large circle of friends who flocked to him for his money, looks, his wit, his tales, his singing and his melodious guitar. He played flamenco like a Spaniard gypsy and the Fado like a Portuguese virtuoso. It seemed for Paulo that the world was sweet and promising, ready to be tamed, controlled and toyed with. I was taken by surprise at my brother's lavish spending habits and wondered where this prerogative would lead.

During his first year in Coimbra, Paulo had frequently asked Mama for additional money in letters written elegantly and convincingly in Portuguese that she read at the dinner table. Later in the year, he had wired about his selection as captain of the debating team, requesting additional living expenses for travel to represent Coimbra University at the Sorbonne. A year or so later, he had written about the trips to Madrid, Vienna, Stockholm, and the need for more money. Mama coaxed Papa to open the coffers. He grudgingly agreed.

In his third year, Paulo wrote a long letter about his selection as a Fado singer in the Coimbra University band. With that came the summer tour to European cities. We were all thrilled, except for Papa who dismissed it with a shrug. Paulo requested a sum of twenty-five thousand rupees—a rather large sum in those days—most of which he owed to the gangster, Angelino de Tor. Papa flatly refused to send him the money despite Mama's tears and Tia Rosita's emotional pleas.

Mama pawned her jewellery set of platinum and gold studded with diamonds and rubies that she wore on her wedding day; it had belonged to her mother and her grandmother before that. She promptly sent the amount to Paulo. But in a terse letter she spelled it out to him, unambiguously, that there would be no extra money forthcoming.

Paulo could not give up his spending habits. He ate, drank, dressed in designer clothes and bought gifts on credit for his friends. He kept on borrowing money from Angelino de Tor, to pay off the debt. He met Angelino in the Algarve, through his brother Raul who was studying law. The brothers, sons of a Cabo Verdeano of Spanish descent, were like different grafts of the same tree. While Angelino wore flashy clothes, drank Johnny Walker Black and Sandeman Port, Raul was serious, studious and a shy type.

Paulo had taken an instant liking to the tall, rugged, testosterone-heady Angelino, whose sycophantic flattery was music to his ears. A few days later, while Paulo was sitting in the café by himself, Angelino joined him and took care of the tab. He was often in the company of an Angolan, who he referred to as *Angolano*. The tall muscular Angolan was soft spoken and showed a great deal of deference towards Angelino and acted as if he were his bodyguard.

Angelino had an import-export business and offered to loan money to Paulo. After a few drinks, he often boasted that he was a long-lost descendant of the Spanish Inquisitor, Tomás de Torquemada, which caused much fear and trepidation in the local circles and earned him the nickname of Angelino de Tor. They often met in bars and in a bordello in which Angelino had a stake and where Paulo usually collected his loans. The bordello was located behind the House of Fados where I heard Paulo sing the last night of my stay in Coimbra. Many of the preferred customers at the Fado House, including dignitaries and military officers, also frequented the bordello.

Late one night, after the singing and dining at the Fado House had nearly ended at almost three in the morning, Paulo and I knocked on the door of the bordello. An older woman, the madam, opened the door. She said that the place was closed for business, but when Paulo mentioned Angelino's name, she asked us to come in for a drink. The bordello was a single-story house, hardly visible from the roadside, with a large oppressive sitting room, dimly lit, with heavily carved mahogany furniture and a piano bar. Across the bar, seated, were half-asleep women in pink and red gowns, a few Portuguese, mostly mulattoes. The Portuguese women were short and heavy set, while the mulattoes were tall, with slim upper torsos and protruding behinds, the female physique the military officers liked.

Behind the gowns, the heavy make-up, the rouge on the fleshy cheekbones and painted eyelids, most of them seemed to be professional women, anxious to please, inciting the desires and fetishes of men. Angelino introduced three of the girls still working to the last customer, whispering each one's specialties as if he were a butcher selling his wares at the market place.

The last customer that night, a naval officer decked in white, took the chosen mulatto woman, walking hand in hand, like a married couple, over red-carpeted circular stairs to one of the upstairs rooms. Subsequently, Angelino, who had his arms around a dreamy, well-endowed mulatto, approached Paulo and handed over a thick envelope.

'Do you guys want to have some fun?' he asked Paulo.

Paulo looked at me. 'Go ahead, my brother,' said Paulo.

I hesitated, embarrassed and at the same time somewhat excited.

'Well, you take the young white one and I'll take the mulatto woman,' he said.

'Take good care of my brother, Branca, it's his first time,' said Paulo and they all laughed. I looked away.

Angelino asked one of the girls to serve us drinks. After stiff shots of whisky on the rocks, we went with the women to their respective rooms. The night was late and with all the excitement of my first sexual adventure, I prematurely finished the act like a quick first swallow of a glass of whisky. It was four o'clock and I was due to leave Coimbra at eight that morning, so we promptly took our leave after Paulo handed some notes he took out from the very envelope that was handed to him by Angelino.

'So how did it go, my brother?' asked Paulo.

'*Porra pa, que foda*—what a fuck,' I said. I simply couldn't confess my inadequate performance.

'The mullato woman—what an ass!' said Paulo.

In the few hours left before daybreak, I couldn't fall asleep. I tossed and turned recollecting the room, its shifting materiality: the damp darkness in there, the soiled bed, the female whiteness exposed by the bedside lamp, the closeness, the smell and feel of naked flesh—these things of a debauched world I had never experienced before. It all seemed so fast and mechanical and yet it carried with it a sordid pleasure. Somehow, I felt empty.

As I sat on the train to Lisbon, the events of the previous night kept repeating in my head like the replay of a movie. I was apprehensive about my brother's friend, Angelino de Tor. I had the distinct impression that he was a shady character, a much-feared gangster with connections. His boasting of his descent from the Spanish Inquisitor, Torquemada, to throw his weight around, befuddled me. No doubt, the image of the bordello with its strange singularity encrypted a sense of forbidden excitement and seductiveness and yet the place also brought on a certain anxiety. I wondered why my brother kept such company and regretted my restrain from expressing my fears to Paulo before I left. Perhaps, it was Paulo's instinct to flirt with danger. Much later, when in Goa, Paulo had mentioned that once one was heavily in debt to a moneylender, it was difficult to break the shackles. 'It's worse than gambling,' he said.

Dona Figueira, who was flattered for her looks and her cooking, was very fond of Paulo. He on the other hand, was spoiled by the many servants in Goa and was messy with his things there. His room was littered with dirty socks and underwear that he was in the habit of shoving under his bed, empty wine bottles stuffed with cigarette butts, opened law books, works of Guy de Maupassant and Bocage and girlie magazines. Dona Figueira did his laundry and meticulously cleaned up his mess, absorbing its materiality and seduced by its decadence.

After Paulo's return to Goa, one day, I questioned him about Dona Figueira. He told me that his relationship with her unraveled after his involvement with her daughter, Ana Sofia, who also had a crush on Paulo, even in her youth, but he treated her as a spoiled brat, often playfully spanking her behind. As she grew up, she rapidly bloomed into a pretty young adolescent with an oval face, a dimple on her chin, a beauty spot on the right side of her cheek close to the lower lip and almond-shaped blue eyes. She often went to Paulo's room with a question or two about her study of geography and literature at the lyceum. At times, she felt intensely jealous when she found her mother in his room, sitting at the edge of the bed, chatting, smoking and laughing away. Needless to say, Paulo enjoyed and thrived on all this female attention: it was like meat and drink to him.

Much attracted to the grown-up Ana, Paulo fantasised about her, but did not show his intentions. But one evening, a few months before he left Coimbra, when she was reciting to him, with gestures, the Canto Primeiro, Verse III of the epic *The Lusiadas* by the Portuguese bard Luís de Camões, she recited:

That I may sing of the illustrious Lusitanian breast
To whom Neptune and Mars obeyed,
Let all end what the old Muse sang,
Another valour, higher, shall rise to mend.

He interjected: 'I cry every night, longing for your Lusitanian breast,' and impulsively buried his face between her breasts. Like an infant's mother, she let him be there; and he, like a lustful boy, fondled her ample breasts. I laughed hilariously at this seduction. It was typical of my brother; only he could conjure up such grand drama—a bohemian quality flowed in his veins influenced by the life and verse of the neoclassical lyric Portuguese poet, Manuel Maria Barbosa du Bocage. How I wished I had some of his seductive qualities. I was too stiff. It was always hard for me to break the ice with a girl. I had miserably failed with Maria while my brother had succeeded without any effort.

Paulo told me that initially, he had moved cautiously, handling Ana like fine crystal, but gradually, as his desires increased, he sought more. A few months later, all of a sudden, she stopped coming to his room. Overnight, she had changed from a pretty young girl into a beautiful, aloof woman. There were other boys now calling on her.

'I was consumed with jealousy after noticing the attention she received when she took a seductive stroll down the roadside, like an indolent cat,' Paulo said. He couldn't fully understand his feelings. He wondered whether he was behaving like a brother protecting his younger sister, or whether he was falling in love with her. Afraid that one of the boys would take advantage of her, he often picked fights with them, scolded them for their bad manners, threatened them and ordered them to stay away from her. It seems Ana Sofia read into his anxiety and secretly enjoyed it.

One day, her mother asked her why she was ignoring all the attention, the gifts that Paulo bestowed. 'After all,' she said, 'it would be a wonderful idea to have Paulo, the Goan maharaja, as my son-in-law.' That same evening, on the doorstep of the Fado House, Ana Sofia had seen a woman talking to Paulo in a coquettish, provocative way, as if they were intimate with each other. She was consumed with jealousy. She answered her mother out loud, angrily, intending Paulo to hear. 'The Goan maharaja doesn't impress me like he does his cheap women friends with his gifts and his singing. I will fall in love with a poor boy and I will make him a prince.'

Paulo heard the conversation from his room. On impulse he cried out in a shrill giggling voice. 'Are you going to fall in love with a frog and turn him into a prince, Princess Ana Sofia? And what about me? Will you turn me into a pauper—a pauper prince—a prince of paupers?'

Stung by his sarcasm, she stormed into his room. 'You big show-off. I know how you spend your evenings. You and your friends visit those women over there in the *baixa*, women of ill repute. And with those same hands and the same mouth you seduce me. *Peito Lusitano!* I will tell on you to my Mama and I will write to my Papa and you'll see when he returns from Macau, he will kill you.'

Paulo fell on his knees and Ana Sofia held his face to her bosom—her *peito Lusitano.*

Her mother hearing the commotion, stormed into his room and pulled Ana Sofia away and forbade her from ever going to his room.

That night, Dona Figueira threatened to throw Paulo out of the house if he continued his ways, warning him that she wouldn't permit any out-of-wedlock involvement with her daughter. He had promised her that he would draw the line and that he wouldn't have Ana Sofia in his room any longer. It was clear to me that Dona Figueira had more than a fondness for Paulo; was well aware of his Casanova charm and yet, was bent on seeing her daughter married to him for status and money.

'After that, we would meet in secret,' Paulo said. 'And then, one day, the day before I left Coimbra, I took her to the top—the Alta of the Coimbra University with a commanding view of the two thousand-year-old city.'

They walked around the campus holding hands and before the tolling of the bells, they ascended the tower of the university. There, Ana Sofia leaned seductively against the wall of the pillar, as if inviting Paulo to come to her. He had stepped towards her, pressing his body against hers. They kissed hungrily. He wanted her more than ever. Urgently. They sank to the floor of the tower effortlessly and there they made love. Hurriedly. And yet it seemed so very natural to them as though they had done it before. In dreams.

'Wow—you are the reincarnation of Casanova de Seingalt,' I said.

'I was truly in love with her,' said Paulo.

Subsequently, Paulo and Ana Sofia entered the Chapel of São Miguel with its gold and azure blue walls and, in front of the statue of Santa Catarina, they prayed. She was seeking forgiveness for the lovemaking. He prayed for a new beginning. He told her he wanted to make a life in Portugal, perhaps Lisbon and maybe even Coimbra. He liked big things like New York and Chicago, Broadway and Hollywood, big pink Chevys and the California surf. One day he would like to go to America and strike it rich like James Dean in the movie *Giant*. He promised her that he would finish law and start practice, or perhaps he would become a writer one day, like Bocage. He told her that he was a restless, adventurous young man.

She talked to him about her father, that she had last seen him when she was twelve and that she remembered him as a rugged handsome man. 'He would sit me in his lap and tell me wild stories of hunting animals in the African bush.' She believed that her father was in Macau and that he had been to Goa during his tour of duty in the military a long time ago before he met her mother. 'Sometimes you remind me of my father… the nose…

the smile... mother says so too,' she had said. He asked her if she had his pictures. She told him that her mother had put them away.

After a long silence, dropping the sentence like a stone in a pond, she told him that her mother liked him. And then she looked at his face, scanning it for an expression to confirm or deny her suspicion. He nodded, unemotionally, allaying her fears. She told him that she loved him and that she was thrilled he would stay in Portugal and not return to Goa for good, as most Goan men did after completing their studies in Portugal. As for America and the things he mentioned, they seemed strange and distant to her. Besides, she wanted to finish high school and become a teacher.

'We talked of marriage, of children and we began making plans like all lovers do when they enter fantasyland,' Paulo said. 'There was a quality of excitement: a sense of running, breathlessly, towards tomorrow.'

'What happened then? Why did you come back to Goa, so suddenly, so unexpectedly?' I asked.

'It's late—let's go to sleep,' said Paulo. There was a tremor in his voice and a sudden fear was written all over his face as if he had seen a ghost in the semi-darkness of the moonlit night. I fell asleep that night wondering what Paulo was hiding.

Eight

Confession on a Harvest Night

September, the harvest month, was upon the Goa villages. The monsoon ended abruptly, as suddenly as it had begun. The sun appeared in a cloudless, glassy blue sky after many weeks behind a curtain of dense-dark monsoon clouds, turning the paddy fields from green to a wavy, glittering, golden yellow. The rice plantings were cut by peasant women, Tulsi among them, with their sharp sickles, then placed around a sunken pole and later trampled upon, repeatedly. Large mounds of golden hay collected on paddy fields where buffaloes and cows grazed and children played. The air was dusty with particles of red mud and speckles of hay.

One September night, Paulo woke up from a nightmare screaming with fear. I woke up startled and ran into his room. He was shouting and tearing at his arms and legs. I shook him from his nightmare. He woke up panting and told me that it was a restless spirit who had encircled and tightened like a noose around his neck. He got off the bed all drenched in sweat and began looking for the bottle of whisky he had hidden under the mattress. I asked him what happened. He took a long draught of the whisky, but seemed reluctant to speak. I asked him again and assured him of my trustworthiness.

'Promise me you'll keep it a secret,' said Paulo.

'I promise,' I said. I could sense that my brother had calmed down and wanted to get it all out. Whatever it was, it had been bottled up for too long a time.

'You remember the story I told you about making out with Ana Sofia at the Alta of the Coimbra University?' asked Paulo, as he lit a cigarette.

'Sure, how could I forget?'

'Well, we returned home separately. I was lying on the bed smoking a cigarette, when Dona Figueira entered my room and told me that a man had come to see me, who gave his name as Angolano. She handed me a note from Angelino requesting that I come and see him urgently.' Paulo's face twisted with apprehension.

Apparently, Angelino had sent word to Paulo several times before that he expected repayment of his loans, which Paulo had ignored. This note had an ominous tone to it; besides it was delivered by the Angolan whose very presence was intimidating to Paulo. A couple of months back, there had been a police raid and the bordello had been shut down. Angelino was arrested and subsequently released and was now in dire financial straits.

The next day, the big Angolan with the hawkish face had come to fetch Paulo, who nervously chain-smoked in the back seat of the taxi as it sped down the narrow cobblestone streets to the Praça Velha. They got out of the taxi and walked up the steps of an old apartment building. On arrival, the tall, imposing figure of Angelino was waiting in a red silk robe with flowery designs and dragons puffing smoke. His big tanned balls hung like de-husked coconuts as he sat on the divan, the blue veins shining in the light as if they were oiled.

'*Ó pá*, my friend, I have been waiting for you since yesterday. *Ó pá*, relax, come have a drink,' Angelino said.

'I have ten contos with me. Take it,' said Paulo, who had borrowed the money from Dona Figueira, as he took out his wallet. 'I promise, I'll pay you back on a monthly basis from now on—two hundred escudos a month—will that do?'

'*Ó pá*, relax, we will talk of money later. *Ó pá*, let's have a good time.'

Paulo felt reassured. He went to the bathroom, walked back and sat on the divan. Angelino, who was drinking whisky straight up, offered him a peg and sat by his side. Paulo gulped down the whisky and Angelino refilled his glass. Paulo quickly gulped that down too and Angelino refilled it again. He asked for some soda and as Angelino was pouring it, he accidentally tipped the glass so that it drenched Paulo's pants. He suggested that he remove the pants and handed him a pink robe with flowers but no dragons. 'I will have the pants washed as soon as the maid comes. She should be here soon,' he said.

He moved close to Paulo putting his arms around him, emitting zephyrs of alcohol and a musky carnal odor. He kissed him on the mouth. Paulo immediately stiffened. Angelino's grip tightened. Then he nudged his arm, holding Paulo's hand and placed it on his crotch. Paulo pulled his hand away.

'At that moment, I didn't know what was going on. My mind was clouded by the alcohol I had rapidly gulped down,' Paulo said. 'I tried to get up, but slipped and fell back on the divan. Angelino turned me around and using his muscular frame he pinned me down. As I tried to struggle, he entered me. Forcefully.'

'What?' I said, flabbergasted. I remembered that night in the bordello, the dark energy in there.

'I screamed,' Paulo continued. 'In one final surge I mustered all my strength, managed to turn and pushed Angelino off my back. I was on my feet, propelled by an adrenaline rush, a dash for survival. Angelino went to grab me again but he tripped and fell. I kicked him hard in the crotch. He doubled up in pain. As he tried to get up, I took a heavy metal lamp that was on the side table beside the divan and brought it crashing down on his head. He fell on the floor. His eyes rolled up. He began convulsing and frothing at the mouth. Then he went limp,' said Paulo, as he took another sip from the whisky bottle and lit another cigarette.

I couldn't believe it—had my brother killed Angelino?

Paulo continued his story: He had been frozen, staring at the limp body until he thought he heard the sound of footsteps. Thinking it was the Angolan, he ran to the bathroom, dressed quickly and ran out through the backstairs. He kept on running till he reached Dona Figueira's home. There, as he packed his bags, he panicked as he remembered the image of Angelino's body lying as lifeless as the dead Goliath. He thought he heard a knock. He hurriedly wrote a note on a piece of paper addressed to Dona Figueira that he had to urgently leave for Goa because his father had a massive heart attack and he had to take the next flight that only operated once a week. He opened the liquor cabinet, took several gulps from a bottle of bagaço, slipped out through the back door and ran down the backstairs onto the street to the train station. Without a thought, he took the train to Lisbon. On the train, the image of Angelino drew closer, settling in, choking him like some fearful monster. He began hyperventilating and momentarily passed out. When he came to, he wondered where he was, as he heard the sound of the train engine, the rattling of the compartment as the train rounded a bend. A female passenger had asked him if he was all right, if he wanted some water to drink, or some eau de cologne. It was then that he felt a sense of relief come over him as he realised that the train was speeding away from Coimbra, from the body of Angelino.

'I wondered whether I did the right thing by running away—the thought briefly crossed my mind,' said Paulo. 'Then I saw the image of Angelino on the floor and fear again crept into me and began circling around like a dense cloud of smoke. I started retching and rubbing my eyes, as if to erase the image. I asked the female passenger for the bottle of eau de cologne that I held to my nose and the retching eased. I fell asleep.'

'I killed a man, Roberto! Now you know why I ran away.'

Paulo banged his head and his clenched fists on the wall. I instinctively hugged my brother, something I hadn't done for a long time. All the jealousy, the colour complex I had felt in the past, dissolved in an instant. And yet, all that I had heard, so descriptively, so many wrongs, so much that wasn't right and so much that was strange: a jumble of weakness and lust, flamboyance and cowardice, that its impact on my mind was a blur of colours, a palimpsest of dark images that left me numbed and jaded. My head spun looking at the tragic figure of my brother.

As I lay on the bed thinking, unable to sleep the few hours left until the dawn would appear, I remembered what Senhor Pissurlenkar, the village historian, had once related: 'Four centuries ago, the Inquisition had raped Goa,' he said, 'destroying its Hindu temples, harassing and even slaughtering some of the New Christians—Jews, Muslims, Hindus and among them perhaps some of my own and your ancestors.'

'How could it all have happened?' I asked, dismayed.

'That was history. Medieval history! Sordid history!'

I wondered how, centuries later, my brother in the very throes of cruel destiny had been raped by a man claiming descendancy to the Spanish Inquisitor. When I had met this Angelino de Tor in Coimbra, I knew that my brother was toying with fire with red-hot shifting eyes. But he had stood his ground and slain the demon. However, he should have gone to the police rather than run away. The poor man was suffering the consequences of his heedless actions.

Nine

War Drums

'Roberto, I have seen them… they look like devils from Dante's inferno,' said Belarmino, a Portuguese sergeant, a friend of mine, with panic in his eyes and a sense of urgency in his voice. He had just returned to Panjim after a two-night vigil at the frontier.

It was December, 1961—the Indian Army had surrounded Goa. The haughty Portuguese soldiers, seeing the Sikh division on the Indian side of the frontier, realised for the first time that the Indian Army was no bunch of satyagrahis. For the Portuguese soldiers, however, Goa was an old relic, a mausoleum of a magnificent epoch in the history of Portugal, where remained interred the visions of Prince Henry the Navigator, Vasco da Gama, Afonso de Albuquerque, Luís de Camões and Francis Xavier, whose entombed venerated body rested in Old Goa.

For the Fatherland and for Mother Church, the Portuguese soldiers would defend Goa to the death.

Nearly a month ago, at my parents' earlier than expected twenty-fifth wedding anniversary celebration attended by Goan and Portuguese dignitaries, my father had discussed the possible outcome of the status of Goa with Senhor Mendes, a high level Portuguese government official. He had expressed concern that India might attack soon. Senhor Mendes pointed out in no uncertain terms that Goans did not want to be a part of India. 'Nehru,' he said at the top of his voice, 'distorts history. The Indian propaganda is a lie. Goa is no colony! Goans are Portuguese citizens and have the same rights as any Portuguese.'

My father argued that the idea of independence from Portugal went back much before Nehru or Gandhi, as far back as 1787 in the 'Pinto Revolt'. Mama was frantically pulling on Papa's jacket and making eyes at him to stop it. She was anxiously waiting to ask Senhor Mendes for a position for Paulo.

Senhor Mendes raised a toast: '*Viva Salazar, Viva Portugal, Viva India Portuguesa!*'

The hall resounded with a '*Viva, Viva, Viva!*'

There were more than two hundred people for the party including a secretary general and the chief justice of the Military Tribunal, the highest positions any Goan had attained during the Portuguese colonial regime in those times. After all the speeches, much gossip and laughter, they all enjoyed the moment, the lavish Goan buffet. Most never realised, or, if they had a hint of it, they were in denial that their world was about to collapse. There were many reasons for this thinking: Nehru's pacifism, Salazar's intransigence and Portugal's membership of NATO, convinced them that India would never attack militarily and things would stay the same as they had for 451 years.

Immediately after the buffet, my mother approached Senhor Mendes and Chief Justice Couto of the Military Tribunal about a position for Paulo.

'It will be my pleasure, Dona Isabella, to appoint your son as an assistant prosecutor. Please ask your son to make an appointment to see me as soon as possible,' said Justice Couto.

When we were tuning our musical instruments for the musical soirée that evening, Mama came all ecstatic to give the good news to Paulo.

It had finally happened: Paulo had landed a prosecutor's job. He enthusiastically sang Coimbra Fados and Malagueña at the party that evening with resounding bravos. I felt somewhat reassured, but on second thoughts I wasn't sure how Paulo would deal with the dark and gloomy incidents that occurred in Coimbra.

Soon thereafter, Indian troops were spotted on the frontier. Fearing a massive military invasion, the government in collaboration with the Catholic Church organised a pilgrimage to the tomb of St Francis Xavier to pray for the safety of Goa.

People in the thousands, Catholics and Hindus, priests and nuns, took part in the pilgrimage. Our family lined up at dawn, on the whitewashed zigzagging steps of the Church of Our Lady of the Immaculate Conception in Panjim. The governor general had invited all the Portugal returnees to accompany him. Amanda, who was initially with the family, excused herself and went her own way.

Paulo was somewhat reluctant to go on the pilgrimage. After the events that transpired in Coimbra that resulted in his abrupt return, he was nervous and anxious in the company of Portuguese officials. Papa's facial expression revealed some suspicion of Paulo's intentions, but he did not express it in words. He had written one letter to Ana Sofia tangentially referring to Angelino, asking whether his brother Raul had come to inquire about his whereabouts. Ana Sofia had written back saying she anxiously awaited his return. He was surprised that she had not mentioned Angelino or Raul in the letter. If the invasion of Goa by India materialised, all contact would be lost with Portugal, no letters would be forthcoming, which meant no news of Angelino. And no news was good news. He almost wished for the invasion, but what then? He felt insecure about the future. The recently offered prosecutorial job would evaporate as well. Either way he could end up being the loser.

'You cannot refuse the governor's invitation,' said Mama. And Paulo had finally agreed to go on the pilgrimage.

The procession went all the way from Panjim along a mile-long causeway with the scenic Mandovi river to the left, salt pans on the right, followed by the emerald green of the paddy fields and shady groves of palm trees, past the village of Ribandar. While some sang religious hymns, others said the rosary led by a group of nuns. Once they passed the village of Ribandar, the ruined towers and baroque pinnacles of the churches of Old Goa appeared in the distance.

The Portuguese governor, dressed in his white military uniform, looked tired as he entered the Basilica. He stared at the immense statue of Ignatius Loyola, as if seeking inspiration. The richly sculpted reredos of gold leaf glowed in the light as if a miracle were about to happen. The governor accompanied by Portuguese and Goan dignitaries made their way to the tomb of St Francis Xavier. Paulo and I, in the company of our father and mother, amid judges, lawyers and some returnees from Portugal, followed behind.

We approached the elaborate tomb, a gift of Cosimo III, the Grand Duke of Tuscany, composed of tiers of sarcophagi in alabaster and Florentine marble. Perched above it lay the gem-studded silver coffin of St Francis Xavier.

The governor took out his key and unlocked the coffin for his personal viewing. On 14 December, the Portuguese dictator, Salazar, had sent an express message to the governor general ordering the Portuguese forces to fight till the last man. He was also ordered to mine and raze to the ground all the bridges and government buildings should the Indian invasion of Goa begin. A man of profound humanity, who embodied the goodness of the Portuguese soul, the governor was unsure whether to carry out Salazar's order. He knelt in front of the coffin and prayed. Then he suddenly rose—as if he had heard a voice—a command—and placed his baton in the tomb. With this symbolic noble gesture, he entrusted the fate of Goa to the saint from the Basque Country. Subsequently, he rescinded the order to detonate the mines should the Indian invasion begin.

After the concelebrated Mass said by the archbishop and the lengthy procession that went around the St Augustine Church, I, together with some of my friends, including Maria, went on a small walk towards the river. Amanda was not around, neither was Paulo. I had seen Amanda briefly outside the basilica with a colleague of hers. I had waved but she hadn't noticed. I wanted to take a look at the man. A friend of mine had seen them earlier, holding hands and strolling on the Colva beach.

As we approached the Arch of the Viceroys through which the Portuguese rulers had ceremonially entered the City of Old Goa in the sixteenth century, I felt a pull on my shirtsleeve and a voice: 'Roberto, *baba*!' I turned around. It was Tucaram in white pants, white shirt and a red tie, all smiles in the company of nuns. We were happy to see each other. We talked for a while. Tucaram inquired about my brethren and my mother but did not mention Tulsi.

Old Goa, besides its historical and serene quality, held fond memories for me. During my childhood, our family went by sailboat for a yearly pilgrimage to the tomb of St Francis Xavier, during the feast of the saint. We stayed as much as a week in the convent, near the basilica, where Paulo, Amanda and I freely roamed the stalls of sweetmeats with our cousins who were also our age, playing hide-and-seek amid the cathedral walls.

As we continued past the arch, I looked up towards the sculpted figure of Argonaut, holding a Bible and with one foot on the neck of a recumbent native. It was an imposing monument to the subjugative power of the biblical God over the native infidel. Many years ago, my father had explained the significance of this monument to me. 'My son,' he had said, 'civilisation is a rather complex undertaking when it is imposed on another culture by the force of arms; and here, in the name of religion, its architecture was once a chimera fed on blood and tears of the Muslim and our Hindu ancestors.'

I pointed out the sculpture to Maria who seemed somewhat surprised, as if she had heard for the first time about the conversion of our Hindu ancestors. I explained to her that after colonisation many Goans lost much of their Hindu heritage. Also gone were their political freedoms and gradually over time, they ended up absorbing the culture of the colonisers. Our ancestors were convinced by persuasion or perhaps by force of the superiority of the White man—their culture, their religion and their language. I could sense that Maria was not pleased at what she was hearing.

'I should add however,' I continued, 'that when the Portuguese conquered Goa, we were under Muslim rule and it was a Hindu ruler, Timoja, who helped Afonso de Albuquerque to reconquer Goa from the Muslims. In this regard, I would like to say that I don't regret my Christianity or my Indo-Portuguese culture; as a matter of fact, I'm proud of it. However, geographically, it is absurd to claim that Goa is a part of Portugal, like the Portuguese would have you believe. We are part of the Indian subcontinent.'

Maria didn't respond. I could sense that she was uncomfortable with my political views. I also noticed that she had changed somewhat: she was less playful, more mature and introspective than the Maria I had known on the beach in Calangute.

We sat on the riverside, drinking beer and munching on samosas. After a while, I asked Maria if she wanted to go for a walk. She agreed. We entered a coconut grove and sat in a shady spot when Maria, placing her arm on my shoulders, said rather pensively: 'I have faith in St Francis Xavier. He will protect our Goa.' I shook my head not knowing what to say and squeezed her hand to reassure her. She reciprocated. These gestures of Maria's: going for a walk with me, sitting by me, placing her arm around me, responding to me with a squeeze, kept my heart racing. At that moment I could see it in her eyes, in the blush on her face, that she was attracted to me. Was I over-reading her gestures? Anyway, it gave me a sense of renewed hope. And yet, doubts lingered in my mind. I suddenly remembered that evening in Calangute when she and Paulo had disappeared behind the sand dunes. I was overtaken by the urge to ask her what had transpired. To my surprise and relief, she told me that nothing had happened between them and that she was only lending Paulo some money, which he had promptly repaid. I was astonished that Paulo would borrow money from her and at the same time, I was so delighted that I promptly hugged and kissed her on the cheeks.

As the crowd left to go back to Panjim, everyone was euphoric. The pilgrimage had allayed our anxieties, at least for now.

More things are wrought by prayer than this world dreams of.

For now, Goa seemed to be in the capable hands of St Francis Xavier.

On 18 December 1961, at about six in the morning, I heard loud roaring noises and sonic booms. I ran to the veranda of the boarding house on Corte de Outeiro, on the southern outskirts of the capital city of Panjim with a commanding view of Santa Cruz and Bambolim hill on the right and the paddy field below. I saw a fighter jet dive steeply and then heard the sound of an explosion. Seeing fire and smoke in the hills where the radio relay station was located, I shouted at the top of my voice: 'They bombed the radio tower.'

The invasion, code named *Operation Vijay*, had begun.

I ran down and put on the radio. Radio Goa was off the air. I kept turning the dial frantically until I caught on to BBC. *Blue Moon*, one of my favourite songs, was playing. The song was interrupted for an announcement:

'This is the British Broadcasting Corporation. Today at 4 a.m. Indian Standard Time, the Indian Army, Navy and Air Force, began the invasion of the Portuguese enclave of Goa. The Portuguese representative at the United Nations has urgently asked for an emergency meeting of the Security Council and an immediate ceasefire.'

Fear and expectation reigned in the boarding house, but my face revealed a thinly veiled excitement.

'Didn't I say they would attack?' I said to one of the boarders.

'Well, it's not over as yet,' she angrily shot back, choking and in tears. 'There is NATO and there is America and they are allies of Portugal.'

By next evening, BBC announced that Goa had fallen without bloodshed; the Portuguese troops had surrendered without a fight. Only the aging Portuguese frigate, the *NRP Afonso de Albuquerque*, which had provided some resistance, was now crippled by the guns from the destroyers *INS Betwa* and *INS Beas*. At that moment, the mood in the boarding house plummeted as they heard of the defeat of the frigate that carried the name of the mighty Afonso de Albuquerque, the *King of Peppercorns*, who once had defeated the elusive king of the Deccan, Yusuf Adil Shah—the *Sabayo*, as the Portuguese called him then.

I decided to leave Panjim and rejoin my family in the village. As I passed Maria's house, I looked up at the window to catch a glimpse of her, but the windows were all shut. I couldn't get her off my mind since that day in Old Goa when she sat by my side. I suspected that she with her family had left the city for the safety of their village.

Back in Loutolim, information was scant and rumours mushroomed. Commandant Videira and his contingent of police officers and a small battalion of Portuguese troops had left for the frontier a few days before the invasion. He had come to the Albuquerque house to wish the family goodbye. The parting was very emotional, particularly for my mother and Tia Rosita, who refused to accept the inevitable.

When I arrived home, I found my father, Paulo, Mr Fernandes, Senhor Tavares, Senhor Pissurlencar, Senhor Gomes, Senhor Miranda and Senhor Palmeira, all local landlords and Father Monteiro seated in the balcony arguing the possible outcome of the invasion.

My father and Senhor Pissurlencar, both strong believers in Nehru's pacifism, felt confident there would be no massacre of the local population. Together, they had calmed the fears of the villagers and other landlords.

Being outnumbered and outgunned, all were sure the Portuguese would be defeated but not without a fight; yet, nobody had any idea how long the fight would last and at what cost. Some landlords expected the intervention of a European power or the United States of America. Paulo seemed certain that any military intervention would be followed by a ceasefire and the battle would be waged in the United Nations Security Council.

'This is not liberation. It is neo-colonialism!' Paulo loudly protested.

I disagreed that NATO powers would intervene. 'India is the world's biggest democracy,' I said, 'and America and England will side with India or profess neutrality. Besides, Portugal has no moral claim to Goa after England had gotten out of India.'

'The world has changed, my friends, the world has changed,' said Senhor Pissurlencar.

Suddenly, Tia Rosita, who was leading a prayer vigil in the church, came running, all excited. 'It has happened—I knew it—it's a miracle of St Francis Xavier. The Americans have given an ultimatum. American fighter planes are on their way from Diego Garcia to attack Indian positions. They say that the aircraft carrier *Vikrant* is already out of commission.'

Father Monteiro knelt down with his rosary in his hand and began praying.

'May God be blessed!'

'Where did you hear this news, Tia Rosita?' I asked.

'It was Peter—the *Bombaywala*. He just returned in a taxi from Margão.'

'I returned from Panjim. It's all over, Tia.' When she mentioned the *Bombaywala*, we all shook our heads. 'Forget it! The man's a liar and a drunkard. Did you sniff his breath?' I asked. Tia Rosita was ready to believe anything that went against the takeover.

Within forty-eight hours of the start of the invasion, the outcome was clear. Goa had fallen without resistance. There was neither NATO intervention nor any reinforcements from Portugal. Adlai Stevenson, the US representative to the UN, criticised the Indian military action and submitted a draft resolution calling for a ceasefire and withdrawal of all Indian forces from Goa and resumption of negotiations. The resolution was co-sponsored by France, the UK and Turkey, but the USSR, India's long-term Cold War ally, exercised its veto.

It was a historic happening; an invisible wall had melted away. A limb long torn apart was suddenly reattached. At last, Goa was part of Mother India.

Many were euphoric: liberation, democracy, self-government and an end to the last vestiges of colonialism on the Indian-subcontinent. There were those who did not know what to make of it all. Others were devastated. 'Goa will lose its identity,' they claimed. 'Hindus or Catholics, we are different,' some said.

And for a few—the last and only hope: a miracle—the re-return of the Portuguese, the Peppercorn Men.

So it was that much had changed in a couple of days; and what seemed to be a permanent condition for centuries was now extinct and riveted with uncertainty. And yet, as in the Indian-subcontinent, things never actually change.

The day after the Portuguese surrendered, most of the members of my family fell into depression. Paulo got drunk. Tia Rosita, rabidly anti-India, was in a state of shock and had to be continuously fanned by Tulsi, ayah Carmina and Mari, in turns. Amanda insisted on going to her school in Margão to catch up with some work. Overdressed and in a hurry as she was, Paulo and I guessed she had a rendezvous at the Colva beach with her colleague, Winnie, with whom we suspected she was having an affair.

Mama played the piano, thinking that Rachmaninoff or Chopin would make her forget the day. She played Rachmaninoff's variations and the waltzes, Mazurkas and Chopin Ballades with intense emotion. When Mama played the piano, the notes fell like drops of soft water flowing over tiny pebbles; like tears that found a vein to her longing heart. It was as if, for her, music was the link to important life events and, like old photographs, it rekindled cherished memories. Besides, for our family, the music of Chopin was always nostalgic. However, this time, the magic failed to work and Mama continued morose. She took some pills to calm her nerves and lay down to sleep.

Only Papa, Paulo, Amanda and I ate dinner that night. The mood was dull and somber as if the house was in a state of mourning. Papa's jubilation seemed drained. Mama and Tia Rosita remained in their rooms. Mari continued fanning Tia Rosita. Carmina went to call Mama for dinner, but found her asleep.

We had hardly begun eating a meager meal of rice and fish curry with *ambli* pickle, when Pedru began his speech:

'Senhor Afonso, Senhor Paulo, Doutor Roberto and Bai Amanda, today, the twentieth of December, the year 1961, Anno Domini, our beloved Goa suffered a great injustice and is no more. In the name of the Great Saint, I proclaim that the invaders will themselves be invaded and ultimately defeated and the Great One will one day return in triumph. *Viva, Viva India-Portuguesa.*'

There were no giggles or laughter this time.

I wondered who was the Great One Pedru was referring to? The ghost of Afonso de Albuquerque, the King of Peppercorns? Like the ghost of Hamlet? I looked at Papa's face. It was stern—an angry flush was visible on the fair side of his dark skin. Pedru waited for some acknowledgment, which Papa had always provided before, but there was none this time. Even in his insanity, Pedru realised that this time he had gone too far. He would never make a speech again.

II

Ten

New Year's Revelations

As Christmas and New Year approached, most of the elders of my family were trapped in a downward spiral of gloom. Likewise, many of the great old families from the south and north of Goa sat in silence in their beautiful and expansive homes. Amanda and I took it upon ourselves to cheer up the old folks, making stars of papier mâché and coloured tissue paper and gathering all sorts of paraphernalia for a nativity scene.

On the twenty-fourth, we went for midnight Mass, after which we gathered around the piano with a guitar and a violin and sang Christmas carols, opened gifts, passed around Christmas sweets and drank port and pineapple wine. Mama, who usually sat at the piano and accompanied the singing, was reluctant to play that night. I took her place, while Paulo accompanied me on the guitar and Amanda on the violin. My family was undoubtedly talented, but the musical genes came from my mother's side of the family, otherwise my father and his ancestors could not distinguish a *do* from a *fa*. Indeed, my mother had the talent required to be a concert pianist.

'See, Mama, cheer up, India or Portugal, Goa will always be Goa to us,' Amanda said. Mama and Tia Rosita continued with their blank looks as if it did not matter any longer, life would never be the same again. Paulo had a faraway uninterested look as if all this was *passé*.

New Year was celebrated with sorpotel, cabidel, *apa de camarão* and chicken cafreal. However, there were additionally two big bombshells and a grenade that were dropped on the table, as if the events of the last few weeks were not enough.

Paulo dropped the first bombshell: 'I have no intention of assuming any position now under India; besides, I don't know Indian or British law.' He hurriedly continued looking at Mama and Papa and addressing Papa, he said: 'I'm going back to Portugal. I will need some financial support in the beginning. I give you my word in a year or two I will be on my own.' Paulo's intentions were received initially with silence as if no one at the table had time to digest his words.

'But, Paulo, I'm trying hard to get you an appointment to the bar association,' said Papa.

'I'm not interested, Papa,' he quickly responded.

Perhaps to sweeten the bitterness of Paulo's announcement, Tia Rosita interjected with some sugary pronouncements of her own. Addressing Amanda, she told her that she had met Dona Carmen, the mother of the doctor from Mozambique and that the doctor had been enchanted by Amanda's beauty and style. He considered her a perfect debutante fit for the African-Portuguese-Goan society.

After pausing to chew a succulent piece of chicken and wash it down with a gulp of pineapple wine, Tia Rosita said that the interview with the doctor and his family was fixed for next Sunday. My mother did not show surprise at Tia Rosita's arrangements, while my father, who was apparently not forewarned, frowned.

Flushed and furious, Amanda got up to drop the second bomb.

'I don't care what he thinks of my beauty and poise. I'm not interested in marrying this doctor from Mozambique and joining the African-Portuguese-Goan society, for that matter. I will not go for the interview.'

The couple of beers I had had, followed up by a glass of Tia Rosita's pineapple wine, put me in a frisky mood. I inadvertently threw the grenade. 'I know why: Amanda is in love with Winnie the Genius—the fisherman's son. Amanda and Winnie, the talk of the town.' And I laughed. I had said it all—the damage was done.

'Shut up, Roberto, you fool! I will never speak to you again,' shouted Amanda, as she left the table and locked herself up in her room.

'I'm sorry, Amanda,' I called out.

'Who is this Winnie and what is this about a fisherman's son?' Mama asked.

Rather upset for the slip, I ignored her question and continued eating lunch.

Mama, who by now was angry and restless, sent Carmina to call Amanda back to the table, but Amanda, who was reciting *Romeo and Juliet*, would not open the door. Tia Rosita tried next, followed by Paulo. The door remained shut. It was useless for me to give it a try.

Amanda was a young woman with a mind of her own. She had schooled and boarded in a convent where she was rebellious, refusing to abide by the strict disciplinary rules of morning assembly, prayer time, study time, dinner time and sleeping time; or by the dress code of polished shoes, short nails and ankle-length skirts. She also distributed sweets and other goodies among less fortunate classmates that Mama frequently sent to her. Because she came from a prominent family, Mother Superior looked the other way at Amanda's indiscretions. Then, one day, Mother Superior used the cane on her and made her kneel in solitary confinement for the entire evening in her office for a crime she said she did not commit. I was not entirely certain about this, for Amanda had a mischievous streak well hidden underneath her pious and sensitive skin.

During the morning assembly, when her class had to file-in in a straight line, with all the playful pushing and shoving that went on, somebody gave a push that sent the girls knocking one over the other. Several of them fell on the floor and the one in the front of the line knocked Mother Superior to the ground. Calmly, Mother Superior asked them who had done it. Their lips remained tightly sealed. 'It's you, Amanda! A devil in the cloak of a saint,' said the wiry Mother Superior, pointing at her with her cane, which she generously used on her. 'I want to see you in my office during the lunch break.' But Amanda remained defiant.

Young Sister Lucia, who taught English composition and who liked Amanda for her vivid essays and poems had interceded on her behalf. She had come for her late that evening and cuddled her sobbing face in her bosom: 'Pray, Amanda, pray with me: The Lord is my shepherd—The Lord is my shepherd—The Lord is my shepherd…' And Amanda prayed with her and they became fast friends from that day onwards.

They read to each other the poetry of Keats, Milton and Browning and Sister Lucia introduced her to Shakespeare. Subsequently, they would see each other secretly, in the garden, in the sacristy of the chapel and sometimes they slipped out of the convent unnoticed. They would play childish games like hide-and-seek and pretend that the Baby Jesus was with them. They would cuddle him, rock him to and fro, change his nappies, until Baby Jesus one day became Jesus of Nazareth who would walk with them, hug and kiss them and they would hug and kiss him and hug and kiss each other. When Amanda came home for Christmas holidays that year, she kept to herself, associating mostly with the servants. She told ayah Carmina that she contemplated becoming a nun after her matriculation. Carmina, alarmed, mentioned it to Mama and Mama to Papa. They brushed it aside. No, not their only daughter! They refused to hear one bit about the nunnery.

And then one day, a couple of months before the summer holidays, Amanda and Sister Lucia were spotted by Mother Superior indulging in one of their games and Sister Lucia was reprimanded and summarily transferred. Amanda refused to go back to the convent. She matriculated from People's High School in Panjim with distinctions. After attending Sophia College in Bombay, the nunnery was forgotten like a discarded dream.

In college, she blossomed like a lotus in a pond but remained moody, closing the petals in the moving shade and the setting sun. She took everything to heart. Profoundly. She often recited Shakespeare aloud in her room with doors closed when she was upset. *Romeo and Juliet*, *Macbeth*, *Hamlet* and *Othello* were her favourites.

And that night when Mama asked ayah Carmina, 'What is Bai doing in there?'

'What else? She is reciting that *Sha-kas-piere*—whatever his name.'

'Hmm, that *Inglez* again? Paulo, convince her to read Camões—far more glorious than that Inglez, *Sha-kas-piere*,' Mama said.

Tia Rosita concurred. Papa laughed his dry measured laugh, hopelessly shaking his head.

'It is Shakespeare, Mama,' I said.

Winnie Fernandes taught English composition, history and civic administration in the same school as Amanda. He was born in a fisherman's family, but his father did not earn his living as a fisherman, except during his teenage years when he would accompany his uncle on late night fishing trips on the Arabian Sea. Winnie's father, a chef by profession, hammered education into his son Winston. 'With education you can buy all the fish you want and the ocean salt water will turn into wine.' He said it almost every day for ten years and those indeed were his final words to his son as he exhaled his last breath.

Winston, soon to be called Winnie, was smart and ambitious. After completing his B.A from Belgaum and an M.A. from St Xavier's College in Bombay with distinctions, he obtained a Ph.D. in English Literature. In Bombay, he was involved with the Indian National Congress and was active in the freedom struggle for Goa, but the Portuguese authorities did not know of his activities. He had returned to Goa to care for his younger sister after the death of his mother. He was the best educated among the fisher-folk class with promising potential, now that Goa was part of India. For some, he was Winnie the Genius, worthy of praise and favours. For others, out of jealous spite, he was Winnie the Fisherman's son. It was rumoured that he would possibly hold a high position in the new government of Goa.

He was a tall charming fellow of dark colour, with a longish face under centrally parted, thick brilliant black hair, thick eyebrows, a fine nose and a well-toned body. He stood out as much for his colour as for his striking handsomeness. He had a laudable knowledge of literature and Indian politics. Amanda took to him both for his intellect and his looks and he took to Amanda for her looks and her status, which he envied like the prize of a pearl. Despite his achievements and the adulation he received from his people, he was a humble chap but suffered from an inferiority complex that often muddied his politics.

At the time, I looked upon the relationship between my sister and Winnie rather lightly, perhaps a passing affair, a reckless fling, but the poetic description of their encounters in her diary spoke of an *Amor fati*.

For months, they had apparently looked at each other, greeted each other and smiled when they passed each other in the corridor, one entering the classroom, the other exiting. Then one evening, while she was waiting outside the classroom on the veranda of the school, looking out at the rainbow after a torrential downpour, Winnie surprised her. 'Hello, Amanda,' he said and followed up with a quotation:

'It gives me wonder great as my content
To see you here. O my soul's joy!
If after every tempest come such calms,
May the winds blow till they have wakened death,

And let the labouring bark climb hills of seas
Olympus high and duck again as low
As hells from Heaven!'

Amanda turned around and blushed. The words barely sank in, but she recognised them. He left the scene hurriedly. He did not wait for a response. Was he embarrassed? Had he rehearsed the scene? Was he waiting for the right moment? She knew, he knew: she was fond of the Bard; she often recited him in class.

A few days later, late in the evening, he was waiting outside the classroom on the veranda looking out at the sun setting behind the palm groves, their comb-like bristles glistening like dangling spears. Amanda was in the library, correcting term papers.

When she heard footsteps and turned around, she saw him approach her and she said:

'The horizons forbid
But that our loves and comforts should increase
Even as our days do grow!'

He responded:

'Amen to that, sweet powers!
I cannot speak enough of this content
It stops me here; it is too much joy.'

So saying, they left the school and walked together to the bus stop. He: her Othello. She: his Desdemona. Did they really understand the meaning of this metaphor or was it just poetry to them?

The morning following New Year's, when Amanda came out of her room for breakfast, Mama confronted her. 'Is it true what Roberto said yesterday? Who is this Winnie? Whose son is he? *Cujo filho é?'*

Amanda remained silent and Mama asked the same question again. Paulo and I stared at Amanda expecting a heated argument.

'Yes,' Amanda finally answered. 'Winnie teaches at my school. He doesn't come from our sort of family, but he is very smart and handsome. He has a Ph.D. in Literature and Philosophy.' Clever Amanda, she had given Winnie an extra doctorate to add more weight.

'We greet each other in school,' Amanda continued. 'We've gone out once or twice to the beach and a few times for dinner. People have seen us together and so you may hear more rumours about us. We love each other and that is as much as I can say. Times have changed, Mama. Though he doesn't belong to our caste, I don't care. I will not go for the interview Tia Rosita has fixed.'

I wanted to say bravo, but kept quiet.

Mama was dumbfounded by Amanda's defiance and total frankness. She impulsively took off her slipper and struck Amanda sharply on the shoulder until Carmina interjected herself between the two. Yes, Carmina—always the shock absorber in the family! Paulo and I separated the two and tempers cooled down. But Amanda stood unrepentant.

'You will not see that man anymore. What will people say?' Mama said, beginning to get worked up again. 'They will laugh at us at weddings, parties and funerals for generations to come. What a disgrace! I will go to the school and speak to the principal and get him fired.'

'Good luck,' said Amanda and she walked out.

'Is that how you talk to your mother? Is this the result of the convent education you received? What is the world coming to? We listened to our parents whether we liked it or not,' Mama shot back angrily.

Papa called out to Pedru to go get some brandy for Mama, who by now had collapsed into a chair and was short of breath. Undoubtedly, she had lost control of the situation.

Papa asked me to run to Senhor Pissurlencar's house and ask him to come right away. After Senhor Pissurlencar arrived and Mama regained her composure, we all went for conference in the oratory.

Papa was against approaching the principal of the school and requesting the termination of Winnie's services.

'Dona Isabella, you have to arrange the wedding with the doctor soon,' said Senhor Pissurlenkar. 'But times have changed. Children today have a mind of their own and now with the integration of Goa into India, all our family traditions are going to be thrown away like spoilt milk.'

'Let's hope Amanda will come to her senses,' said Papa.

'I'm going to see the principal and if I meet that man Winnie, I will have a word or two with him,' said Mama.

'I will not be a part of this,' said Papa.

'No, Mama, you cannot do this,' Paulo and I unanimously interjected.

'What should I say about the interview I've arranged? If Dona Carmen comes to know… Oh my God! In the name of the Father, the Son and the Holy Spirit,' said Tia Rosita looking up at the altar in the oratory and making the sign of the cross.

'Send a letter saying that Amanda is sick with the flu and request postponement of the interview,' said Senhor Pissurlencar. 'Say that Amanda would like to wait a few months to consider such an excellent proposal. You have to leave the door open, Dona Rosita.'

'Senhor Pissurlencar, this is bad,' said Papa. 'Marriage to a fisherman's son! A stain on our family! It will affect the marriage opportunities of Paulo and Roberto. She is my jewel, my only jewel and what's the use of a jewel if not cast in gold?'

'Son of a fisherman for my niece? Never!' said Tia Rosita stamping her feet.

'All this is going to kill me and Isabella,' said Papa.

'*Arre Ram, Ram!*' said Senhor Pissurlencar. 'It's your liberal Catholicism that is to blame. In our Hindu Brahmin families, this would never happen. Our boys and girls know from birth not to mess around with people of the lower caste. But you Catholics, your education is different—too much of freedom. I guess it's the Christ thing: equality, compassion, these things gradually seep in. Let's hope Amanda will come to her senses.'

'She is stubborn, very stubborn just like her mama,' Papa said. 'But worse, she is smart and idealistic like the Albuquerques' and over-sensitive like I don't know who. Always a bad combination in a young woman.'

Mama and Tia Rosita went to draft the letter.

A few weeks later, after the Christmas holidays, Mama and Tia Rosita went to the church to pray. After the Mass, they approached the vicar, requesting his assistance. The presence of a padre would come in handy; it was after all a Jesuit school that Amanda taught at and Father Loyola, the principal, was a Jesuit of Spanish origin. Papa suggested that I accompany them—perhaps as an informant. I was reluctant to go, but Papa insisted and so I went. It was a big mistake. Amanda hated me for it. She felt I had aligned myself with the elders.

Mama was dressed in a black pleated skirt and a white blouse. Tia Rosita was in her usual black dress that skimmed her ankles. Both entered the crowded bus with the fisher-folk smelling of sardines and the Kundbi with loads of green and red vegetables.

We took off for Margão to confront the principal. Despite the bus being full, its conductor kept pushing in more and more people like sardines in a can until they could hardly breathe. Father Vicar and Tia Rosita were behind Mama and I was behind them all. Seeing our plight, the bus conductor found the vicar a window seat and arranged one for Mama beside a fisherwoman. Mama immediately took out her embroidered handkerchief and held it to her nose. I wondered what was going on in Mama's mind: could this woman be Amanda's future aunt or cousin? How could Amanda stand such a smell? She who had been brought up with European perfumes and the smell of sandalwood.

Mama marched into the school like a general determined to win the battle. Tia Rosita, the aging vicar and I followed behind. The first person Mama met in the corridor near the entrance was a tall, dark-skinned handsome man clad in a white Terylene bush-shirt with whom she inquired the whereabouts of Winnie. To her surprise, the answer was: 'I am Winston Fernandes.' He said it with a lot of confidence and pride. The three looked like midgets compared to him.

Mama, who had come armed with poisonous darts, was dumbfounded. Words she had prepared to humiliate Winnie with seemed glued to the roof of her mouth. 'Well, can you show me the way to the principal's office?' she asked.

'Go straight and take a left after the third classroom. The office is right there. I believe Father Loyola is inside. Good day,' said Winnie.

We continued down the hallway, but Mama's composure and self-confidence had been rattled. To make matters worse, the vicar interjected, 'A fine-looking boy, Dona Isabella.'

At first sight, I did not take a liking to Winnie. Perhaps it was a feeling that a brother has towards his sister's boyfriend—a protective shield against predators.

As soon as I knocked on the office door, a tall heavyset priest with a long grey beard appeared. The introductions made, Father Loyola invited us in to his office and arranged for tea.

'Please sit down. How is Amanda?' he asked, as he rearranged the chairs for us. Sitting in his swivel chair, stroking his long gray beard and staring at Mama, he continued: 'I received a note that she's down with the flu. I hope she gets well soon.'

He told us that Amanda was doing a superb job with the students. Since she and Winnie Fernandes joined the school, the grades had gone up. In fact, he was considering promoting Amanda to teach the matriculation class. He was unsure how much longer Winnie would be around, as he was over qualified to teach at a high school. He expected Winnie to be offered the position of head of the English department in the soon-to-be-opened Panjim College.

'Who knows, one day he could even become a minister in Goa's new government,' he said. 'Amanda and Winnie are preparing a production of Shakespeare's *The Merchant of Venice*. I'm confident the play will be a success. Your daughter and Winnie make a fantastic team. Now what can I do for you?'

I was relieved, even overjoyed, at hearing so much praise for both Winnie and my sister, but Mama seemed dumbfounded again.

Finally, after taking a sip of the tea, Mama spoke: 'I am here to talk to you about my daughter and this Winnie Fernandes. It has come to my attention that this Winnie is seeing Amanda even outside school hours—you know what I mean. I am here to request that you stop any further contact between the two. This Winnie, he doesn't come from our kind of family and is totally unacceptable. He is unsuitable for my Amanda.'

The vicar and Tia Rosita nodded their heads in agreement. I sat there ashamed by all the pomposity.

'Oh Dona Isabella,' Father Loyola said, with a wide grin on his face. 'Winnie is a fine young man. And your daughter is a fine and decent young woman. It is really not in my hands. It is a decision for the two of them and the will of God.' And abruptly turning to the vicar, he asked, 'And who are you, Father?'

'I am the vicar of the village.'

'Oh how wonderful, a secular.' After this rather sarcastic remark, he looked at his watch.

'I have to leave now. I have a class to give in two minutes. Please stay and finish your tea. It was wonderful seeing you, Dona

Isabella and you, Dona Rosita. Well good-bye now, Father Vicar. Go in the grace of God.' And he left.

With heads stooping like vanquished scarecrows, we left the school. It was clear to me that in Father Loyola, Mama had met her match. Once outside, Mama remarked in a tremulous voice: 'I don't believe what I heard. How could he make a joke of such a serious matter? And this man is a priest and principal of one of the best Jesuit schools of Goa? This is not over. I will go to the archbishop. And see, he was making fun of you, calling you a secular.'

I saw an element of anxiety in her drawn face and in the dulling of her eyes. It seemed as though she felt defeated and lonely in her quest for a quick victory.

'Dona Isabella, he is a liberal Jesuit. And a European! These Jesuits—they are a troublesome lot—the intellectuals of the Church, some say. At one time, the Portuguese had kicked them out of Goa. They are too liberal! They encourage social mixing, social justice, education for the poor and the underprivileged. Not that all this is bad, but in moderation. Their views are controversial. Some, however, label them as the conscience of the Catholic Church. I must confess there is some truth to that,' editorialised Father Vicar.

'*Tatswat-a-titiss* then, Jesuits!' said Tia Rosita rather upset. 'We have lost Amanda.'

As if on second thought, Father Vicar muttered in between his teeth: 'But, Dona Isabella, the man is handsome and, maybe, he could become minister some day? Don't you think you should reconsider?'

'What did you say?'

'No, no… I was just thinking aloud.'

'That sounded like good advice, Father Vicar,' I whispered. 'Why don't you stress it to my mother once again? Winnie has a PhD. He may be nominated as head of the English department in our newest college. He may even become a minister in the new government of Goa. Isn't that enough for my mother?'

Mama wasn't listening however. She had walked away angrily. The vicar wasn't listening either.

Suddenly, Mama turned around and walked back towards us as if she had made a discovery that would save the day.

'Wait a moment—I almost forgot—Father Loyola said that Winnie may leave to take a position in the new college,' she said, emboldened. 'This is a silver lining, Father Vicar. What is going to happen with all these new colleges opening up? Soon everyone will want an education and there will be no cooks, no carpenters, no cleaners and the wages will go sky high.'

'Total chaos—*tatswat-a-titiss*,' Tia Rosita said.

When we returned home, Mama went straight to her room with a faltering swagger and locked the door. Tia Rosita stopped at the church to pray. I recounted to Papa the encounter with Winnie and Father Loyola.

'I'm not surprised in the least,' said Papa. 'It was immature to go to the principal. Leave it to the women and they will turn the world upside down.' I could sense he was hurt.

After this brief exchange with my father, I left for Panjim. I was, however, upset with my father. He was a passive man, an intellectual, more concerned with his estate and issues of politics. Domestic affairs he left entirely to Mama. He should have put his foot down and stopped Mama from meeting the principal of Amanda's school. However, I wondered whether it would hold her back. Once she made up her mind, there was no stopping her.

Eleven

Mama's Predicament

I had come upon an entry in my mother's diary, penned on 24 January 1962, after the incident with Amanda:

I sat on my bed rather restless and contemplated what had transpired. Opening and closing the drawer of the mahogany dresser, not knowing what I was looking for, I found the jewellery box containing the gold ring my mother had given to me, with its fine, Belgian-cut diamonds surrounding a heart-shaped ruby, the colour of cocum. I wore it for my wedding and was going to pass it on to Amanda. This now looks like a remote possibility.

Will my dream of a big wedding for my Amanda ever materialise? Will she run away with this Winnie? And who is he to take her away from me? Where would I even find her now that Goa is part of India and India is so vast? What's the use of this beautiful ring if not to pass on to my beautiful daughter?

I placed the ring back in the box and closed the drawer. I looked at myself in the mirror; the puffiness of my eyelids showed the strain of the last few days. I called out to Mari to fill the English porcelain basin with hot water. I washed my face, combed my hair, which when let loose fell in waves now tinged with gray. I opened the almirah, took out a light pink Macau robe and changed into it.

Not since the encounter with the Captain have I looked at my body in front of a mirror. Today I felt a need to do so. Perhaps I wanted to understand Amanda, to act out her feelings and this could be the bridge that would link the past to the present. After all, wasn't I once in love like she is now? Is history repeating itself?

I let the robe fall to the ground in front of the mirror.

I noticed my sagging breasts. Beads of sweat rolled down my neck like pearls through the tunnel in between them; a few continued their roll down below my waist over the creases left over from childbearing. It is a different body now, not the body, the once loved body, enshrined in mystery, that was oiled with sandalwood oil the day before my wedding, bathed in saffron-coloured coconut milk and draped in silk and marigolds. I have aged in flesh and blood; my passion subdued and burnt out.

Will I deny love, like love was denied to me first by fate and then by duty and honour to a family name?

I put on my robe and lay on the bed. I fumbled with the embroidered bed sheets; straightened out the pillowcases. For a moment I shuddered. Fear gripped me at the thought of losing my children. Soon, Paulo and Amanda would leave and maybe even Roberto, who is so like my husband, Afonso; perhaps he will stay home, doctor in the village and take over the reins of the estate. But it is my Paulo that concerns me most—he is so anxious to leave for Portugal and I may lose him again, this time perhaps for good. No—I cannot let it happen! And Amanda will be disowned and lost to the family if she marries this Winnie.

I too had once loved like Amanda and did not want to go for the marriage interview. But did I have a choice? We listened to our parents then; they knew what was best for us. Obediently, I went for the interview and under pressure from my mother and my cousins and for the sake of the family name, relented to marry a man I did not love.

It is true I had sinned and this was my punishment, my life-long penance. After all, hadn't He died for us on the cross? What was my suffering as compared to His? I had prayed to His bleeding crucified image in the chapel. I felt stronger. With His grace I went on with it.

I went through the wedding ceremony as if I was walking in a fog not knowing what was on the other side of the clearing. And what a wedding it was, replete with an embroidered dress made to order from

Portugal. The bridal train was twenty feet long with filigreed filaments of silver and gold and white pearls. There were a dozen page girls dressed in pink. More than half a dozen chefs and a dozen assistants attended to the cooking. Makeshift kitchens were built in the patio behind the Albuquerque house. The buffet was long and lavish with more than fifty different dishes: an assortment of whole fish and shellfish, fowl and turkeys, beef and piglets and even wild boar. More than four hundred guests arrived from all over Goa in carriages driven by oxen. The drinking and the dancing and the singing went on till the early hours of the morning. The Governor General and the Archbishop of Goa were in attendance. It was the grandest wedding the village had ever witnessed.

I waited for my husband in my embroidered nightgown after the reception. He wasn't intimate with me on the first night. Was he very shy?

It was very hot and humid the following night and I had left the window open. There was a pale fuzzy moon and in the faint light of this moon, I saw two big eyes like opals staring at me and moving rapidly from side to side. At first I thought it was an owl and owls were a bad omen and this wedding was surely a mistake. Then I saw a tail and realised that it was a monkey. I let out a scream and the whole house was in my room at my bedside and my husband was there as well. Carmina calmed me down.

'It is only a harmless monkey,' he said. 'He will bring us good luck; we have many of them in the village.' I was disgusted. There were no monkeys in my village of Aldona. 'Perhaps all the Salcete people are monkeys like my husband,' I had whispered to Carmina. 'Chee, Bai, don't speak of your husband like that,' Carmina had scolded me.

After Carmina left, my husband realised I was shaken and held me close for a moment. He seemed embarrassed. We lay side-by-side in the darkness. I lay still, like a log of wood. Turning towards me he began tenderly stroking my face; then he placed his hand on my breast and rapidly withdrew it as if a hot burning coal had scorched his hand.

I felt his hand on my thigh. It was the sign I was waiting for. My mother had instructed me well. I heard him breathing fast. I felt him come on top of me. He was gentle. There were no kisses. Perhaps he did not know how to kiss. I shut my eyes tight. The act was done. The marriage was consummated. He was like a clock—it was mostly once, sometimes twice a week, in the darkness. There was no intimacy during Lent, on Sundays, first Fridays and on holy days of obligation.

He never saw my body. I never saw his. It did not seem to matter. I never rode the crest of the wave like I had with the Captain. Sometimes I wondered where in the world he had moored his ship. But with time, the memory of the wave would end. Somewhere in the ocean it would find a home, perhaps it would rest like the Titanic. The heart of a woman is like the bottom of the ocean, a graveyard with sunken memories pickled on the seabed.

My Afonso may not be passionate, but he is kind and respectful and well-liked, a man of character. Though it took some time, I do love him. I learned to love him. A love of understanding, of familiarity, a love that seeps in by a slow process of osmosis. A love that lacks fire and the crest of a wave, yet a love that endures, reared in the Catholic tradition for better or for worse, in sickness and in health, until death do us part. Amen.

How to tell my Amanda that life goes on and it does get better, without betraying my past? Arranged marriages do work. She can't know this at her age. Nor could I have known back then.

Amanda must break off the affair. The family name must be upheld.

Twelve

The New Order

1963

It was the day of my graduation and together with the other graduates I attended Mass at the *Escola Médica* chapel where the reverend preached to us new doctors about the need for self-sacrifice and compassion in the great medical profession. He administered the Hippocratic oath and blessed the new stethoscopes that would soon go about hearing: 1) the gallops and coos of hearts; 2) the whispers of drowning lungs like the crackles of trampled autumn leaves; 3) the tympanic tunes of trumpeted intestines and 4) the eerie silence of dead motors.

We were handed diplomas that to our sheer disappointment were not worth their weight in gold. The *Escola Médica* degree, *Médico-Cirurgião*, was not recognised in the rest of India, beyond the borders of Goa. The new Goa Medical College would be opening soon, superimposed on the old one and fashioned according to the Indo-British system.

There was a mood of elation as is usual on such momentous occasions, though for the most part the future remained uncertain. I had passed with distinction, obtaining the highest aggregate grade of eighteen out of twenty; but unfortunately, it did not matter any longer, the scores would get me no further. My intention had been to go to Portugal and specialise in tropical medicine and return to Goa. With my grades, I had expected to be the recipient of a scholarship. All this changed after the integration of Goa into India. However, unlike many college-age teenagers who studied at the Portuguese lyceum and did not speak or write much English, as was the case with my brother and Maria, my integration into the new Goa was a relatively easy task since I spoke and wrote fluently in both languages and was well-versed with India and Indian ways.

After much internal debate, I finally settled on the USA. First, however, I decided to do the condensed MBBS (Bachelor of Medicine; Bachelor of Surgery) course in Bombay and to sit for the American entrance examination, even though I knew my father would vehemently object to my leaving for America. My parents had planned my future: general practice in the village.

A party for family and friends followed the graduation ceremony. My cousin, the professor and director of the now defunct Portuguese medical school, Dr Pagão, raised a toast over the last drop of Portuguese port. He welcomed me to the most honourable of all professions, attesting to all and sundry that I had a brilliant future as a man of medicine. Regretting that almost all positions in local government—including within the medical school—were occupied by out-of-state Indians after the 'liberation of Goa', he said: 'Roberto, a true Goan of our traditional families, will raise the Albuquerque name and that of Goa to unprecedented heights,' as though I was a Sputnik destined for outer space.

Dr Kodpo, the village general practitioner, stood up to say a few words: he praised me for my intelligence, adding that unfortunately I was too smart for a village doctor and wished me the best in the big city of Bombay or Delhi or 'maybe, even the USA!' he proclaimed, raising his voice an octave and stabbing his finger in the air.

My father was proud of me, but upset at being told that the possibility of family practice in the village was out of the question.

After lunch, the guests retreated to the drawing room. The women reminisced about the good old days of Gouda cheese, olive oil, Portuguese codfish and peace. They were distraught at the rising prices, higher wages, the busloads of cheap Indian tourists and the dirt and filth on the city streets. 'Look at Vasco and Margão and the scenic and beautiful Campal—they are littered with squatting men and boys from other parts of India relieving themselves shamelessly. Rua Heliodoro Salgado, lined with acacia and palm trees, now stinks of urine,' said Mama with disgust.

'Worse,' said Tia Rosita. 'Soon we are going to be like the Americans and the Europeans. We will have to do our own cooking and cleaning!'

'Who's for brandy and who's for feni and who's for a few hands of rummy?' asked Papa of the elder men, handing Pedru the silver tray with a bottle of Portuguese brandy and a bottle of feni. The mood of the elders turned sour when Senhor Madeira, a testy local landlord, announced that he had heard that some politicians intended to introduce land reforms and a Tenants Act in the near future.

'Now wait a moment, things are not so bad. The roads are being tarred, we are getting electricity in the villages,' said Senhor Pissurlencar. 'Why the panic?'

'You have hardly any tenants on your properties—you have no right to speak. Look, before you know it, our tenants will claim our lands,' retorted Senhor Madeira with much cynicism.

'*O'pa*, so what's to be done?' asked Paulo who was savouring the brandy.

'I'm selling all I have and then *ta-ta, cheerio!*—I'm gone to Portugal,' Senhor Madeira pronounced loudly, gulping a shot of brandy.

'I'm with you; I have nothing to sell, so I am going, going, gone,' said Paulo, floating his hand in the air and gliding it like an airplane.

From the far corner, a few words were delivered softly from the contemplative village philosopher, Senhor Gomes: 'There is nothing we can do my friends. *The old order changeth, yielding place to the new.*'

'*Merda*, this man has started philosophising,' muttered Senhor Madeira, bitterly.

'There is no doubt that the ones who left Goa for Portugal were the lucky ones,' said Paulo.

'Well... but those with a strong connection to the land like our family and many others have stayed and adjusted,' I said. 'Some of the initial shock of integration was psychological.'

'It is easy for you to say that,' said Paulo. 'You have both a Portuguese and English education.'

'Well, anyway, get your guitar—let's go to the hall and make some music,' I said, trying to change the mood. The two of us got up and left the room. Soon others joined. After a chorus of Portuguese, English and Spanish songs, Amanda and I sang the Mando—the local love songs; Paulo accompanied us on the guitar, while our parents and cousins danced.

Mama and Papa dressed for the traditional courtly dance. She wore the *panu-baju*, a gold-embroidered red sari cloth worn as a skirt and a top over a long-sleeved lace blouse, with a white silk sash over her shoulders and had an embroidered silk fan in her right hand. Papa wore a tuxedo with long tails and held the ends of a silk handkerchief stretched between his hands, one placed above and the other below his head.

They stepped forth and like two courting peacocks, circled around and around each other in the traditional Mando dance sequence. Just as the dancing was coming to an end, Father Vicar appeared with a grave, disconsolate expression on his face.

'What is it, Father, what's happened?' I asked.

'You haven't heard the news? It is doom all over the world. President Kennedy was assassinated.'

The sudden news of his death left us bereft. It was as if a living myth was prematurely felled. For some time we all sat in the hall in a somber mood. Tia Rosita finally suggested a rosary for the assassinated president and his family. After the rosary, she suggested that we start a petition for Kennedy's canonisation and sainthood. We winked at each other at the naïveté of our holy aunt Rosita.

Two weeks later, I was to attend the medical college ball at the Mandovi Hotel in Panjim. Paulo suggested we go together, but I preferred to go by myself. Maria would be there and I did not want to hustle and compete with my brother, not now, after my graduation. Since her warming up to me, I was more determined in my quest than ever. It was clear to me that Maria felt that Paulo's interest in her was merely flirtatious; besides, she was probably turned off by Paulo's drinking. Though whatever happened in the past seemed trifling, the memory of that painful night, of Maria dancing cheek to cheek with Paolo, remained. Then again, I was a doctor now and it imbued me with an aura of confidence, a sense of importance. I agreed to my brother's request. Perhaps Paulo sensed my apprehension—he promised to stay away from Maria. We left in a taxi for Panjim.

Paulo and I immediately went to the bar to get drinks. Amanda, who was dressed in a green sari with a gold embroidered border and a matching jewellery set of emeralds, sat with Maria who looked stunning in a pink sari with a red border; a pink rose bobby-pinned into the thicket of jet-black hair. Since India's takeover of Goa, the youth had given up gowns and dresses in favour of the bold, multi-colour Indian saris and sarwar-kameez now in vogue. Mama and Tia Rosita disapproved of this new mode of dress.

Paulo never left the bar most of the night. Mama and Papa were concerned about his drinking and had had a chat about it with him. He listened without a word, as if he couldn't care anymore. His return to Portugal seemed like a pipe dream that resurfaced on and off. None of his friends were there, most having left Goa; he was out of place and out of rhythm. The dance floor was noisy and flooded with medical students and tipsy tourists who shuffled their feet for a foxtrot, a cha-cha-cha, or a rock-n-roll dance. The debonair charm of the medical ball during the Portuguese times now seemed to have been replaced by a cheap decadence.

I danced five dances with Maria, including the last one—the dance that mattered the most. I was not a good dancer like Paulo. 'I'm sorry, Maria... I'm sorry,' I kept apologising for missing steps and stepping on her feet. She did not respond. Sometimes her gaze shifted towards Paulo who was at the bar, drinking. I wondered whether she was tempting Paulo to dance with her. Was she imagining she was dancing with Paulo and not with me? Had she noticed Paulo's melancholy expression, the threads of glistening gray that had appeared in his dangling curls? And did she feel an urge to glide on the floor, to tango with Paulo and to kiss his pain away? These disturbing thoughts raced through my mind. Paulo, on the other hand, kept his distance; yet, his mere presence was distracting and unsettling.

Dr Lobo and Winnie were indulging in a tug of war for Amanda. The doctor did not know about Winnie and every time he went to ask Amanda for a dance, she told him she was booked. Finally she danced one dance with him while Winnie managed many more.

On our way back home, Amanda told us that Dr Lobo had tried to impress her with talk about the high society life in Lourenço Marques, Mozambique. He described it as the garden city by the sea where the skies are blue and the nights are star-studded and gay.

'So?' said Amanda. 'The skies are blue in Goa and the nights here are also star-studded and gay. Just go to the veranda and look outside.'

Dr Lobo talked of the beautiful beaches of Portugal: of Caparica, Sintra and the Algarve, where he would take Amanda vacationing in style.

'Fortunately for us,' Amanda responded, 'we don't have to go that far. The beaches of Calangute, Colva, Vagator and Baga, are better by far.'

Paulo and I laughed at this comic interlude.

A few months later, I left by train for Bombay. Anxious to impress the professors there, as soon as I found a comfortable seat, I immersed myself in the latest American medical textbook. Just twenty pages into the chapter on infectious diseases, I yawned, closed the book and fell into a reverie of the future. I saw myself boarding Air India for America. Trepidation, a fear of the unknown and the thought of Maria made me question my priorities. I had so much here—friends and family, influence and affluence—why emigrate to America? But I didn't want the easy way out; Goa was too provincial, I needed to go out into the world. And if knowledge was the fuel that kindled the fire within, where would I seek the fuel if not in the USA? While ruminating on these thoughts, the train left the mountains behind and rolled over the plains like a huge cradle swaying side-to-side, spitting fiery pieces of burning coal into the dark of the night, lulling me to sleep.

At Londa, I boarded the train to Poona for the second leg of the journey to Bombay. As the sound of the coal engine and the urgent train-whistle became louder and louder, the acrobatic coolies sprinted on the side of the rails with bedding in their hands and a trunk on their red-clothed heads and jumped onto the running train to find me a seat. I arrived in Poona the next morning and there, boarded the Deccan Queen. When that elegant express entered Victoria Terminus in Bombay, the big-city excitement took hold of me.

I roomed at my cousin's in Mazagaon and attended at the J.J. Hospital where I took refresher courses in Anatomy, Physiology, Medicine and Surgery. The crush of bodies on the daily railway commute, the beggars lining the road to the hospital, the heat and humidity, the smells of decaying flesh, excrement, perfume, sweat, food, rotting garbage, all mixed together in a fuming cauldron, was dizzying and often brought on my fainting episodes. Amid the peace, serenity and affluence of Goa, the ferocity of life and the teaming poverty of India had been abstract ideas to me. But it was here, in Bombay, at J.J. Hospital, that I began to have a sense of mission about probing, investigating and discovering the mysteries of disease: how the human body resists, conquers, or succumbs to the onslaught of micro-organisms and viruses. I considered pursuing clinical and basic research in infectious diseases.

After six months in Bombay, I returned to Goa to finish my studies there. Undoubtedly, my return was partly prompted by my quest for Maria.

Thirteen

Night of the Full Moon

They began arriving like locusts: white men and women of a different kind. Unlike the Portuguese, they dressed in lungi, the kaxti and strips of cotton cloth or nothing at all and before anyone realised it, they had swarmed all over the secluded beach strips.

The American hippie invasion had begun.

Some were pathetic to the eye: rickety and diarrheal, like burnt-out cattle in the sub-Sahara; while others were all flesh and ass. Secluded strips of Calangute, Baga and Vagator were their naked haunts. They lived in makeshift huts on the golden sand with the starry sky for a roof, bananas and chapattis for food and opium, hashish and acid for a high. In due time, Goa became the tourist attraction for the rest of India. Maharashtrians, Keralites, Delhiites and Punjabis would roam the beaches with binoculars or eyes wide open like wide-angle lenses looking to see a blonde or a red pussy. The locals as usual took all this in stride.

'Ye pishe mure!'—these crazy people—the fisher-folk humorously decried. There was a hippie gathering with loud Beatles' music (*I Love You Yeah Yeah Yeah*) on the Anjuna beach of rock and silver sand with swaying coconut palm groves on the night of the full moon. Americans high on hashish gyrated around bonfires, floated on crystalline ocean froth and meditated on sand dunes: *Ommmmmmmm Shanti Ommmmmmmm, Ommm Shanti Om.*

They fucked under coconut palms, beside the hulk of fishing boats and played volleyball under the moonlit-starlit skies, their breasts and blue-veined balls bouncing to and fro. They slept naked, covered by the mantle of starry skies. Their mothers and fathers—high on the greenback in faraway New York City or LA, on the shrink-couch, in sterile bedrooms, in their designer clothes and stretch limos—were totally oblivious to the proclivities of their precious progeny.

On the night of the crimson full moon, when the silhouettes of palm trees hung motionless like black sickles in the warm midnight air, Paulo and I walked into the hippie circle. A bit tipsy after whisky-sodas we'd had at the birthday party of one of our cousins, we sat unnoticed in an opening by the bonfire.

On my right was a bronzed woman sitting in the lotus position with long red hair that spread around her waist skirting the sand. Her forearms rested on her knees, her hands dangled in the oppressive night air, the third finger of each hand barely kissing the tip of each thumb. Her skin, glistening from the luster of coconut oil rubbed that evening, glowed in the crimson moonlight. Her glazed eyes stared into oblivion.

To the left of Paulo, a man was preparing a chillum. He emptied tobacco from a cigarette onto the painted side of an Indian mirror and held a lit match under a lump of Afghani hashish that broke into bits. He sprinkled the hashish onto the tobacco and with his tobacco-stained fingers, mixed the two ingredients and filled the chillum with the mixture. Then he wrapped a tobacco-stained rag around the base of the chillum, took three matchsticks from the matchbox and lit it. He took a draught through the rag as he inserted the nozzle of the chillum in his mouth and passed it on to Paulo, who put the chillum in his mouth without the rag covering the nozzle, took a draught and coughed hard. The guy showed Paulo how to take a deep draught and how to hold it in. And Paulo took another draught, a big deep one and held it in, then passed the chillum to me. The pungent smoke burned my lungs; I could hardly catch my breath. I passed it to the woman by my side. The chillum and the acid pills came round and round.

I remember falling asleep. I woke up with the morning glare and shook Paulo who was still asleep. Startled, the body next to him moved and sat up. 'Oops, I must have fallen asleep. What a trip! Shit, those strawberry pills blew me to smithereens.' Her American accent fell on deaf ears. Paulo woke up startled as well and was rather surprised at the presence of the woman. He asked her name.

'Uma,' she said, yawning.

'I'm Paulo and this is my brother, Roberto. He's a doctor.'

'Uma what?' I asked.

'Does it matter?' said Uma. 'Who cares?'

'But you're American,' I said. 'With an Indian name?' The name she had taken—Uma—was the name of the Hindu goddess of beauty and sunlight, the wife of Lord Shiva.

'I'm not proud of my American name what with all that's going on in Vietnam—all that napalm shit!' She sat up wide-eyed.

'Are you native?' she asked Paulo.

'Yes,' said Paulo. 'I've travelled widely: Portugal, Spain, Paris, Berlin, London—studied law at the University of Coimbra for four and a half years. You know Coimbra?' She shrugged her shoulders.

'I'll be leaving for Portugal hopefully soon and one day perhaps to America,' Paulo said.

'Why do you want to leave paradise and jump into hell?' Uma asked.

Paulo didn't answer. Somewhat angered by her attitude, he was about to get up and leave, when she placed her hand on his shoulders and gently pushed him down onto the sand. 'Man, what a trip. Do you want to hear about it?'

She didn't wait for an answer. I was about to leave to attend the surgical clinic at the medical college, but as she began speaking,

I became interested and somewhat amused.

'The sand we were sitting on became a dune—then a mountain with peaks and each one of us around the bonfire occupied a peak,' she said. 'The ocean gushed in and disconnected us from land and we floated over this sacred ground on these grains of sand and below us was a sparkling ocean infinitesimally vast—all sound, all colour, with an intense clarity. The peaks kept swaying wildly, side to side and we in the circle kept fusing and birthing and separating.'

We stared at her, mesmerised, while she continued talking as if to herself, oblivious to our presence.

'I sprang from this ground,' she said after a deep breath, as she took a handful of sand and let it flow like liquid mercury and when all the sand was gone, she kept on repeating the sequence and continued talking.

'I travelled to the Himalayas and there I saw Shiva. I placed my hands on his eyes (placing her hand on Paulo's eyes), when a great flame burst from his forehead and the third eye as bright as the sun opened... I glowed in its rays. I can see it all like this sand in the palm of my hand... life flows... it flows... like the sand.' She looked dreamy and far away saying these words as if there was another being altogether within her speaking. Then unexpectedly she became agitated.

'It was a fantastic trip. Did you try the stuff?' she asked, getting up and dusting off the sand.

'Yes,' Paulo replied.

We were intrigued with Uma, quite certain that she was describing her own hallucinations. But the things she said about India and Shiva seemed strange coming from an American woman of exquisite looks. Paulo had no interest in India or Hindu philosophy. For him Europe was the pinnacle of culture and he was part of it. I did not know exactly where I belonged; many young Goans felt that way during this time. I was nationalistic, but like Paulo and most if not all Goan Catholics, I was ignorant of Hindu religion and philosophy—the faith of our ancestors. Catholicism was deeply ingrained in us and difficult to shake off like a close family connection. For us, however, America was the centre of power and wealth and we were all pro-American.

I wondered why Uma had turned against her own and sought solace in another culture. I was about to ask her this very question, but I became distracted by her ravishing beauty. She was a tall woman with long slim legs like a gazelle; her skin tanned from the sun had an almost metallic bronzed colour, while her red hair fell straight like that of a mare to cover her naked breasts and back, almost to the waist and her dark green eyes sparkled like African emeralds. She slightly covered herself with a saffron-colour lungi and I immediately turned my head away. A quarter of the original circle was still asleep, sprawled on the beach; the rest had left.

'Hey, Uma baby, you were dead stoned,' said the man everyone called Indy, coming towards us from behind the rocks. 'Wow, man, what a trip! Hey, that was some good shit, right? You looked stoned too, man,' he said, addressing Paulo.

Paulo shook his head. 'What is he referring to as shit? Shit is *merda.*' I did not understand their lingo either. We hung around until the scorching sun would no longer permit it. Uma got up to go with Indy and asked Paulo if he wanted to join them. Paulo hesitated.

'Well if you change your mind, we are going to Baga. We have a commune in a cave behind the chapel on the hill,' said Uma and they left.

It was almost noon. Paulo and I sat chatting in a shack and ordered a cold beer, gulped it down and ordered another. Paulo felt an urge to go looking for Uma, but felt apprehensive like he had felt in Coimbra when Ana Sofia had changed into a beautiful aloof woman.

Obviously attracted to Uma's singularity, he smelt a challenging conquest. Mr Handsome was certain he could have her, but couldn't fathom her like he fathomed Ana Sofia. Uma belonged to another world, a strange anachronistic world. With Ana Sofia he felt like a man, but in front of Uma, he was a boy. He recollected the hours he spent with Ana Sofia at the university tower in Coimbra. It was as if he felt her breath, her lips, the almond scent of her body and Uma receded from his mind.

As Paulo reminisced about his life in Portugal, he saw in his mind's eye, in the distance and beyond the ocean waves, a vision of the *três irmãos*—the three cliffs bathed in hues of red, orange and black, in the fading sunset that marked the Algarve—the land beyond the West. Without his friends who had all returned to Europe, Paulo was lonely. Besides, Goa had lost its meaning and was fast becoming a strange and foreign land. He felt a strong nostalgia for Portugal, for barbecued sardines in olive oil and the smell of her salty breath.

Oh, why should the ageing mind of man remember acts of love, of life, of death?

What stands today—tomorrow is spent in a grain of sand.

As soon as we arrived home that evening, Paulo approached Papa about his departure for Portugal, but Papa was in no mood to debate the issue. 'I have to attend a meeting to discuss the formation of the village panchayat. We will talk tomorrow,' he said. The next day, Papa did not bring it up, but Paulo insisted that they talk about his departure. Papa, rather annoyed, responded by reminding him that he had got him a bar appointment.

'Why don't you start a law practice? After all, the Portuguese Civil Code still governs the judicial system in Goa.'

Paulo angrily pointed out that those who were staying were already entrenched in the system. Papa was not convinced and an argument ensued wherein Paulo accused Papa of being a filthy miser. Then came the pronouncements that would sever their relationship. 'You are my eldest son but you have set a bad example for Roberto and Amanda. You have disappointed your mother and me to the core,' he said.

Papa's words, said slowly yet purposefully in a low tone of voice, sliced like a sword spilling blood in the air. Paulo was humiliated and wounded, perhaps more so because I was a witness to this heart-wrenching confrontation. He stormed out of the house. I caught up with him and we walked together to the village square. I tried to convince him that Papa never meant what he said. We went to Ferrão's bar where after a whisky-soda, Paulo felt more relaxed.

'Boy, the hashish and those pills made me hallucinate,' he said.

'I just fell asleep with all the whisky and a drag,' I said.

'I'm not sure whether I was awake or half-asleep. I was seeing these things—everything was so vivid and real,' said Paulo, all excited. He had seen an orange moon dancing on the ocean's edge, bouncing on the water and braking into pieces like spherical bubbles that fused and enlarged and fragmented into multiples of the previous moons. He could count the sequences from four to sixteen and the fusing sequences made a bigger and bigger moon, until it took up the entire ocean and like a ball of fire came rolling and spinning to the shore. 'It was amazing—I wasn't afraid,' he said. His eyes, like two prisms, split the light of the moon into multiple colours. He kept running faster and faster towards the oncoming moon when he saw Uma by his side. 'The moon sucked and devoured us and we spun as one rolling like a ball into infinite space.'

'Wow!' I exclaimed.

'It was a great feeling, Roberto, a feeling of infinite speed. I want more of it. I'm going to Baga to look for Uma.'

I returned home alone, rather distressed at Paulo's heedlessness; in the evening, I went looking for him in Baga.

Fourteen

Krishna, Krishna, Hare Krishna

After arriving at Baga beach, the high tide prevented Paulo from crossing to the other side of the river to meet Uma. He decided to wait till after sunset when the low tide would arrive. He hung around in the lone bar next to the river. I caught up with him there. We decided to take a walk through the sand dunes. It was almost dark. I noticed the silhouette of a woman, cross-legged, squatting naked on top of a sand dune meditating. I pointed her out to Paulo.

She was inside a circle of burning incense sticks that emitted sinuous and circular whorls of fragrant smoke that lingered around her body like a cloud of divinity, before being snatched violently away by the ocean wind.

Her wide green eyes stared into nothingness. Her tanned face was a mask of oblivion. Her long hair caressed the sand, covering her nakedness. It was as if the twilight was about to release her image into darkness.

'Uma!' Paulo shouted. But she didn't stir.

'Uma!' Uma didn't move. Paulo climbed the sand dune and shook her out of her trance. She was quite miffed at being disturbed.

'You shouldn't have done that, man,' she said, shaking her head as if in disbelief. 'It's the hour of *aarti* when the gods are praised with fire and incense. It took me almost an hour to get into the state of kundalini—you just shook me out of it!'

Paulo did not understand much of what she said, but apologised.

'Hey, I forgot your name.'

'Paulo.'

'Paulo? Let's call you Krishna.' She laughed. Then in a serious tone, folding her hands and bowing in obeisance, she incanted: '*Krishna, Krishna, Hare Krishna.*'

Paulo did not say a yes or a no. For him all this was as alien as Greek and a little worse than Latin. Besides, he did not really care anymore. It amazed me how Uma could be so detached at one moment and so engaged the next. Undoubtedly, she was attracted to Mr Handsome. It was uncommon for the hippies to associate with the local crowd—they usually kept to themselves. I wondered where all this would lead to.

She got up, tied a piece of cloth around her waist and took Paulo by the hand. Bare-breasted, she began walking the short beach strip. She asked me if I would like to join them. I told her that I would have to leave early, since I had to attend the clinic in the morning.

We waded through the river to the other side of Baga and began climbing the hill towards the Retreat House. Momentarily, as night settled in, Uma brought out a flashlight from her bag as we climbed down the mass of rock on the ocean side. We walked down narrow steps of rock to an opening with a cave, below which was the *chor baim*—a rogues' well that was formed by ocean waters surging into a space in the rock formation, producing currents and eddies with a powerful undertow.

I barely noticed the figures of the three women and three men already in the cave. A cotton curtain with painted mandalas covered the entrance. I looked for a familiar face and recognised Indy reclined on a Rajasthani cushion, smoking a bidi and strumming on a guitar.

'Hey, Uma baby, did you get the hash?' asked one of the men.

'Yeah, it's in the bag. He gave me a couple of rolls; wouldn't give me any hot stuff—only to Indy,' she said. 'Hey, Indy, that was some shitty contact.' Indy did not acknowledge her remark. She emptied the contents of her bag: two joints, chunks of yellow and red hashish, a few opium balls, a ball pen, a pair of knickers, silver bracelets, anklets and amulets.

'Hey guys, this is Krishna,' Uma said. 'He's local, lived in Europe—and that's his brother. He's a doctor.'

They all nodded, except for Indy, who was not amused and seemed displeased with our intrusion. We sat on a tattered spread surrounded by oil lamps and incense sticks emitting the scents of champak, sandalwood and pinewood—the dizzying fragrance, when mixed with the fresh smell of the ocean air, made the heavy air in the mini-cave easier to breathe. The glow of the lamps, the multi-coloured, mirrored Rajasthani spreads on the floor and walls of the tiny cave, the thick cloud of incense mixed with ganja and Beatles' music gave the place a psychedelic atmosphere. Paulo had never seen anything like this before, nor had I. '*Épa? Que fantasia!*' he remarked in Portuguese, when the tall and rickety Kash, who was squatting trying to search for a joint in his bag, almost fell on him. Kash handed a joint to Yogi, who abruptly left the cave. He was the oldest of the pack and the shortest of the men. He wore a dark red lungi and a Banares mirrored pillbox cap to cover his balding head.

Uma was lying on a cushion with her eyes closed. A saffron-colour strip of cloth was tied around her waist. Paulo and I kept watching her, digesting her wild beauty. There was a seductive quality to her features: her lips were full, her emerald eyes, cat-like. Her red hair changed colour with the glow of the lamps, like a flame.

All of a sudden the music stopped playing. The unbearable silence in the mini-cave was broken by the repetitious, monotonous sound of the waves, like rising peals of distant mourning. The effect was surreal.

I approached one of the women who was sitting alone and asked her name. 'Hi, I'm Suzy,' she said. She was thin with big breasts and freckles on her face. Multicoloured beads hung around her neck and her waist, around which she had wrapped a red piece of batik; silver bangles adorned her ankles. I then turned to the left and asked the names of the other two women sitting nearby. They had an almost Indian physique—full-bodied, a bit on the plump side with a narrow upper torso and round buttocks above short brown legs. They were blonde twins locked in an embrace like they were in their mother's womb. High on drugs, one barely moved her lips, a whisper I did not comprehend. Suzy, pointing to them, identified the slightly taller one as Laxmi and her twin sister as Sita.

Suddenly, Indy got up and began to undress. Unconcerned, he stripped off his lungi and exposed himself. His strong arms revealed colourful tattoos of naked women and on his chest was tattooed Ananta, the serpent whose heads fanned just below his navel. One head, the middle one, made its convoluted descent to his shaved pubis wrapping around the base of his phallus. Uma got up and approached Indy and kneeling in front of him, she bowed; the others followed.

She chanted, as Indy stood there like a deity.

'Brahma-murari surachit lingam, nirmal bhakchit shobhita lingam
Janma ja dukha vinashaka lingam, tat pranamami sadaa shiva-lingam.'

Smearing him with saffron and lotus petals, she continued:

'Kumkum chandana laypit lingam, pankaj haar sushobhita lingam
Sanchit paap vinashana lingam, tat pranamami sadaa shivalingam.'

Spraying water and milk and now circling around in a frenzy:

'Kanak maha-mani bhuchita lingam, phanti-pati veksh-tita shobhita lingam
Daksha suyagya vinashana lingam, tat pranamami sadaa shiva-lingam.'

Paulo and I stared at this spectacle in awe. I didn't know what to make of all this. It was all new to us: this apotheosis of the carnal.

After the Shiva-lingam ceremony ended, Indy dressed in a pair of patched jeans and a Rajasthani vest, tied a bandanna around his forehead and a silver belt around his waist, which hung low on his hips (like that of Yul Brynner in *The Magnificent Seven*), from which hung a kukri, a long curved Nepalese knife. He seemed transformed into one of the desperadoes in Westerns. Paulo and I were certain that Indy was the leader of the pack, but unsure of his relationship with Uma. Indy's power and demeanour reminded Paulo of Angelino de Tor in Coimbra; he was uncomfortable in his presence.

'Hey, Krishna, do you have some dough? Hey there—I'm talking to you,' said Indy pointing to Paulo.

Paulo was puzzled. 'What's dough?'

'*Dineiro*—money,' I said.

Indy waved a rupee in the air. 'You've got to pay for your keep, man. I need some dough for the dope.'

'He's my guest!' said Uma.

'Okay, okay. Anybody have some dough here?'

'Here, take it Mister Indy,' Paulo said. He handed him fifty rupees.

'Hey, thanks, man, you're a cool dude,' Indy said. The others added to the pot. Uma gave a bunch of ten rupee notes and Kash finally unearthed some change from the bowels of his bag. Indy left abruptly and he returned within an hour or so with plenty of booze, hash, opium, strawberry pills and vials containing a thick liquid. Immediately after, Yogi came with a local kid. He had his arm around him. It was Tucaram! As soon as Tucaram saw me, he took off like a bird.

'What is Tucaram doing with Yogi?' I asked Paulo, who just shrugged his shoulders, as if unconcerned.

It was almost eleven at night. I told my brother in Portuguese that I wanted to leave. Paulo insisted that I stay at least for a while; besides, it was doubtful I would find transport to the town at this late hour.

The music played. The booze and the chillum passed around and the orgy began. Paulo and I had sips of the feni liquor and several droughts of the chillum. I was sitting by Suzy and Suzy was all over me. My poor tolerance to alcohol quickly made me high and woozy. Afraid I would black out, I lay down on the Rajasthani spread and, before I knew what was happening, a blur of naked bodies moved like serpents in the psychedelic pit.

I woke up sweating and breathless with the weight of Suzy's leg over my chest. I did not know where I was; naked bodies were sprawled on the floor and the air was heavy with a stale acrid smell of sweat and weed. It all seemed like a dream. I looked at my watch. It was eight in the morning. I abruptly left the cave into the early morning sunlight.

On my way back to Panjim, as I began recollecting the events of that night and the fogged-out images flashed back, I was overwhelmed and did not know the moment I would talk to Paulo about it. The drugs and sex were new to us—it was undoubtedly restricted to the hippies, but I wondered how long it would take before the locals got a taste of it.

A few days later, I went to the orphanage where I was informed that Tucaram had run away. On my way back, I came upon Suzy at the jetty in Panjim. We went for a cup of chai. Suzy told me that she had taken a year off before joining medical school at Columbia University, in New York City. She had been all over Europe and crossed over into Afghanistan, into Pakistan and India. She had been to Nepal and Rajasthan, Delhi and Poona and there she met up with Uma. She knew her as an undergraduate student at Berkeley. Uma's mother had pushed her to achieve, private tutors and Ivy League and her father showered her with gifts. She was fed up with the American teflon society, the materialism and the competition, the war in Vietnam and actively led the student antiwar protests at Berkeley. Uma, however, still kept in touch with her father. She only had to send a telegram asking for money and it arrived. That's what she did when she ran out of gringo stuff to sell at the Anjuna fair. But she was generous with her money, supporting her friends at various times. To them, India provided an escape into a spiritual world and dope provided what reality could not. Suzy and Uma had spent time in Jabalpur with a guru before they came to Goa. While Uma planned to settle in Goa and open up an ashram in Anjuna, Suzy seemed anxious to return to the US. I was uncertain whether Uma was for real—the Karma type—passing by like the others and whether the idea of an ashram in Anjuna was another fantasy.

'There is nothing much between Uma and Indy—she is dependent on him for the dope. But your brother has to be careful of Indy,' Suzy warned. 'Indy may ask him to smuggle dope to Europe and blackmail him to achieve his end. Your brother is quite a gullible chap.'

'My brother's departure for Europe seems more and more like a pipe-dream,' I said.

'I love India,' Suzy said, as she sweetened her second cup of chai while chewing on paan. 'Despite the poverty, there is an inner joy among the people I have never seen anywhere else in the world. And Goa is so different than the rest of India. I will come back here for a holiday, perhaps after medical school.' I felt Suzy was goal-oriented, so different from the others; for her, all this seemed passé.

I told her my plans and my intention to specialise in the US. Suzy wanted to hang around with me, to visit my home in the village. However, I gave excuses saying that I had to attend a clinic rather soon and that I was too busy studying for the American exams. That evening, I had a date with Maria. I was in a hurry to refresh myself.

As I walked to the boarding house at a rapid pace, I wondered about Suzy's impression of India. She seemed honest on the surface, perhaps somewhat romantic and yet awfully self-deceiving. For me there was no room for equating poverty and hunger with inner joy in the teeming humanity in slums and slime. And yet, I was intrigued by her viewpoint. Years later, however, when driving on the streets of Harlem and Brooklyn's Flatbush, I was introduced to a different kind of poverty and hopelessness: of anger, drunkenness, lassitude and drug addiction... the grayness of wrecked, burnt-out buildings one might find in a war zone... a landscape devoid, it seemed, of any joy, outer or inner. It was then that I understood what Suzy had meant.

It was almost five o'clock when I arrived at the boarding house. I immediately had a bath and studied myself in the mirror, with my tailored terylene trousers and a bright-red silk kameez. I applied Vaseline to my hair and parted it to the side. I tried out various poses in the mirror. My long side burns and a newly kept thin moustache gave me an aura of handsomeness and a romantic hauteur. A little Clark Gable perhaps? I was ready for the conquest.

Modes of dress had rapidly changed after Goa's integration into India, but the social mores remained deeply ingrained. Dating was not permitted before engagement, so I had arranged to meet Maria at the Copacabana, an expensive bar and eatery mostly frequented by clandestine lovers. I waited for her anxiously, walking the street up and down, hoping that no acquaintance would see us enter the bar together. I looked at my watch. She had promised to be there at 6.30 and it was already 6.50. Had she changed her mind? Did something I said hold her back? Was she still infatuated with my brother? And then I saw her walking rapidly in a plain, pink cotton sari, her hair done up in a bun. We entered the bar separately and were seated upstairs where there were two other couples. Maria had told her parents that she would be home by 8, at most by 8.30. She had also told them that she was going to study with a friend, with whom she had arranged the alibi. I quickly ordered beer, with samosas as appetisers and tandoori chicken and rogan gosh as the main dishes—this was an entirely new cuisine for Goa and the two of us.

We talked of the upcoming elections, the referendum and the tragedy should Goa merge into the neighbouring state of Maharashtra.

'If it comes to pass, I'll leave the country,' I said. 'However, I feel confident that the merger issue will be rejected. We met yesterday with Jack Sequeira, the leader of the United Goans Party and everyone was cautiously optimistic.'

'I heard that Paulo has taken up with the hippies—is it true?' Maria asked. I shook my head.

'What a shame. What a waste of a promising life,' she said.

I had no desire to discuss Paulo. And the conversation came to a sudden end. My heart began pounding as I placed my hand on Maria's shoulders and drew her close to me. We looked at each other. Deeply. And then I pulled her towards me and kissed her. We kissed each other again and again. I wanted to touch her breasts. I could see her engorged nipples through her flimsy silk choli, but restrained myself.

Paulo finally returned home after living with Uma and her friends for several weeks, but within a few days, he left again with some of his clothes, sporadically returning home for a few days to request pocket money. This went on for several months.

Paulo's consorting with the hippies was a source of much consternation in our family. There was much prayer and penance, the offering of masses and novenas to St Jude and St Anthony by Tia Rosita and Mama. And Mama blamed Papa for driving Paulo into the devil's arms. Finally, Papa scolded Paulo in no uncertain terms for keeping company with the hippies. Paulo walked out and did not return home. The family was concerned. And the novenas to St Jude and St Anthony began all over again.

Many of my classmates and colleagues in medical school often made derogatory remarks: 'Hey, Roberto, your brother has become a hippie!' said one. 'Someone saw him in a lungi,' said another. And they burst out laughing. I was embarrassed and did not know how to respond. Someone else commented: 'He is fucking the red-haired one. Can you ask him to arrange a hippie for me?' I was about to punch him in the face when another classmate separated us. I turned around and walked away. Paulo's behaviour was not only inappropriate and headless—it was demeaning to the family, particularly to Amanda and me. We often had to explain his behaviour to cousins and friends. I felt the need to take upon myself the responsibility of my older brother to uphold the honour, the dignity and the name of the family. I vowed to myself that I would excel in my endeavours and make my parents proud.

It was nearly a month since Paulo had last been home. On Mama's and Amanda's coaxing, I went to Baga to look for him. In Baga, I saw Tucaram sitting in a bar with a hippie. This time Tucaram approached as soon as he saw me. He confirmed that he saw Paulo often with the red-haired American, but that, he hadn't seen him of late. I decided to proceed to the cave and asked Tucaram to accompany me. On our way, Tucaram told me that he worked as an errand boy for the American hippies, who paid him generously for his services. I scolded Tucaram for running away and told him in no uncertain terms that I expected him to study and make something of himself. Tucaram did not answer and I did not persist, for my concern at the moment was obviously for my brother.

As we made our way to the cave at sunset, a thick mass of clouds reflected bright rays from the salmon sun onto the ocean waves as if the sun wished to make its last statement of its power on this side of the earth. Then, in a few minutes, the sun tumbled down the sky and sank into the ocean. A broken circle was barely floating on the waves and in a moment it was gone, leaving an afterglow of orange and yellow on an ornamental mass of clouds, painting the ocean waves in dazzling streaks of liquid gold. Atop the rock, the Retreat House with its towering crucifix jutted into the sunset, a dark silhouette as if proclaiming: this is God's country—the land of Christianity.

According to an ancient legend, Lord Krishna had come to the shores of the Konkan, centuries before Christianity arrived and was enchanted to find women bathing in the sea and drying themselves on the *sopanas*—the steps that lead from the shore to the hilltop. He had enticed them with his magical flute and these shepherdesses—the *gopikas*—had danced for him with their well-fed cows. He had named this land Govapuri, after them. It almost seemed that Lord Krishna remained hidden behind mud-walls, impregnated into Mother Earth for four-and-a-half centuries of Christian reign. But now, Lord Krishna sprouted everywhere like a sun-ray, in the masks of his recently arrived Western devotees.

We found no sign of Paulo or Uma and her gang behind the Retreat House. On my way back, I asked the owner of the bar in Baga to inform me if he spotted Paulo.

One night, well after eleven, I picked up my guitarist friend, El Rei, the well-known Goan Segovia, and we walked to the Rua de Ourem to serenade Maria, whose birthday it would soon be. The Rua de Ourem was empty and our footsteps echoed in the stark silence of the night. The night was chilly, the street lamps reflected in the serene waters of the rivulet. El Rei and I sat on the riverbank softly tuning our guitars. The serenade was a surprise so we made as little sound as possible.

When midnight struck, we walked to a spot below Maria's window and began the serenade: *'Deus ti hai dado la gracia del cielo, Maria Dolores—en sus brazos...'* Guitar chords resounded and my voice echoed through the night as if it would shatter the stars. I briefly looked up; the house remained asleep. Was her sleep so deep that she was oblivious to my singing? Or was she lying in bed wide awake, afraid to come to the window? I began singing again, in a lower key, as El Rei began the prelude to *Manhã de Carnaval*, Maria's favourite song.

'Manhã, tão bonita manhã... de um dia feliz que chegou...' I sang.

It was then that the lights came on—a shadow passed by the window. My heart palpitated with the rhythm of the music, as if to the rhythms of a Brazilian carnival. Maria was standing on the first floor balcony, alongside her father and mother. A chill went up my spine, a brief tremor found its way into my tenor voice; I looked down and looked up again and saw them smile. I felt relaxed, the tension dissipated. When the song was over and El Rei continued strumming the minor Brazilian chords, I heard claps and her father's voice: 'Please, come up for a drink.' It was as if her father approved of the music and in turn approved of me. My vocal repertoire had recently changed: Elvis Presley and *Jailhouse Rock* had receded from memory as Paulo had instructed me on the Spanish and Portuguese songs he knew.

As I was about to climb up the stairs to Maria's house, I heard somebody call out my name. It was Anton Martins. He had alarming news: Paulo had come down with fever and diarrhea. Uma, who tended to him, finally decided that his family should be notified and she and her friends carried Paulo all the way to Anton's bar, in Baga. Having made Paulo as comfortable as he possibly could, Anton drove his Morris Minor to my boarding house and my landlady told him where he might find me this late into the night.

I asked him to wait for me as I climbed the steps to Maria's house. Maria came bearing a tray with a bottle of Johnny Walker, several slices of bebinca and two glasses. El Rei and I poured ourselves a drink of the Scotch whiskey, which we drank in between morsels of the sweat-silky bebinca. I quickly excused myself saying that I had an emergency at the medical college. El Rei was happy to linger on sipping pegs of the precious Scotch, which was now a rare and much sought-after commodity. As I left Maria's house, she accompanied me down the steps, thanked me for the serenade and kissed me on the lips. It was a long kiss that would linger on my lips for a long time to come.

Anton and I immediately took off for Baga.

Flushed with fever, dried out and semi-comatose, Paulo looked like death itself. I called out to him but he did not respond. Uma was sponging his body with cold compresses. Needless to say, I felt that my brother had a relationship with Uma and noticing her physical beauty a third time, I thought that perhaps Paulo's present state was worth it after all.

'I'm very sorry this happened to your brother,' Uma said. 'We love the man—he has my karma now—he'll be fine.'

As the Morris Minor sped off in a cloud of red mud and sand, a few stray dogs sleeping in the middle of the street lazily got up and made their way to the side of the road with a slanting disdainful look, as if to demand why their sleep was being disturbed in the early pre-dawn hours. A bunch of crows perched on a guava tree, suddenly and noisily, clapped their wings and took flight.

I suspected that Paulo had typhoid fever and took him to Goa Medical. By morning, Paulo began responding after receiving intravenous fluids. He tried to utter some words, but he was too weak. I called the England-returned Dr Savelkar, who had an excellent reputation as a diagnostician, to consult on Paulo. He confirmed the diagnosis of typhoid fever and started him on intravenous antibiotics. He also prescribed intravenous sedatives, fearing he might suffer withdrawal symptoms.

That evening, I went home to inform my parents. Mama was beside herself and blamed my father for Paulo's illness, while my father called all this a disgrace to the good name of the Albuquerque family and blamed Paulo's misadventures on my mother for spoiling him. Paulo remained hospitalised for almost two months, ayah Carmina constantly by his side. When he returned home, he looked like one of the burnt-out hippies. In Carmina's care, Paulo recovered speedily with daily coconut oil massages and chicken broth.

Paulo stopped drinking for a while, but not for long. He missed Uma, who left Goa for America during the monsoons months. She was different from other women he had known, someone he had no control over, who was into things beyond his comprehension, but he loved her company nonetheless.

Fifteen

Amanda's Tribulations

Since Amanda's row with Mama, nothing much had changed. Winnie and Amanda continued their secret rendezvous in beach bars and on secluded beach strips. But after Winnie joined the Maharashtravadi Gomantak Party, which stood for the merger of Goa into the neighbouring state of Maharashtra, Amanda and Winnie's relationship soured. At about the same time, Winnie assumed the position of head of the English department at Panjim College and moved back to his village of Calangute.

Mama wrongly assumed that it was over between them. My opinion of Winnie took a slide after his political flip-flop, as I believed that Winnie had switched parties for power or money or both. I had an argument with Amanda about it, when Paulo interjected, saying that matters of politics should not be mixed with issues of the heart. Amanda was upset, but tried to contain herself and not show it outwardly; like the rest of the family, she, too, was strongly against the merger.

A few days after the announcement of Winnie's change in political affiliation, I came to know from her diary that she met Winnie in Panjim at the Copacabana Bar, at about three in the afternoon. Winnie had consumed a few beers by then and was a bit tipsy when she arrived. They kissed as soon as they sat down on the upper floor of the restaurant where there were no other customers. After she had a few sips of beer, she felt his hand underneath her pleated skirt. She pushed his hand away. Disappointed and chagrined, he apologised, telling her that he had been fantasising and had decided to muster greater courage and boldness in his advances. As she laughingly turned her head to the side, she saw the waiter watching from behind.

'Another beer, sir?' asked the waiter.

They stiffened up, but it was too late. Embarrassed, she dropped her glance and told Winnie, rather angrily, that they better leave. He left some money on the table and they abruptly left, hailing a taxi for Dona Paula.

In Dona Paula, at the roadside tavern, they stopped for *pão-chouriço* and bottles of beer, after which they climbed the rocky hill on top of which was an elegant gazebo; and there, they ate the spicy-pungent bread with sausage, washed it down with beer and waited for the sun to set on the Arabian Sea.

The event at the Copacabana, the waiter quietly watching, had visibly upset Amanda. Now standing on the headland, looking straight down, she felt mesmerised by the crashing waves and remembered the legend of Dona Paula, whose name the place carried. She felt cold, her teeth clattered and her body shivered as she was gripped by a sense of tragedy—for legend had it that the lady Dona Paula, betrayed by her lover, committed suicide by leaping off the cliff.

'What's wrong, Amanda?' asked Winnie.

'It's the waves—I always get mesmerised by the waves—they have a magnetic pull on me.'

'The waves?'

'Never mind, Winnie. Perhaps it's Dona Paula's ghost lurking in the ocean breeze. I have the shivers, let's leave this place.'

They came down the steps and walked onto a nearby short secluded strip of beach and there, Winnie embraced and kissed her. He whispered in her ear that he was longing to make love to her. She told him that it was not the right time. He insisted.

'I will give myself to you on the day we marry,' she said.

'How does it matter between now and then? What matters is that we love each other,' he said.

'Perhaps nothing matters to you?' she said. 'Maybe that was the reason you joined the Maharashtravadi Gomantak Party? How can you support that party's agenda? They will merge Goa into Maharashtra. Don't you see they're using you?' She could see the tension in his face, but she carried on: 'Look, most of the educated Goans: lawyers, judges, doctors, government officials, have left for Portugal, the Goan diaspora to Portugal has ended. But if Goa is merged into Maharashtra, those of us still here, who are nationalistic and attached to this land, will leave as well. Besides, whatever is left of our unique culture, our identity, will be lost forever.'

'Wait a second—I'm fed up with the accusations and insinuations.'

'No—you wait—and listen: your heart is burst. You have lost half your soul.'

'Bravo,' he said, clapping his hands. 'That was a great quote from *Othello*. I should hire you to teach literature.' And then angrily he piped: 'Shit, Amanda! I'm not responsible for what's happening to Goa and so what if Goa is gobbled by Maharashtra? Weren't you the privileged class during the Portuguese years? Your mother and your aunt and that priest still think I'm no good for you. Fuck it—at least once in four hundred and fifty years you elite people, *nobres* as you like to call yourselves, need to have your ego blasted like they blast the land for iron ore.'

'Stop it, Winnie. We all could end up empty-handed and powerless under Maharashtra. Just look at the freedom fighters that gave up their youth behind bars. Now they're alienated, powerless, feasting on leftover crumbs.'

'The privileged class is scared shitless. Who cares about your culture?'

'I cannot believe what I'm hearing. So that's what it is, *hmm*—an inferiority complex?'

'Despise me, then. I know my price. I'm worth no less,' he responded tersely, clenching his jaw, his arm rising in a semi-threatening pose, but he managed to restrain himself. She knew then that the remark had landed where it hurt most.

Remorseful, she instinctively hugged him. He remained stiff and suddenly, he doubled up and clenched his belly in agony. The furrows on his forehead, the perspiration and the contracted muscles in his arms revealed intense pain. He slumped on the sand, staying there with his head in between his hands for several minutes. Nervously, she once again put her arms around him. After a while, he got up and wiped his forehead with a handkerchief.

'It was only a belly pain. Must be the *chouriço*. I'm okay now. It's late, we better go.'

On the way back to Panjim, they did not speak a word. Their silence sat in between them like the encroaching night. At the jetty, Winnie stepped out of the taxi and took the ferry to Betim, while Amanda continued to Altinho to a cousin's house.

Next morning, she went to meet him at the college that was temporally housed at the old Portuguese lyceum, but when she got there, she changed her mind and went home. They had parted in a state of tension and confusion; she wasn't sure whether to make up with him, wondering whether they loved each other enough for their love to survive the difficulties that lay ahead.

Paulo and I were sitting on the steps to the house chatting, when the daily bus arrived from Margão. Amanda stepped out and ran into the house in tears. She did not even say hello to us. I chased after her and asked her what was wrong, but she did not answer and locked herself in her room, reciting Shakespeare. At times she felt better after sobbing uncontrollably; at other moments she felt consumed by pain, overtaken by a terrible solitude. Ayah Carmina kneaded and massaged her feet and fed her with her own hand morsels of rice with her favourite pungent sour fish-curry—*the amott-tikk.*

After giving her some space to calm herself down, several hours later, we knocked on her door. Surprisingly, she let us in.

'You look troubled. Were you crying?' Paulo said and embraced her, kissing her on the forehead. She remained detached and far away as if lost in her own thoughts.

'What's bothering you? It's Winnie, isn't it?' I said.

'Yes,' she said. 'We broke up. I met him yesterday at the Copacabana. I arrived late and he had already consumed a few beers. He made some bold and aggressive advances that upset me.'

'He made sexual advances towards you? The bastard!' I exclaimed.

'Calm down, Roberto,' said Paulo. 'Go on, Amanda.'

'Who does he think you are? Paulo, we need to have a word with this man,' I said.

'No, Roberto, please don't meddle in my affairs. You have already messed up my life by mentioning Winnie on Christmas day. I can take care of myself.'

'I'm sorry, Amanda.'

'*Merda* on Mama and Papa,' Paulo said. 'Who cares if they don't approve of your relationship? The pressure will lighten if you see each other more often and in the open. Amanda, you're too young and beautiful to be sad.' Amanda seemed surprised at his advice but did not reject it. And as if to change the topic, she asked him about his own plans.

'Why don't you make a life in Goa now that you have a bar appointment? Forget Portugal once and for all!'

After a long silence, Paulo spoke in a soft voice as if he was looking at a distant time. While dragging deeply on a cigarette, he told us about Ana Sofia. 'I wrote her so many letters,' he said. 'The only answer I received came before Goa's takeover, even though mail between Portugal and Goa has been restored. There are other things in my life, very bad and confusing things, that

I cannot speak about. But hopefully soon, I will receive a letter from my friend who promised to inquire about events in Coimbra since my departure. Then, I will decide about my future. I have no interest in practicing law in Goa. As a matter of fact, I never had interest in law—it was Papa's idea.'

'Didn't Mama give you any letters?' Amanda asked, rather surprised. 'There was a letter that came for you about five months after you returned and subsequently, maybe six months back or more, there were at least three letters from Portugal. I saw the Portuguese stamps and your name written in large capital letters on one of them.'

'Mama must have read my letters. She knows. I am disgraced. Now I understand her change in attitude,' he said.

'What do you mean by disgraced?' asked Amanda. He did not respond but walked briskly out of the room. Turning back, he told me that he would like a word with me in private.

'Did you spill our secret?' he asked.

'No, absolutely not!' I said. Paulo then went to confront Mama and ask about the letters. I followed behind.

Mama and Tia Rosita were sitting in the balcony chatting with our neighbour, Dona Alcina, who had a great sense of humour and was good at telling jokes about the village freaks. Tulsi was sitting on the steps on one side of the balcony and Carmina was sitting on the other. It was dusk. The four were laughing at Dona Alcina's description of the village imbecile's infatuation with her maid. Our entry abruptly interrupted the laughter. But with so many people around, Paulo felt it was not the right time to confront Mama.

Later, after dinner, Paulo, Amanda and I, took a long walk on the riverbank. We sat on a rock under a coconut tree and watched the dark waters of the river glide downstream. A school of baby shrimp suddenly burst though the surface, exploding in the moonlight as if in ecstasy; some spilled over the riverbank and met a premature death. We waited for night to settle and then went home and to bed.

Amanda was restless and couldn't fall asleep. She tried to read but lacked concentration. It was then that she decided to write in her diary all that transpired between her and Winnie; after which, exhausted, she fell asleep. That night she had a dream: she was all alone in the gazebo at Dona Paula, looking down at the crashing waves, when the same urge to jump came over her. The spirit of Dona Paula came prodding in the shape of a mermaid and they both made the plunge. She floated on the waves—and the motion, the rising and falling, felt peaceful, a water bed that put her to sleep.

Sixteen

Missing Letters

A few weeks later, when the postman arrived on his bicycle, we were sitting in the balcony.

'Hand me the letters, Caetan,' Paulo ordered.

'No, Baba, I have to hand them to your mother.'

'You have been handing my letters to my mother and receiving a bribe,' Paulo said. 'I could get you into a lot of trouble—even get you fired.' Caetan looked nervous as the threatening words rang out. He stammered, spraying saliva all over, asking whether the landlady was at home, scratched his bald head and fumbled in his pockets as if searching for a treasure that had escaped though his khaki pants. Paulo approached him threateningly. The postman swirled the leather mailbag to the front of his chest and produced a letter for Paulo. Hearing the argument, Mama came running from the bedroom.

'What is it, Paulo? Why are you shouting at poor Caetan? He is only doing his job to feed his nine kids.' Without making eye contact, she began walking to the bedroom and sat in her rocking chair. Paulo followed her and struck back.

'What have you done with my letters, Mama?'

'What letters?' she asked as if surprised, tilting back in her rocking chair.

'I know that there were letters that came from Portugal. Amanda saw the postman handing them to you.'

'So you and Amanda are ganging up on me now?'

'Where are my letters, Mama?'

'Oh yes, now I remember. There were letters for you. *Hmm...* I must have forgotten to give them to you. They must be in that drawer in my escritoire.' She got off the chair, unlocked the third drawer of her secretary and produced three letters. They had possibly arrived at the same time since at least two of them must have been held back in Portugal after the military invasion of Goa.

'But where are the letters I received after I returned from Portugal?'

'I don't know what you are talking about. This is all I have. And you see, I have not even opened them. I just forgot to hand them over to you.'

'I cannot believe you did this, Mama.'

'I have always defended you, Paulo, protected you, given you money without the knowledge of your father, pawned jewellery to support your spending habits, paid all your debts that keep on mounting and what have you done with your life?'

Paulo took the letters and walked out.

From Mama's diary

That night, when I was combing my hair before bedtime, I looked at the letter addressed to my son that lay on the dresser. The return address stated in bold letters: Ana Sofia, Rua dos Estudos 45, Apartamento No. 3, Coimbra, Portugal.

The letter, from Dona Figueira's daughter, Ana Sofia, made me curious. Besides, my husband and I were suspicious of Paulo's unexpected return, believing him to be not entirely forthcoming about the real reason. With some reluctance, I carefully inserted the ivory letter opener in an attempt to cleanly open the letter so that I could later close it flawlessly. But the heavily glued envelope tore. I read its contents and was shocked. If Paulo knew, I felt certain he would immediately leave for Portugal and that would be the end of him and my dreams for him. I went to the kitchen and flung the letter in the smoldering wood fire and buried any thoughts of what I read, not confiding with anyone, even my husband.

A few days later, I reluctantly instructed the postman to deliver all the letters for Paulo to me, placing two one-rupee notes in his pocket. Caetan assured me with a nod and placed his index finger across his lips. The next two letters from Ana Sofia requested Paulo's return and expressed surprise that he had not addressed the issue she had raised in her previous letters.

I was overcome with guilt, but felt that my action was morally justified: Ana Sofia and her mother Dona Figueira had planned all of this to ensnare Paulo. After all, he was a big Goan fish and Dona Figueira was a Portuguese peasant or a lady of marginal means; otherwise, why would she have kept boarders? I mentioned the letters and its shocking contents to Father Vicar at the confessional and he assured me that I did the right thing. 'It is a mother's duty to protect her children,' he said.

It was my obligation to see to it that Paulo wouldn't leave for Portugal to marry that girl. It would come to no good. Besides, how would he support a family? I could convince my husband to let Paulo have his part of the inheritance. But what then? How long would the money last, considering Paulo's spending habits? And what would happen when the money was gone? Portugal is no Goa. No, I had to protect him under my wings like the mother hen protects her chicks. Suffused with remorse, I did not read the remaining letters, which arrived a good time after the Indian takeover of Goa. For a long time, during and after the takeover, the mail between Portugal and Goa had been suspended.

Now I sit on this rocking chair, contemplating the chaos all around me. What is all this talk from my children about the need to discover their own identities, to find their place amidst a remoulded society? Whatever happened to our family traditions? I had fantasised a different world for Paolo: He was to be a judge and I dreamt of attending weddings, receptions and even funerals by his side. My cousins, the villagers and the dignitaries would adore Paulo and, in the process, I would relish my position as the proud mother of an accomplished son.

Of course, my husband was an accomplished man. A mayor and subsequently an administrator, but a rather docile one, often withdrawn, a private person for whom political receptions and protocols were an ordeal; a man who seemed uncomfortable in the job. But not Paulo: he was tall, handsome and fair, a man of the world. By God, he would look like a god in a black judicial robe.

That evening, after confronting Mama, Paulo went to his room and opened the letter that was just delivered by the postman. This was the long awaited letter from his friend, Alberto.

Dear Paulo,

I am writing to you in a hurry and I am sorry for the delay. I stayed in Lisbon and Oporto for six months and, subsequently, I spent a month in Paris with my cousin who sends you his regards. He was asking me about you and was very surprised that you were still in Goa. I also spent a few months in Madrid with my brother, the petrochemical engineer, who is married to a wonderful Spanish woman.

If things do not work out for me in Portugal, I may move to Madrid. Spain at this time offers better opportunities than Portugal. Besides, my sister-in-law has many contacts. I'm sorry for boring you with the details of my life, but now you can understand why I delayed so long to write, since it took me almost a year to make it to Coimbra after I left Goa.

I found out through a friend of yours, Florêncio Pimenta, who has started a law practice, that both Raul and his brother Angelino, the men you were concerned about, have gone back to Cabo Verde. Apparently, Angelino was in jail; he wouldn't tell me why, but your friend Florêncio managed to commute part of the jail sentence because of an underlying medical condition, an epileptic fit that Angelino had.

The second issue is about Ana Sofia. Here things got very complicated.

I went to the house and an older man met me at the door. He ushered me to the living room and asked me very politely who I was and what was my business. In the living room there was a toddler, a moreno with brown curly hair, playing with a motor toy on the floor. I told him that I had come to see Dona Figueira and her daughter Ana Sofia and that I had a message from Paulo Albuquerque. He had barely started speaking, saying that Ana was not at home, when a woman, I presume her mother, stormed out.

'Did I hear the name Paulo Albuquerque and a friend of his has a message for us?' she said. 'Vá-se embora, Vá-se embora—get out! Get out!' she shouted at me, gesticulating like a wild woman with her threatening hand. I hurriedly got up and left; she slammed the door after me.

I am very sorry if I couldn't be of more help. I hope to see you soon in Coimbra. Best wishes, Alberto.

'He is alive! He is alive!' Paulo screamed and jumped up and down.

'Who is alive?' I asked.

'Angelino is alive!' He came and embraced me and heaved a sigh of relief.

'Angelino is out of the way in Cabo Verde,' he said.

Obviously, the convulsion that Angelino had experienced was probably an epileptic fit. I told him that Angelino's unconsciousness following the epileptic fit was a post-convulsion state and was unrelated to the lamp blow he had dealt him on the head on that fateful day in Coimbra.

'What a horrible mistake I made,' Paulo said, as he stooped with his head in the palms of his hands. I should have gone to the police, rather than running away. And even if Angelino de Tor had died from the blow after what he did to me, it could be classified as self-defense. I acted precipitously. Foolishly. The fact that Ana Sofia in her first letter hadn't mentioned him or his brother Raul perplexed me. I considered the possibility that he might be alive but thought it impossible. All these years of uncertainty—the pain and suffering and all the anxiety—for nothing! '

'You must have panicked,' I said. 'Without feeling Angelino's pulse or his heartbeat there was no way you could say with certainty that he was dead.'

Paulo did not know what to make of the second part of the letter. Why was Dona Figueira mad at him? After all, he had sent her the money he owed. And who were the middle-aged man and the little boy?

Paulo took out a Charminar cigarette and lit up.

Since his illness and during the monsoon season when Uma and her gang dispersed to different corners of the world, he often sat by himself in the veranda at sunset with nothing to do, but sadly await the still silence of the village night.

Finally, Paulo went to his room and tearing open the three envelopes, all from Ana Sofia, he began reading them in the order they were written.

My love,

I am mortified at not receiving your letter and you not responding to the letters I wrote to you after I came to know that I was pregnant. How could you ignore me at the very time I needed your emotional and financial support? Whatever happened to all the promises you made at the statue of Santa Catarina?

The letter I received from you after you unexpectedly left does not even refer to my second and subsequent letters. I simply cannot understand it. You cannot imagine what I have gone through these months. And not a single response from you to the three letters I wrote.

Mother threw a tantrum after she came to know of my pregnancy. I managed to keep it from her for nearly five months, but after that I had no choice. She said that she would have taken me to England or to Germany to have an abortion if she knew before. In the beginning, I did not realise I was pregnant. Only after I missed my period for two months in a row I became suspicious. I prayed hard that my suspicions were not true. I believed you would marry me as soon as you came to know of my condition. I thought you would want the child as much as I wanted it.

Perhaps you ignored my letters because you are already married to a Goan girl? I told my mother that you would never abandon me. I was wrong and my mother was right.

In a couple of months, I will deliver. I don't know what I am going to do. I have stopped studying. I feel terribly ashamed. I don't know how I am going to support my child.

All my love,
Ana Sofia.

'Oh my God,' Paulo said. 'Ana Sofia was pregnant; and the child, the boy Alberto refers to in his letter, is obviously my son. Mama, knowing all along, probably felt that if I knew about the pregnancy, I would have left for Portugal to marry Ana Sofia and she couldn't accept that. She read the letter and destroyed it, leaving the others unopened to cover up her guilt; yet, hiding them to keep me ignorant.'

Now he understood why Dona Figueira was so mad at the mention of his name.

Sick to his stomach, he did not read the second letter, which was written a few months after the first. He walked out of the house towards the church. I accompanied him. After a couple of whisky-sodas at Ferrão's bar, he calmed down.

As we were leaving the bar, the bus from Margão arrived and Amanda stepped out. We walked home together. Paulo told Amanda about the letters.

'Poor Ana Sofia,' said Amanda, all teary. 'I cannot believe Mama could do this. I wonder whether Papa knows.'

'Paulo, you better read the remaining letters and decide for yourself,' I said.

That night after dinner, Paulo mustered the courage to continue with the letters. The second letter was written in January of 1962.

My dear Paulo,

I don't know whether this letter will reach you or not. We were shocked with the Indian invasion and the takeover of Goa.

We read in the newspapers that Goa remains occupied by Indian troops and the Indians are treating the Goans very badly. Is it true that they have taken all the government posts? What a shame!

I hope you and your family will migrate to Portugal soon. I am very worried about you. I received your letter mailed just before the invasion. Again, I am surprised that you make no mention of my pregnancy. I now suspect that you may not be receiving my letters, otherwise why would you even bother to write?

I had made up my mind to come down to Goa. My mother, after much begging, had agreed. I wanted a name for our child, if nothing else.

I had fixed the date of departure for 2 January and as I was about to write to you that I was coming down, then came the tragedy of the invasion and now I am unsure what to do.

There are no diplomatic relations with India and I will not be able to get a visa. Perhaps you can find out more about this? Maybe your family has influence and contacts with the Indian authorities.

My due date is past and I am very nervous and anxious and so is my mother.

I will pray to Santa Catarina that you may receive this letter.

Love, Ana Sofia.

He began reading the last letter.

Dear Paulo,

Our son is called Paulo Junior, but I have not baptised him for lack of a surname. I have not received any letters from you; perhaps they have been lost or just thrown in the garbage by the postal authorities. In the meanwhile, my father returned from Macau for good. He sustained shrapnel wounds in Angola, which have left him with a bad limp.

He was very upset and angry with mother and me. He felt very strongly that I should have gone to Goa immediately after I came to know I was pregnant. He blamed my mother for not keeping a close eye on me and has threatened several times to go to Goa and look for you. He feels that it is your responsibility to provide your name for the boy and financial support.

Because I could not bear to hear my father's curses when he drank, it is a little more than a year now that I left for Lisbon after securing a job as a nanny for an American family.

I kept Paulo Junior with my mother and I visit him often on weekends. The American, who is an executive of a company, treats me well. He has a two-year-old son who reminds me of our son and it makes me cry.

I have given up hope of ever seeing you or hearing from you. I feel in my bones that you are already married to a Goan, as my mother predicted. I know now that I have to make life on my own.

To some extent, I feel better and stronger after I took this job. I could not live anymore in Coimbra with my father and my hysterical mother. But I miss little Paulo very much. He has your colour and your hair; the rest I think is mine.

Yours, Ana.

Paulo felt reassured that Ana Sofia was working and would be able to support herself and Paulo Junior was well. This seemed to ease his guilt. He was disturbed by the possibility of Ana Sofia's father coming down to Goa to look for him. However, he thought it unlikely that that would happen; it was doubtful the man would get a visa.

He felt like writing back; but first, he had to muster the courage to ask Papa for his part of the inheritance now and not after his father's death, which was the traditional way of doing things. His part of the inheritance would be substantial even if divided equally among the siblings. He would sell the properties, send money to support his son and Ana Sofia and with the rest, he would be gone.

He wondered whether his father would consent to it and now he couldn't count on Mama either. His return to Portugal seemed more and more like a distant illusion.

Paulo chain-smoked Charminars as he rocked on the chair. My room, which was by the side of his room separated by half a wall, was filled with smoke. I asked him what was wrong. He opened the window to let in some air. There was a silvery crescent moon that night that lit the garden on the west side of the house. A serpent wound itself around a mango tree, inching slowly where a red-crested chameleon lay upright, sheltered by a green peppercorn vine. The chameleon's light green body was well camouflaged, but the crescent moon's silver sheen betrayed its hiding place. The snake gobbled it in one stroke like a swallow of hot tea. The hungry jackals began their macabre howling and today, for unknown reasons, there was no response from the village dogs.

Just before we retired to bed, I asked Paulo if he wanted to go for a walk. He agreed.

'Can we have a drink?' said Paulo.

'Not me. If you want one, sure,' I said.

We entered the roadside tavern with a window and a draw of locally brewed liquor bottles of cashew feni, urrak and coconut feni. One-eyed Kakodcar and his bent-over wife owned and worked the tavern and lived in the room behind. As we entered the tavern, the wooden sign dangled and knocked on the foreheads of half-drunk peasants leaving late at night. The broken sign, with missing syllables like fallen teeth, still read in Portuguese: *'Ta e na Li enc ada, Prop: Su il Ka odkar'*—licensed Tavern. Proprietor: Sunil Kakodcar.

After Paulo had a shot of feni liquor, we proceeded to walk on the riverbank below. It was then that Paulo told me all in great detail: about the letters, about Ana Sofia's pregnancy and his profound anxiety and insecurity since his return that had taken its toll. He also related his dreams and nightmares: of a big bird pinning him down and how he would wake up struggling and tearing at the bed sheets. How he would stab the big bird as it lay dying on its back, its wide wings flapping, its shrill cries full of agony piercing his ears and how he would wake up screaming, all splattered with blood.

'Now you will understand why I drink and keep on screaming in my sleep.' I saw tears in Paulo's eyes, as he covered his face in the palms of his hands and whispered: 'My son, my son, I don't even know when I will hold him in my arms.'

We talked till midnight, but mostly I listened to what Paulo had to say and it aroused mixed emotions in me. I felt warmth for my brother like I had never felt before. For the first time I even felt as if I was the older brother, pitying him, witnessing a deep vulnerability, a spiralling destructiveness, an unravelling of his life. And yet, to some extent all this was anti-climactic and disdainful. I believed all along that Paulo was destined to accomplish great things, to soar to great heights. His charm, his looks, the debonairness that was so much a part of his persona would serve him well. Little did I know that in the long run, appearances did not matter much. It was in Paulo's nature to take risks. His life was an adventure—and the price he was paying was irrevocably high.

As soon as we returned home, I saw Paulo trembling while we entered his room. He insisted I go back to sleep. As I left Paulo's room, I saw him frantically searching for the feni bottle hidden under the mattress. Likely ayah Carmina had taken it when making his bed.

Paulo decided to look for some liquor in the pantry. There were carafes of feni and urrak in there and Carmina kept the keys of the pantry; sometimes, the pantry door remained unlocked, as often happened, Carmina forgot to lock the door.

Paulo lit a kerosene lamp and proceeded through the hallway into the large dining room, past another long corridor and tried the door of the pantry, slowly and gently lest its creaking sound wake up the servants. Finding the door unlocked, he looked for the carafes amid mounds of *chouriço*, dried red chillies, sacks of black peppercorns and rice, jars of pickles and preserves and bottles of the homemade soft drinks, the *orxata* and *xarope de brindão*. And there he found them like temples of gold, two carafes and a bottle. Paulo uncorked the bottle of Madeira, a 1956 Bual Adegas de Torreão and emptied it in his mouth. It was the last bottle left over from the Portuguese days and, when he finished with it, it was less than half-full. He uncorked the carafe of feni, took a long drink from it and emptied some into the bottle of Madeira up to the brim like when he was a teenager and played all sorts of pranks. He managed to find his way to his bed amid the shadows created by the fading kerosene lamp and fell into a deep stupor.

He slept till almost eleven in the morning when I came to wake him up. The lieutenant governor was expected in the village together with some dignitaries of the governing political party and a short visit to our house was on the agenda.

Mama, who was gradually but reluctantly accepting the realities of the new order, had seen to it that the house was in tiptop shape. A light lunch consisting of sandwiches of chicken and coriander chutney, *bajji puri* and chicken *xacuti* made by Tulsi the Hindu way and pomfret *rexead*, *arroz refogado* and shrimp *balchão* were on the menu. There would be bebinca and flan for desert, Carmina prepared it; Tia Rosita, still bitter about the invasion, remained in her room, refusing to lend a hand. For drinks they would be served Coca-Cola, Fanta, whisky-soda, beer and for the special dignitaries from India, a taste of the fine Portuguese Madeira served in the drawing room. Mama and Papa wished to impress upon their Indian hosts the ways of the Goan noble folks and so they took out their most elegant china (*loiça de galo* from Macau) and Parisian crystal.

The acting lieutenant governor's party arrived two hours late. The introductions made, my father and I took the party for a tour of the house, after which we sat for drinks and the buffet lunch.

After lunch, to Paulo's surprise, Papa asked for the bottle of Madeira and in crystal glasses poured some for the non-teetotaler Indian dignitaries he led into the drawing room. Paulo was about to tell his father that the Madeira was bad. It was too late. Papa raised a brief toast, commenting on the progress (the newly tarred roads and electricity) made in the village by the newly elected democratic government. He then introduced the Madeira as an excellent Portuguese reserve and the last remaining bottle. Their eyes lit up at the very thought of such a precious elixir.

For prohibition-wary Indians, Goa was heaven on earth not because of its sun and sand and hospitality but because of the booze. They could drink to their heart's content. And drink they did: Paulo's cocktail with smiles and smack of the lips until the last drop of the precious elixir was licked from the rim of the crystal glasses like dessert-crossing, thirsty cowboys feasting on drops of moonshine.

That night after the rosary, at the dinner table, for the first time after long, we laughed at the events of the day and, just like in the old days, we seemed like a happy family once again. After dinner, Paulo, Amanda and I sat in the balcony and Paulo told us about his Madeira concoction that some of the Indian dignitaries drank. We laughed and laughed until we teared.

'They deserved it—these neo-colonisers,' Paulo said with some satisfaction, as if he had his unintended revenge.

Seventeen

Paulo's Redemption

The news that Angelino was alive finally sank into Paulo's consciousness, like a divine revelation releasing him of overpowering guilt and the subsequent euphoria that went along with it. The very reason for his binge drinking was now an afterthought. But the demons would not leave him. Not yet. They were deeply rooted in his brain like seafarers in a fable lost in the innards of some sea monster. One day, a week or so later, after re-reading the letters from Portugal, he called me to his room after breakfast.

'That damn Angelino is alive and out of the way,' he said, tapping me on the back. 'What a relief.' There was a tone of self-confidence in his voice that had been shattered a long time ago. I felt happy for him and contended that he had again taken me into confidence.

'But what about Ana Sofia and your son?' I asked.

'That's a big problem. I have to think about it. I have to find a solution,' Paulo said, after much thought. There was anguish written all over his face as the conversation changed from Angelino to Ana Sofia. And yet, he seemed to be in an upbeat mood, ready to take on the challenges that lay ahead. On the same day, in the evening, I left for Panjim. I had finished my condensed MBBS course and landed a registrar's job in the department of medicine at the medical college. Finally, I was practicing the art of medicine as well as teaching medical students.

I returned a couple of weeks later on a Friday evening to spend the weekend, when I found Paulo waiting for me at the bus stop. After dinner, Paulo suggested we go for a walk on the riverbank. Usually, Paulo stopped at the roadside tavern for a few shots of the local liquor. It took me entirely by surprise when he bypassed the tavern.

'Have you stopped drinking?' I asked.

'I haven't touched alcohol for the last two weeks,' he said. I found it hard to believe him, but gave no hint of my doubts. By now I knew that Paulo's actions were mostly impulsive without serious consideration of the consequences. I rather casually suggested that he might see a psychiatrist at the medical college to get a better grip on his drinking and his dreams. However, Paulo did not respond to it positively and I did not insist. After all, in Goa, in those days, psychiatry and psychotherapy were not in vogue; only two psychiatrists were servicing the whole of Goa.

'I have stopped drinking and I can slay the demons all by myself,' he said, confidently.

During the last few weeks, rather uncharacteristically, Paulo had been ruminating on all that had transpired since his return to Goa. He knew he had to make a radical change and take hold of his destiny. He decided to practice law, or to at least give it a try, although whatever law studies he had completed had been long forgotten. Perhaps he could start as an assistant, a junior partner to an established lawyer? He talked about it to Mama and at her suggestion (and upon much coaxing), approached Papa. They were both forgiving and even ecstatic at the idea.

'Give him a chance,' she said. 'After all, what do you have to lose?'

Soon, Paulo together with Papa approached our lawyer cousin in the city of Margão, who agreed to take on Paulo as his assistant without hesitation. This change in Paulo's fortunes was a cause for celebration at our house. Mama and Tia Rosita immediately claimed that it was their prayers and novenas to the Saints that had brought redemption. And more masses were offered and more candles were burnt in gratitude—with rice and coconuts offered as alms to the few village beggars—and more novenas were started to our favourite Saints: St Jude, St Francis Xavier and St Anthony.

The issue of Ana Sofia and Paulo Junior seemed more difficult to tackle. He wrote a long letter to Ana Sofia explaining everything (leaving out the more sordid details) and offering his financial support. He raised the possibility of her coming down to Goa for a holiday together with his son. He wasn't sure about marriage to Ana Sofia; however, he was willing to consider it. There was no return address on Ana Sofia's last letter from Lisbon, so he addressed it to her mother's house in Coimbra, hoping that her mother or father would hand it to her. If he was unhappy at practicing law in Goa, there was always the possibility he could return to Portugal, his long lost Ithaca. However, he wasn't sure how Mama and Papa would react to his leaving again. Not to mention the fact that he had no money of his own. Besides, he hadn't brought up the subject of Ana Sofia with Papa; let alone the fact that she had a child by him. He had only confided his intentions to me and to Amanda. The thought of what our parents might say to this scenario was something he wasn't ready to confront, not yet.

Paulo gained weight, grew a beard that had tinges of grey and became his usual ebullient self. He started attending the district court with our cousin and Tia Rosita and Mama marvelled at his poise and demeanour in the black robe. Papa purchased an Ambassador car, mostly for Paulo but also for family use. Whenever our cousin had cases to argue, Paulo went to court in his chauffeur-driven black Ambassador; the rest of his time he spent reading English law books, with which he had much difficulty. Often he asked Amanda to translate. He joined the United Goans Party and wrote an incendiary letter in the local newspaper questioning the legality of the military annexation of Goa by India and the agenda of the opposing party to merge Goa into the neighbouring state of Maharashtra. This article was much talked about, winning Paulo both friends and foes.

Eighteen

Goa for Goans

1967

Since Amanda and Winnie's falling out, they had not seen each other. A few weeks before the opinion poll, a referendum commissioned by the central government in New Delhi to decide whether Goa should merge into the neighbouring state of Maharashtra or remain as a separate entity, Amanda received a telegram from Winnie asking her to meet him in Panjim.

'Have an important announcement,' he wrote, '...will make you very happy.' As a prominent member of the Marashtravadi Gomantak Party, which was for Goa's merger, Winnie's switch to the United Goans Party, which was against the merger issue, had made it to the newspapers. The newspaper story speculated that the switch was related to disagreement regarding the administrative role of Maharashtra in the government of Goa, should the merger move succeed.

Winnie promised Amanda that he would work tirelessly to defeat the merger. Amanda was thrilled.

Twenty-four hours before the opinion poll, an eerie silence fell all over, as often happens the day before an election. The honking, the blaring of messages on loudspeakers announced by passing vans, taxis, buses and private cars had come to an end. The trees seemed still, the crows relentlessly called out their *caw-caw* and the air was heavy with the burden of an uncertain future. A sullen mood of expectation and fear had descended over Goa. If Goa merged into the state of Maharashtra, it would be reduced to a nonentity. There were no pre-election polls those days and no one knew what the outcome would be.

On the day of the poll itself, I, together with Paulo, frantically roamed in our car the south of Goa, together with some of the United Goans Party workers, making sure that those in remote areas voted.

The following day, the vote counting began at the Instituto Menezes Bragança in Panjim. It was done by hand and the results for each constituency were read on loudspeakers and posted on a blackboard written out in chalk. Some carried placards that read: *'Amchem Goem amka zai,'* which meant: Goa for Goans. While others carried those that read: *'Zalach pahize'* that meant: Merger is a Must.

Large crowds gathered around the Instituto and cheered and jeered as the numbers went up. I was there in jeans and a black T-shirt with a beach sunset painting under which was written: *Goa for Goans* together with Amanda and Maria, both in salwar kameez, holding large placards against the merger. Paulo was there as well, all dressed up in a Goa-tailored white cotton suit with a reporter from Reuters who was in Goa during the invasion and had come back for a follow-up story. Paulo was giving him some bad accounts and painted a bleak picture after the takeover.

'They have no business deciding whether Goa should merge into Maharashtra after more than four hundred and fifty-one years,' Paulo said, as the two of them took off for the Mandovi hotel where the reporter was staying.

Most of the initial vote-counting was from north Goa, where the majority was for the merger. The following day, we anxiously waited for the count from south Goa.

Amanda looked for Winnie but there was no sign of him. He had told her that he would come to the Instituto at about four o'clock. She thought that perhaps he was at some strategy planning meeting. When I saw Amanda and Maria's apprehension, I tried to reassure them. 'Don't you worry,' I said. 'We'll sink them soon into the Arabian Sea. Just wait for the vote from the South.' Maria, who was with Amanda, remarked, pointing at her heart: 'If you say so, Roberto—I believe and have faith in you.' Accidentally, the placard she was holding slipped out of her hands. I bent down to pick it up and for an instant our hands touched. I felt her warm breath on my face as her pink lips parted in a smile.

Turning towards Amanda, she said, 'I really appreciate Roberto—he has tirelessly worked against the merger.' Did she say it loud enough for me to hear?

'Has Maria all of a sudden lost her heart to you?' Amanda whispered in my ear. I shrugged, though my cheeks flushed.

At almost 7.30 in the evening, the returns from south Goa began trickling in and before the count was closed for the night, it was clear that merger with Maharashtra was rejected. Cheers, tears, bear hugs and plenty of firecrackers followed. The battle for Goa was won.

Maria approached and hugged and kissed me for the hard work and invited me for a celebratory lunch the following day at her house. It was a great day for me: the merger issue was defeated and Maria gave me her dreamy look.

I took a deep breath, savouring the double victory.

As I passed the Mandovi hotel on my way home, I spotted Paulo at the entrance of the hotel. He asked me to join him at the party attended by Indian and foreign reporters. We celebrated the rejection of the merger with whisky-sodas, after which we went home. I asked Paulo about his law practice and whether he had received a response from Ana Sofia. Paulo shook his head and seemed withdrawn.

Nineteen

Winnie's Illness

Following the results of the opinion poll, Amanda spent the night at her cousin's in Altinho. Rather surprised at not seeing Winnie the previous day, Amanda inquired at Panjim College the next morning, only to learn that he was in critical condition at the Ribandar Hospital where he had undergone emergency surgery by Dr Balldesai.

She immediately left for the hospital where she found Winnie unresponsive, with tubes coming out of his orifices and some going into his belly. As Dr Balldesai passed by the corridor, she ran up to him. He told her that Winnie's condition was critical, that she should wait in the sitting room and that he would see her soon. Amanda sat stunned amid moans, groans, coughs and odours of antiseptic and disease all around, of gangrene and open sores. In about fifteen minutes, Dr Balldesai called her into his office.

'He had a mass in the belly. Now we'll have to wait for the pathology,' said Dr Balldesai.

'Mass? Is it a tumour? Is it cancer? Did you remove it?' Amanda asked, rather alarmed.

'It was a cyst, I'm sure. But there were nodes, which I removed,' he said, folding his hands as if in prayer and shaking his head to and fro.

Amanda began to cry and shake all over. After Dr Balldesai came to know that she was my sister, he reassured her that all would be well and offered her a cup of tea. He told her to go home and that he would discuss Winnie's medical condition with me. She came to see me at the medical college and described her conversation with Dr Balldesai. The word *mass* stuck in her mind like an ugly sore. I assured her that I would speak to Dr Balldesai.

Amanda took the bus to Old Goa. There, in the Basilica of Bom Jesus, she started a novena to St Francis Xavier and made a *vow* that she would marry Winnie if he came out of the illness alive.

The next morning, I met Dr Balldesai, who related his findings to me. On the day of the opinion poll, Winnie frantically travelled around in north Goa to see to it that villagers far from the voting booths were provided with transportation to vote. In the car, he vomited and the intermittent belly pain intensified. Though he began sweating profusely and could not retain any food or fluid, he persisted in travelling from one village to another.

By two in the afternoon, his weakening condition prompted his co-workers to take him to a local clinic, but he insisted on going home to Calangute. He spent a sleepless night as the pain worsened. Finally, at about two in the morning, he sent for his neighbour, asking him to get his friend, Dr Balldesai, a general surgeon—a know-it-all, well into his sixties who also practised internal medicine, a bit of dermatology, a whole lot of gastroenterology and a tiny bit of cardiology. He was famous all over Goa and its neighbouring states for his ping-pong ball therapy for pulmonary tuberculosis. He was no ping-pong player, but he was an expert at filling lung cavities from tuberculosis with ping-pong balls long after others in the field had abandoned the procedure. His actual surname was Desai however, due to his association with ping-pong balls, he was nicknamed Balldesai.

Dr Balldesai found Winnie febrile, dehydrated and with a belly that was like a wooden board. At his touch, Winnie winced with intense pain. Dr Balldesai took him to the Ribandar Hospital where he started intravenous glucose feeding and prepared him for the operating room. Dr Anil, my senior, who was a junior registrar studying for his master of surgery, assisted on the case. As Dr Balldesai opened Winnie's abdominal cavity, he saw a large mass like a melon straddling the top of his stomach and pancreas. The stomach was attached to this mass with a lot of adhesions.

'Pseudo-cyst of the pancreas, Anil. Have you seen anything like this before?'

'No, sir, no!'

The abdominal cavity was messy with small bloody pimples on the inner flimsy lining called the peritoneum, normally, the texture of cellophane. There was plenty of fluid that had the looks of soapy-foamy water. Dr Balldesai looked alarmed. Sweat began dripping from his forehead onto his eyeglasses and onto the surgical mask. He was not sure of himself, wondering whether he should remove the mass in the presence of inflammation of the pancreatic gland.

'What is it, sir?'

'Acute pancreatitis on top of chronic pancreatitis on top of pseudo-cyst of the pancreas on top of perforated stomach ulcer,' Dr Balldesai answered rapidly and authoritatively.

'Many on tops, sir! How many tops do we scoop off the top, sir?'

Dr Balldesai ignored the question and went on dissecting, until the bleeding became uncontrollable and the blood pressure began dropping precipitously. The anesthesiologist cursed as Winnie slipped.

After three blood transfusions and clamping and cauterising, the bleeding came under control. Dr Balldesai removed several of the nodes and left Dr Anil to do the closing. He entered the OR lounge reserved only for doctors and asked the peon to fetch two cups of strong, daylong-nightlong boiling tea. He took one cup and offered the other to Dr Anil. He looked tired and washed out. Dr Balldesai, however, tired or lemon fresh, always had a washed-out look. They both emptied their teacups into their saucers and slurped on it as if imbibing power and energy.

'What's the use?' he said, shaking his head in utter frustration and hopelessness. 'Winnie is a young man with a bright future. One day, the man could be the chief minister of Goa.'

'There is always possibility of reincarnation, sir, and maybe another chance at the chief ministership,' said Dr Anil, a close friend of mine and a bright and very funny bloke. After a long silence, as they were called back to the OR, to operate on a farmer with gastrointestinal bleeding, Dr Balldesai commented that Dr Anil would be better suited to be a Hindu priest than a surgeon. *'Tum bhott mure,'* he said.

Amanda returned to the hospital the following evening and was happy to see that Winnie was conscious and recognised her. A sliver of hope trickled in and she smiled.

Slowly, Winnie began to recover, although he lost a lot of weight. The pathology of the node was read as cancer of the stomach, but Dr Balldesai did not disclose the information to Winnie. He would tell him when he was about to leave the hospital.

Winnie spent a long time in the hospital. He developed diabetes and was receiving daily insulin shots. Amanda visited him often. Mama, Papa and Tia Rosita knew of the visits.

One day, at the dinner table, the conversation had turned to the opinion poll and the Chinese invasion of India. Tia Rosita made her usual proclamation that the Chinese invasion was a punishment from St Francis Xavier for the Indian invasion of Goa. She added Winnie to her punishment theory as well. When Mama commented that Amanda's visits to the hospital were scandalous, Amanda stormed off from the dining table. She told Paulo and me that she would marry Winnie as soon as he was discharged from the hospital.

The day before Winnie's discharge, Amanda was surprised to see him looking sullen and depressed. She asked him what was wrong. He looked out towards the street and the river beyond. After a long silence, still looking at the river, he told her they had no future.

'What do you mean, Winnie?' she cried. 'I want to marry you—you know that! I cannot live at home anymore. I will seek a teaching job in Panjim and we can rent an apartment in town or a house in Santa Cruz, or Caranzalem.'

'No, Amanda, I'm not in a condition to marry. Look at me... I am all scarred. Are you sure you want to marry me now? What kind of a future will you have with me? Besides, I am seriously thinking of migrating to Brazil. I've had it here! Uncle Cajetan keeps on writing to me to come. Why don't you just forget me, Amanda? That Dr Lobo will be delighted. He is crazy about you, heart and mind and family put together all bundled into one. He is just waiting for a nod of your head. He has started a practice in Saligão and given up on Mozambique just because of you.' She burst out laughing, brushing the issue aside. Winnie continued, serious. Amanda did not want to press the issue any further. She thought that perhaps Winnie was just feeling sorry for himself.

The previous evening, Dr Balldesai had come to Winnie's room to tell him that the lymph node biopsy had shown cancer of the stomach. With a puzzled look, he said that he was not sure whether it had spread; there was a possibility that it had invaded the pancreas, causing pancreatic inflammation, which gave rise to the cyst. He told him that he might need additional surgery and suggested that Winnie go to Tata Memorial Hospital in Bombay in due time. Winnie was stunned. After a long silence, he asked if it could be a mistake.

'Wouldn't it be wise to send the slides to Bombay, I mean to Tata Hospital?'

'Of course, Winnie, of course, we can do that. But our Dr Pereira is a good and reliable pathologist trained in Bombay at

Tata Memorial Hospital, the best cancer hospital in India. I was myself surprised with the diagnosis and requested Dr Pereira to look at it again. There's no mistake.' Winnie kept silent.

Twenty

An Act of Compassion

As Mari combed Mama's coconut oil-suffused hair, while she leisurely dozed in the balcony and Tulsi sorted through rice grains in a pan looking for tiny stones, she saw a priest climbing up the steps. 'Bai, look—somebody is coming—it's a priest!'

Startled, Mama jumped off the chair and saw Father Loyola. She ran inside, calling out to me to ask the priest to take a seat in the balcony and to get Carmina to open the hall. She proceeded to her room, changed into a dark brown dress and came to meet Father Loyola, while I ushered him into the hall.

'Good morning, Father Loyola. What brings you to my humble home?' said my mother.

'You are being very modest, Dona Isabella. You have a palace here,' he said. 'And, Dona Isabella, you need not have gone through the trouble of opening the hall. I only needed some privacy with you. We could even talk on the balcony...'

Mama, however, insisted on taking Father Loyola into the hall, which had a large main sitting area abutting the right wall and four semicircular sitting areas in each corner. Carved chairs lined the two walls. To ensure privacy, she chose the corner farthest from the door.

'Perhaps you know the reason for my visit,' Father Loyola said, placing his hand on her. 'Dona Isabella, I think Amanda is depressed. I certainly don't want to interfere in your family matters, but I thought you should know. She has requested me to intercede on her behalf.'

'I agree with your assessment, Father. I, too, think Amanda is depressed,' I said.

Mama, obviously irritated, shook her head stiffly. 'If it is something to do with that Winnie, I don't want to hear about it, Father. Neither she nor you can change my mind. We know that Amanda has been visiting him in the hospital in Ribandar. Scandalous! Scandalous behaviour, Father. What is our world coming to? If she is depressed, I'm not surprised. She eats very little and sometimes, she skips dinner. She sits in her room with the door closed reciting that Inglez: *Shakaspierre.* She will get over it as we all do. There is no sense in crying over spilled milk. Besides, that man is sick. I heard that he has an incurable illness.'

'Where did you hear about the seriousness of his illness?' he said, with a tremor in his voice, obviously surprised at Mama's outburst.

'Oh, I overheard a conversation.'

'He had acute pancreatitis and a cyst and has now developed diabetes,' I added.

'I hope this man has told her the truth. Perhaps then she will come to her senses,' said Mama.

After a long silence and hot steaming tea, Father Loyola tried once again to spell out the real purpose of his visit. 'Whether you want to hear about it or not, it is my Christian duty to bring it to your attention,' he said with authority as if he was lecturing one of his pupils. 'If it is your rejection of Winnie depressing Amanda, then you should reconcile with her and let them go on with their lives. If they want to get married, the earlier the better for them and for you; otherwise, the frustration and the ill will mounts. Please, Dona Isabella, seek to reconcile with your daughter; she is, after all, your only daughter. I care for them very much. They represent the future of Goa.'

'Future of Goa? What about the future of my family?' snapped Mama. 'Marriage with this Winnie is out of the question. She cannot count on my blessing and I can speak for my husband as well about that. Father Loyola, we are Church-abiding Christians. It is best you do not interfere with our personal affairs. We have our own parish priests that are well suited to provide advice and God's grace.'

This time around, Father Loyola knew he was licked. Tipping his hat, he left. His stiff and brisk departure reflected his profound irritation with my mother.

'Please, Mama, listen to Father Loyola,' I pleaded.

'You are too young to understand these matters. I will not have the family name in ruins,' said Mama.

As Father Loyola was getting into his jeep, I caught up to him and requested that he go speak to Winnie and that I would be happy to accompany him. I hopped into Father Loyola's jeep and we took off for Panjim, where we were informed that Winnie was on sick leave and nobody knew when he would be back. We decided to go to his home in Calangute.

When Amanda visited Winnie the previous day, he looked dishevelled and rather strange. He had already received a letter from Tata Memorial Hospital in Bombay that the slides of the lymph nodes confirmed the diagnosis of cancer of the stomach. This destroyed his last hope. Besides, the pain had also returned, but it was dull and more of a feeling of discomfort in his mid-belly. Amanda was seeing him for the first time after the results of the biopsy had arrived. She had previously implored him to go to Bombay or to Vellore to seek another opinion and she also raised the issue of marriage several times.

She had written in her diary: *We sat in his bedroom looking at each other and then his gaze drifted towards the floor. I approached him and kissed him on the lips, but found him distant. He looked haggard: the unshaven face, the glazed eyes, the dishevelled hair mirrored an inner vulnerability of illness. I moved closer to him, my hand tenderly caressing his body. He had frozen like a statue that desired no physical contact. How different from the man I had known. Unable to fathom his aloofness, the impenetrability, I withdrew, looking down at the cold, cemented floor.*

That night, I was restless—tossing and turning in a semi-sleepy state; and again, the dream of floating on the waves came back and, finally, lulled me to sleep.

Amanda left with a heavy burden, a burden of not knowing what was going on in Winnie's mind, plummeting her into the depths of uncertainty. And so it was that they lived in a time, in a space, where minds and bodies exist, loving, bordering each other, like rivers meandering through forests on fire, both unknowingly moving in separate directions as if towards their own calamitous end.

When Father Loyola and I arrived at Winnie's doorstep, his sister ushered us into the sitting room. Winnie, who had shortly before sent off a telegram requesting a meeting with Father Loyola, was surprised to see us.

'Father, you received my telegram so soon? That's impossible—it was sent just thirty minutes ago,' exclaimed Winnie, kissing his hand.

'Which telegram, Winnie? We left Margão at ten.'

'Then you two came on your own?'

'Of course, of course—but why the telegram? Did you want to discuss some important matter?'

'Yes, Father, I need your help.'

'It is the will of God.'

Winnie told us everything there was to tell about his illness: the cancer and Amanda's obsession of marrying him as soon as possible.

'What's the use of marriage, Father? Why spoil her chances?

Why destroy her life? Mine is over.' At that moment, I felt sorry for Winnie and more so for my sister.

'She has to be told the truth and soon,' Father Loyola advised. 'Suspense is the worst torture, it corrodes like acid. She's very depressed and on the brink of a nervous breakdown.'

Father Loyola, who had sensed Winnie's dilemma all along, told him that he was willing to break the news to Amanda. Winnie's eyes flushed with tears. It was as if a yoke was lifted off his shoulders.

The next morning, during the school recess, Father Loyola summoned Amanda to his office. I imagined her tugging at the hem of her skirt, something she always did when fraught with anxiety. He told her everything Winnie had told him and that he had spoken to her mother and related that her mother refused any compromise on the issue. He was surprised that Amanda showed no emotion whatsoever. After he had spoken for almost half an hour, the silence was unbearable. She just looked right through him as if in a waking dream like a *petit mal* state.

'I will pray for a miracle, dedicate every Mass I say for the two of you. But you need to reconcile with the reality of Winnie's cancer.' Amanda looked down at the floor as if resigned to her fate. 'I will do anything for you Amanda. I will support you and Winnie all the way. Go now in the grace of God,' said Father Loyola.

The following day, as Father Loyola was leaving the classroom, Amanda approached and asked whether she could have a word with him.

'Do you want to come to the office?' he asked.

'It's not necessary, Father. Will you marry us?' asked Amanda, abruptly. The question startled Father Loyola, who pondered for some time and then nodded. She went into her class with a sad smile on her face as the orbs of a few tears rolled down her cheeks.

That evening, Amanda went to Winnie's house in Calangute. She wrote in her diary:

Winnie was not at home, nor was Winnie's sister there. I waited for him in the balcony. At about 6 in the evening, when Winnie returned, I flew into his arms. We did not exchange words, but cried together streams of tears, as the emotions of the last few months came pouring forth like a torrential rain shower. As we walked towards the sea, the night was upon us, the ocean was calm, the sky, a crystal black. I could see far beyond... a lonely boat with a flickering light, without sails, without oars, disappear into the horizon.

Twenty-one

The Sting of Peppercorns

A few weeks after Amanda came to know of Winnie's cancer and decided to marry him nonetheless, I learned that a white man had visited our home. At the time of his visit, I was in Bombay taking the American Educational Council for Foreign Medical Graduates (ECFMG) examination.

Before I left for America, I tried to find out from my mother about the white man. She stated that he was a Portuguese friend of Paulo's who came on a visit. Tulsi, who had seen him, initially spread the news around like butter on bread and then subsequently denied it. It is likely that my mother bought her silence. The white man's identity remained a tightly held secret, like one kept in a safe at the bank. I did not pursue it any further. I was too busy preparing for my departure.

There was a main road to this story and there were also alleys and deadends I often got lost in, where my emotions played hide-and-seek. After reading my mother's diary, my sister's journal, the letters Paulo received from Portugal, the police report and the deposition by Captain Borda de Mar, I had tried to piece everything together, quilt-like, before coming back to Goa on this visit, after so many years. I was also surprised at the abrupt end of Mama's diary after her row with Paulo about the letters from Portugal. I wondered if there was something missing: a secret perhaps? Today, I was determined to sew it all together.

Now, ayah Carmina, after returning from the store, walks into the oratory with a tray. As she serves me cream-cracker biscuits with cheese and pours a chilled glass of Kingfisher beer, I ask her whether she knows anything about the white man, the mystery man and what his mission was. Carmina begins relating the events of that fateful day.

That afternoon when Mama, Tia Rosita and Paulo were in their respective rooms napping, a man knocked on the door and asked for Paulo, so Carmina immediately sent Mari to wake Paulo.

'Baba, Baba, wake up,' Mari said, tugging at the ends of Paulo's pajamas. Paulo turned around in his bed, half-asleep and quite irritated to be disturbed from his siesta.

'There is someone to see you, Baba. He is sitting in the balcony,' Mari insisted.

Paulo dressed up and reached the balcony at about the same time as Mama, who had also been alerted by Mari that there was a white man at the door looking for Paulo.

Paulo became upset at the sight of Mama, but did not protest her intrusion. The visitor, hearing oncoming footsteps, got off the chair and faced them.

Carmina saw him but did not recognise him right away. She stayed behind the front door that was partly closed. After seeing the visitor, Paulo had a startled look as if he had seen his own, aged ghost. Mama looked at the man and immediately recognised Captain Borda de Mar, despite the gray beard. He had aged—his countenance bore the effects of alcohol: pouched eyes, a swollen nose and a flushed complexion. Oddly, it seemed that the vices of hard drink and tobacco had had their decaying effect on both: the Captain and Paulo.

'Have I met you before?' he asked Paulo. Paulo shook his head and identified himself and introduced Mama.

The man introduced himself as António, the father of Ana Sofia and kept staring at Mama.

Mama was speechless. She had seen the resemblance between the man and Paulo and Paulo had seen it too. Each stared at the other for a long time. Time froze. Then, like a flash of lightning, he snapped his fingers, saying in Portuguese: '*Sim, Chopin,*' while moving his long tobacco-stained fingers as if he were playing the piano keys. He came towards her and pointing at her, he said: '*É—I-s-a-be-be-lla? Isabella!*'

He recognised her as he stepped back into a time when he had been the captain of the police station in the village of Aldona; the memory like a cascade of distant images probably flashed in front of his eyes. He kept staring at Paulo, perhaps struck by the resemblance. In a tremolo, Mama called out to Carmina to open the hall. She walked into the hall with the visitor and Paulo behind her. Paulo asked the captain where he had met his mother and the stranger, now no longer a stranger, said he met her many years ago in the village of Aldona.

As they sat in the right corner of the hall, Mama called out to Carmina asking her to close the door. Having done so, Carmina went to the other side of the hall where a door led to the study. She stayed behind the Chinese glass partition from where she could see and hear the conversation.

'What did you see and hear?' I ask.

'They were tense moments,' Carmina says. 'They kept staring at each other. It was then that I recognised him. He was like a ghost that had appeared out of the past. I instinctively turned my face away, like I had done almost thirty years ago. I made the sign of the cross and prayed.'

The captain was uncomfortable. He seemed at a loss for words. Mama looked at the mosaic floor and Paulo stared at the captain with an appraising look. His puzzled face, mouth semi-agape, dispelled an expression of surprise and astonishment, as if he had unearthed a mystery: that he was looking at his own aged face, as if in a mirror.

'At that moment, I think he made the link. He realised that the captain was his real father,' Carmina says.

'Oh my God… my brother was the captain's son and Ana Sofia was his half-sister?' I say. 'I didn't know all this until now. Carmina, why didn't you tell me before I left for America?'

'I had promised your mother I'd keep it a secret.'

I'm overwhelmed. For a short moment after I read my mother's diary and the captain's deposition, the thought had briefly crossed my mind but was summarily rejected. I feel apprehensive and dismayed and above all, a sense of empathy for my brother's despair and pain and the subsequent events that transpired. My eyes flush with tears; I feel hot and clammy. I cover my face with the palm of my hands. Afraid that I'll faint again, I take a few deep breaths and lie on the couch nearby. Carmina brings me some soup, with which I gradually feel much better. I think of the misgivings of one's own intelligence, one's self-deception and one's ability to take for granted what is irrelevant, turning a blind eye to what is obviously there. We conform to and mould into the world we were born in—our minds refusing to consider the horizon beyond and in-between.

'After the captain left,' Carmina now interjects, 'your mother made me swear that I would not tell anybody about this until her death. I would have told you when you came down, but you left immediately after your Mama's funeral.'

'Did my mother know all along that Paulo was the captain's son? Perhaps that is the very reason she always favoured and protected him? And did my father know?'

'If she suspected, she never told me. I didn't know, neither did I suspect,' Carmina quietly utters. 'Yes… Paulo was very fair, like a *pacló*, but so many Goan Hindus and Catholics are fair. Besides, your Mama married your father about a month and a half after the encounter with the captain.'

I now wonder whether my mother subconsciously knew and was in denial all along.

When Paulo realised what had gone on, the lies, the deceptions, he lost his composure and sense of reality. He felt as if a candle light had been extinguished by a gust of sudden wind. He felt faint. Darkness came over him, as it had on the train ride from Coimbra to Lisbon after his encounter with Angelinho de Tor. He took out his handkerchief and wiped his face. He took a sip of water and tried to steady himself. He gradually managed to absorb the reality of the room and saw an opening. He had to assert himself. He angrily twisted in the chair, then abruptly got off it and addressed Ana Sofia's father in a determined tone of voice.

'I didn't know until very recently that Ana Sofia had given birth to my son. I swear. And I didn't desert her.' He went on to tell him that he had not received Ana Sofia's letters. He then asked him whether he was here to seek financial support for Ana Sofia and his son. 'Well, you can discuss the issue of money with this grand lady... they can hand over all my inheritance to you for all I care,' said Paulo.

He asked Mama if he could have a word in private and they both left for the drawing room. Both, shaken; both, without much grace or fluidity.

Paulo asked her point-blank whether the captain was his father. Mama did not answer his query promptly. A long uncomfortable silence fell between them like a dark curtain descending in a dim theatre.

'I didn't know... my son... I didn't know,' she softly said, dropping her gaze to hide her liquid eyes. She reached for him, but he stormed out of the drawing room, through the hall and out of the door. He re-entered the house through the back door to collect his things and then went to see Carmina in her room and told her what had transpired.

Mama walked back into the hall with an unsteady gait and an angry expression on her face. Looking the captain in the eye she asked: 'What is it that you want, *Capitão*? You have absolutely no right to barge in here after so many years.'

'Yes, Isabella, I'm sorry, I didn't have the foggiest idea that Paulo was your son.'

At that moment, the looks on Mama's face apparently spoke a thousand words.

'Oh my God, yes—our son, Isabella.'

'I was innocent and you took advantage of me,' she said.

She went on to tell him that with him gone out of her life, all her feelings died. It was the only way she could go on living. She thought of him night and day. She cried ceaselessly. She did not want to marry, but had no choice.

'I drowned you in the depths of the ocean and went through life in a cold, unemotional way,' she said. 'Yes, sometimes when I played the piano, you came back—sunken memories surged like the tide.' After she paused for a deep breath and to wipe her tear-filled eyes, she told him that she couldn't deal with the consequences of their affair. She never fully realised until today that the event of that day, that fleeting moment, had a lasting consequence: a life.

Then in a louder and distressed voice, she said: 'You killed the twenty-one-year-old Isabella and another Isabella was born. An Isabella I did not want.'

She had tears in her eyes for the first time since those days when she had cried in Carmina's lap and they had cried together. The captain, with eyes moist and glazed, got off the chair and embraced her, but suddenly, her body seemed to burn with anger and contempt, unyielding, rigid like iron and she pushed him away. He lost his balance and almost fell back on the sofa. She wiped away her tears and then all emotion left her, vanished into thin air and she was again Dona Isabella, the imperious landlady, always in charge, always in control.

'So what is it that you want, *Capitão*?' she asked again. He seemed dazed and did not answer.

'If it is marriage between Paulo and your daughter—that is out of the question! May God forgive us all! So what is it that you want, *Capitão*?' she asked again.

'It's nobody's fault, Dona Isabella,' he finally responded after regaining his composure. 'It is only fair that my daughter and her son should be provided with financial support. I'm requesting a lump sum in the amount of fifteen thousand dollars. Even ten thousand will do for now. I believe this is a fair and equitable sum.'

Getting off the chair and raising his voice threateningly, he continued: 'I would like to have it as soon as possible. I will leave you the address of my hotel and you can have it delivered there. And I will be out of your life, Isabella. I know how uncomfortable all this must be to you.'

Mama seemed surprised at his demand. She felt the sum was too steep; besides, the lump sum to be paid to him with such urgency was totally unacceptable.

Then she snapped.

She told the captain that she did not have fifteen or ten thousand dollars in the bank and even if she did, she wouldn't hand it to him just like that. 'I don't even know what it amounts to in rupees,' she said. 'Besides, in India, one cannot exchange rupees for dollars. It is a very complicated process that requires permission from the Reserve Bank in Bombay.'

She then told him that she would have to speak about the matter to her husband and that he may agree to sell what belongs to Paulo and let him have the proceeds. 'It is up to Paulo to use that money for the support of his son and your daughter.'

She categorically stated that it was doubtful that any money would be handed to him just like that. She felt quite sure that Paulo would want to remit checks to Ana Sofia on a monthly basis.

'You forget that Paulo is a lawyer,' said Mama. 'He is an adult and he is not our responsibility. I will have to speak to Paulo when he calms down. I would advise you that under the circumstances, you should not deal with my husband directly. It is best that you leave Goa as soon as possible.'

The captain turned pale. He couldn't accept this.

'You can leave now, *Capitão*,' said Mama. Blood rushed to the captain's face as he lit another cigarette.

'I could tell your husband what happened,' he said, trying to pull a card for one last stroke of luck. Mama flushed with anger. Clearly, she felt ashamed of the illegitimate affair, but what riled her the most was that the captain had devised a scheme to use that shame as leverage.

'If you are not out of Goa within seventy-two hours, you will rot in the Panjim jail for six months, maybe more, before you are deported to Portugal,' Mama responded. Then she called out to Pedru to escort him out of the house.

The captain was shocked at Mama's insolence. He walked out, taciturn, with an unsteady swagger, as if he had bitten on a chilli pepper that stung.

When Papa, who had been visiting Senhor Pissurlencar, arrived home, Mama took him to the bedroom and recounted the visit of Ana Sofia's father. However, she did not tell him that Ana Sofia's father was Paulo's real father, but related to him that he had visited earlier and was seeking a large sum to be paid, as soon as possible, for his daughter's and Paulo's son's upkeep. She advised him that he should let Paulo have his inheritance and he should be free to exercise his wish. She did not mind if he sent Ana Sofia money on a monthly basis. She advised him not to give the money to the captain even if he had the amount in the bank. Her instincts told her that he was not to be trusted.

'I told you so,' Papa exploded. 'There was something unredeeming and terrible about Paulo that was going to fall on our heads. Oh my God, to think of it, he got this poor girl pregnant and left the country. What a shame,' he shouted at the top of his voice. 'What disgrace. I will disown him.' Obviously, Papa's integrity and sense of morality was shattered. He had never faced a personal dilemma of such magnitude in his entire life.

He tried to leave, but fell back into the chair he was sitting on. Mama told him that Paulo had not known that Ana Sofia was pregnant when he left Portugal. Papa was not convinced.

'Why did he run away from Coimbra like a beaten dog?' he said in a defeated voice. Mama was at a loss for words. She had no knowledge of the incident in Coimbra with Angelino de Tor that had prompted Paulo's return. She felt that only Senhor Pissurlencar, his close and trusted friend, could convince Papa to give Paulo his inheritance. Besides, she urgently needed his advice. She immediately dressed up and left for Senhor Pissurlencar's home. She wanted to catch him before he left for Bombay, but it was too late; Senhor Pissurlencar was already on his way to the airport. Mama became desperate. She had to act soon now. She went to the house of Police Inspector Andrade who owed her many favours. During the Portuguese colonial regime, Andrade had been imprisoned for his association with the freedom movement and for bombing a police station, a charge that was never proved. My father, at Mama's coaxing, had finally secured his release from the Aguada prison. Besides, his wife was bed-ridden following a car accident and Mama often sent Carmina to help. Consequently, Carmina became a confidante of the inspector's wife. Lucky for Mama, she caught up with Inspector Andrade as he was about to leave for Panjim.

The next morning, as the captain was putting on his trousers to go to the cafeteria of the Tourist Hotel in Panjim for breakfast, there was a loud knock on the door.

'*Um momento, um momento!*' he shouted in Portuguese. The knock continued, but was louder and more forceful. He ran to the door and opened it. There were three men dressed in khaki uniforms, one was taller than the others and wore a turban. He immediately introduced himself.

'I am Deputy Superintendent Singh of the Panjim Police and this is Deputy Inspector Pereira and this is Inspector Andrade. You speak English, Captain Borda de Mar?'

'*Não, não*, only little *Inglez*!'

'Okay—good—Captain Borda de Mar—Inspector Andrade here speak Portuguese. Inspector, tell him purpose of visit. *Challo*—must see passport first. You under arrest! Take him to police station *far* booking. *Challo ya*.'

Inspector Andrade took the stunned captain aside and asked to see his passport. The captain quickly composed himself. He protested softly, saying that he had a legitimate visa issued by the Indian Consulate in Hong Kong. Inspector Andrade told him that he better surrender the passport and come with them to the police station. He said they knew he was in the Portuguese Army, that he was the commandant in-charge of the Aldona police station in Goa during the colonial regime; that he served in the army in Angola and there was information he was currently a spy for the Portuguese secret service: The PIDE. The captain protested loudly and angrily in Portuguese, saying he was here on business and to visit friends. He categorically stated that he was not a spy; and that he would be leaving soon.

'You under arrest... *Challo ya*... take him to police station *far* booking,' said, Deputy Superintendent Singh, tapping the captain on the shoulder.

Then, without any warning, the captain suddenly went for the throat of the deputy superintendent of police. A fight ensued, but the aging, limping captain was no match for the three police officers, particularly the tall and muscular sardarji. He was soon wrestled to the ground and handcuffed. His suitcase was searched; his camera and passport were confiscated.

'*Chalo*, Borda de Mar, you under arrest for spying, for resisting arrest and for assaulting a police officer on duty,' said the deputy superintendent of police.

Inspector Andrade handed the passport to Deputy Superintendent Singh, who, after dusting his uniform, straightening his turban and twirling his well-greased moustache, pocketed it and abruptly left. The Portuguese captain was stunned and subdued; it was as if he just realised that he was in a big jam. With head bowed, he requested Inspector Andrade in Portuguese to remove the handcuffs. He apologised for losing his temper and assured him he would accompany them to the police station.

Deputy Inspector Pereira and Inspector Andrade escorted the captain to the police station. They passed the Secretariat, went past the expressive statue of Abbé Faria, one of the earliest practitioners of hypnotism, towards the riverside boulevard passing the steamship dock, the State Bank of India, the Hotel Mandovi, towards the Instituto Menezes Bragança.

They entered the walled enclosure of the nineteenth century army barracks that now housed the Goa police headquarters. As they walked past the archway, two policemen guarding the main entrance saluted the inspectors. They crossed the dusty parade ground where battalions of policemen were marching, 'left-right-left,' practicing for the coming parade. They stepped onto the colonnade behind which were a row of offices with wide open doors. Clerks, peons, policemen in and out of uniform lounged on dilapidated benches and chairs, smoking bidis and drinking chai. They stared at the captain, probably thinking he was some big-shot smuggler accidentally caught and stood at attention saluting the inspectors as they passed.

They entered a room that was dark and dusty with cobwebs on the walls and tables and chairs with broken legs. They passed a long, dark corridor into another large room, bright with flickering fluorescent lights, where half a dozen police officers were busy interrogating handcuffed criminals. Twice as many clerks just sat and three times as many peons stood, some idly, most chatting. Inspector Andrade told the captain to sit on the wooden sofa, called out for two police officers to stand guard and told the captain that he had an important errand to perform; it would possibly take an hour or so before he could attend to him. Finally at about noon, Inspector Andrade appeared, took the captain into his private office and sat behind a large table that was littered with files and stacks of coarse yellow paper. A fan buzzed above the inspector's head as he interrogated the captain. He called out several times to his secretary, Rukmini, who appeared on the double all sweaty and panting and sat behind her typewriter. 'Sorry, Sir, sorry—just having a cup of chai, Sir.'

Inspector Andrade was a short, rather lean man with a bald head and a small classical Indian paunch, like he was five months pregnant, which he tapped often with his police stick that had a flap at the end. He had a pock-marked face that he kept wiping nervously with a soiled handkerchief. When not tapping his stick, he ran his hand over his shining, coconut-oiled bald head, as if the massage would one day miraculously sprout some hair. He questioned the captain regarding his movements after he left Goa.

In the deposition that Rukmini typed out, it is clear that captain António Borda de Mar lived the life of a soldier of fortune. He had not risked his life warring in Angola or as a mercenary in South Africa or Tanganyika. He mostly free-loaded on the wealthy in the overseas Portuguese provinces where his rugged handsome looks and Casanova charm made him a sought-after lover boy.

At the request of Inspector Andrade, Captain Borda de Mar detailed his movements: After he returned to Portugal from Goa, he was sent to Angola where he stayed for several years, serving in the army. He returned to Portugal and married his friend's widow, Dona Figueira. After a couple of years in the Portuguese secret police, he went back to Angola and worked for a rich Portuguese widow, managing her plantation. He then started an import-export business that took him frequently to Macau, where he befriended the Chinese divorcee of a Hong Kong businessman. He ultimately moved in with her. Often, he visited Angola for business and holidays. When he was there on one of his trips, the Chinese woman was killed in a car accident.

He seemed to have come into his self-assured ways, when he related in his deposition that he loved Africa, the countryside, the animal safaris and talked about the free sexual habits in the Portuguese colony.

When the captain rather appealingly suggested a vacation for the inspector in Africa, saying that he would make all the necessary arrangements, the church-going devout inspector became enraged. 'Stop trying to bribe me with a holiday in Sodom and Gomorrah,' he said, tapping his stick violently on the table.

When the encroaching guerrilla movement in Angola became too dangerous, the captain decided that it was time to return to Dona Figueira and his daughter Ana Sofia, in Coimbra. After being informed that his name was mentioned in the Chinese woman's will, which until then was being contested, he left for Macau to claim some of her wealth. But she had left him a paltry sum.

He vehemently and repeatedly denied that he was in Goa to spy.

After the captain had detailed his movements, Inspector Andrade insisted that he had reliable information he had been a spy all along for the Portuguese secret service. He told him that his trip to Mormugão Port and other towns and villages where he had taken pictures, confirmed that he was spying. Inspector Andrade removed and confiscated the film in the camera. He finally told the captain that they could jail him indefinitely; besides, he would be additionally charged for resisting arrest and for assaulting a police officer, for which he could spend years in jail. He would have to post a bond of two thousand dollars for his release; that it had to be in dollars, that rupees wouldn't do and it could take a long time before he came to trial, perhaps six months, maybe more. If he left tomorrow, he would still have to pay around five hundred dollars to the inspector. He told him that the money would be used to make the necessary arrangements: the bail, release orders from the judge, the police fees and the like. The captain did not realise that the large sum was essentially a bribe. The inspector assured him he would speak to Deputy Superintendent Singh requesting him to drop the assault charges.

The captain again denied the charge of espionage and stated that he did not have the money to post the bond. He added that he had a return ticket to Hong Kong and, as previously mentioned, one thousand dollars in traveller's checks and about five hundred dollars in cash.

'Please check my story with Dona Isabella,' he pleaded.

'I know the story. You come here and try to blackmail this poor old lady? Hmm? I know this is just a front. Your real purpose here is to spy,' said the inspector, once again hitting the cane on the table. 'You think you're a big man? Hmm? Your white skin will not work here any longer.'

The captain realised it was useless. Dona Isabella had not only kept her promise, but worse still, she had shortened the ultimatum by more than forty-eight hours. As he sank into the concave chair, Inspector Andrade advised him in a stern voice that was disproportionate to his diminutive size to leave Goa within twenty-four hours. His passport would be handed to him at the Dabolim airport. A seat had been secured for the flight to Bombay. He did not mention who had purchased the ticket, but this was obvious to the captain. He accepted defeat with a bowed head.

'I'll leave tomorrow,' he said.

Inspector Andrade got off his seat, towering over the sitting-sunken captain. Wagging his finger, he remarked in Portuguese, a last parting shot at the Captain: 'I was jailed at the Cabo. I was put there by your people on suspicion of my association with the freedom fighters. The trial was a sham. I was jailed for two long years. I'm going very easy on you my friend.' He had a sly smile of mischief and hidden content. He took out his wallet, flashed a ten-rupee note and ordered Rukmini to ask the peon to get a chilled Kingfisher beer and two glasses.

Twenty-two

Paulo's and Amanda's Foreboding

That evening, after the visit of Captain António Borda de Mar, when Amanda returned home from school, the house was suffused with a strange silence. At the doorstep, Tulsi greeted her with a look of inquisitive apprehension. She had seen a tall white older man with a resemblance to Paulo come out of the house all agitated, and after about fifteen minutes, it was Paulo rushing down the steps with a concerned look on his face. She had inquired from Carmina and Mari about the white man's identity, but Mari did not know and Carmina wouldn't tell. Amanda wanted to inform Paulo about her secret wedding plan and ask him to be best man, but Paulo was nowhere to be found.

The next morning, I returned from Bombay, very pleased with my effort in the American examination, only to find the house sunk in gloom. Amanda was in her room with the door closed; Tia Rosita was saying rosaries non-stop, while Papa had left for Margão to seek advice from a trusted lawyer cousin.

I found Mama visibly upset with dark pouches of sleeplessness underneath her eyes. During lunch, Mama asked me to go searching for Paulo. I was too tired from the journey and reluctant to go. 'He can take care of himself,' I grumbled. 'Anyway, why all the interest in Paulo all of a sudden?'

'I'm afraid he is with those hippie friends,' said Mama. 'Do please go to Baga beach and see if you can find him there.'

'Did he and Papa quarrel?' I asked. Mama did not answer.

'Day after tomorrow is the dance and the Miss Goa Contest at the Tourist Hotel in Calangute,' I said. 'I'm going to the affair. I'll inquire about him when I'm there.'

After Paulo's encounter with the captain and the heart-wrenching exchange with Mama, he walked out of the house not knowing where he was going or what he was going to do. He had briefly entered his room through the back door, packed a bag with clothes, taken all his money and jewellery: the gold tie pins studded with a diamond, ruby and pearl given to him by his grandparents for Holy Communion, Confirmation and a birthday or two.

He hadn't forgotten to say good-bye to Carmina. She had taken care of him unselfishly like she had taken care of everybody else in the family, treating all equally. If there ever were a cast of a saint, she would fit it perfectly like Christ on the Cross. He found her in her room sitting in a corner. He told her that he was going to Baga beach and that he had no intentions of returning home ever. He told Carmina that there was nothing left for him at home. He felt cheated and robbed of his inheritance and disgusted with Mama and Papa and his real father. For him Goa was long dead; now, he felt that Portugal was dead as well. He felt alone in the world. Alienated. A man without a family; a man without a country! It was as if life was an uncontrollable spirit constantly metamorphosing, while he, a mere pawn, seemed caught in between its crushing wings.

He hugged Carmina for a long time and left through the back door.

There was only one place where Paulo could seek refuge. After crossing to Betim from Panjim by ferryboat, Paulo took the bus to Mapuçá. There, in the bazaar, he sold all his jewellery. He then took a cab to Baga beach. He asked for Uma, but nobody knew who she was or her whereabouts. The place had changed dramatically. There were now hippies in the hundreds, not only Americans but also Europeans; and there were the Indian tourists happily bathing in the waters of the Arabian sea with their clothes on. Ample stalls with rugs and silver and brass knickknacks, bronze and copper statues of Buddha, Shiva and Kali abounded, amid chai stalls and bars that cropped up on the beach like coconut palm trees. The old faces seemed to have disappeared or perhaps were lost in the crowd.

Paulo walked the entire length of the beach searching for Uma. He waited for the sun to set when the hippies with long hair and beards, in lungis and saffron robes, and the bronzed sanyasis would meditate and chant their Oms. He met a group stoned on hash and smack. He tagged along with them for a party and there, he bought vials of the potent acid and strawberry pills. He slept with them that night and the following night. On the third day, late in the evening, he saw Uma. She was in a saffron-coloured robe, her head shaved, sitting alone in a crowded, noisy bar, sipping on lemonade. She told him that she had just returned from Poona and that she was working hard to get the ashram going. He asked her about Indy, Kash and the twins.

'Oh them?' she answered nonchalantly. 'Kash is back in the US. The twins, I last heard, were in Thailand; and Indy is rotting in a Turkish cell. We are all dispersed. I haven't kept their company for some time now.'

At that moment, Tucaram, who had gained height and muscle and looked like a hippie himself, an Indian one with long hair tied in a ponytail, was also sitting in the bar with his hippie friend. They joined Paulo and Uma at their table. After they shared a joint and Tucaram left with his hippie friend, Paulo suggested to Uma that they go to the cave.

'I am totally lost,' he said.

'Is it your parents again?' she asked.

'It's much more than that.'

'Okay, let's go and talk. We have rented a house in Anjuna—I'm moving in tomorrow. You're welcome to come and stay with us.' As he got up to leave, he popped a couple of pills.

Paulo knew to swim only a little. The three of us, Paulo, Amanda and I, had learned to swim in a small quarry in the village supervised by a dozen or so peasants, whose swimming feats were suspicious to say the least. Indeed, although surrounded by a golden coastline of sun and sand, we hardly ever swam in the Arabian Sea, contenting ourselves with paddling in the shallows. But now Paulo must have felt euphoric after all the dope. He probably thought he could fly.

He began wading across the Baga river. After covering a space of about fifty feet, the currents began pulling him out to sea. He lost his footing. He struggled and with one last effort, managed to lift his head above the water, shout for help and then he sank. Uma, who was an excellent swimmer, was almost on the other side when she heard his cry. She immediately swam at a rapid pace as Paulo held on to a jutting rock. Like a tugboat, she pulled him to the other side.

That afternoon, when Mama and Papa were taking a nap, Amanda slipped quietly out of the house and took a taxi to Old Goa. There, Father Loyola secretly married Amanda and Winnie in the Basilica of Bom Jesus. Father Castellino, who assisted at the Mass and would be the witness as well, sang the *Ave Maria* in his baritone voice that resounded in the Basilica. Amanda wore a simple white silk dress with a pearl necklace. The wedding ceremony was quick and small with only four people in attendance—that is, counting the bride and the bridegroom.

When Winnie was in the hospital, Amanda had come here to pray for a miracle. She had started a novena to the saint and pledged that she would marry Winnie if he came out of the hospital alive, no matter what his illness. Today, she was keeping the *vow* she had made. The vow was an act of intercession for the life of the man she loved and perhaps a prop for her own will to marry him. Right until the very last moment, Father Loyola had tried to persuade Amanda that she did not have to go through with the marriage, no matter the vow to the saint and that God was all forgiving. But Amanda wouldn't relent.

After the ceremony, Amanda began sobbing and Winnie and Father Loyola tried to console her. Perhaps the emotion of the event was overbearing, or she was overrun by the new fleeting realities she soon would have to face. Gradually, she managed to compose herself as they entered the taxi and left for Winnie's home in Calangute.

She had written in her diary the night before her secret marriage: *I am torn between my love for Winnie, the preservation of honour to the family name and my commitment to the vow I made to the saint. I feel like a cornered Christian in a Roman pit with guilt and commitments tearing me apart from all sides. My Winnie will soon be gone. I will never be able to return to the nesting warmth of my home. I will be looked down on, made fun of by cousins and friends. If this is the price I will ultimately have to pay for my refusal to conform to social dictates, so be it. Oh my God, I don't know what tomorrow will bring.*

In her writings that night, she had agonised about lovemaking, of how she had rejected Winnie's sexual advances on the beach strip in Dona Paula and how she had been consumed by guilt when he had suddenly doubled up in pain. She had gone on to write how she intended to love and be loved on the night of her marriage on the sandy beach, as if she intended to make up for what she had denied Winnie on that day in Dona Paula.

The last entry in her diary was a poem she wrote that night.

Amanda had crossed into forbidden territory, rupturing long-held, centuries-old strictures regarding love and marriage. She married Winnie for the ideal of love even though the cause seemed doomed. And so it was, that love having competed for primacy, was victorious at the end; but the victory seemed hollow, a transient one, that would soon fall out of the sky like a soaring bird shot dead by a passerby.

Twenty-three

The Sea Claims What Is Hers

It was almost dark when Paulo and Uma walked up the hill. The silhouette of the Retreat House with its crucifix stood tall against the darkened sky with its last few strips of orange and yellow highlighting the scattered clouds. They sat on a rock below which was the rogues' well that could swallow all things with a powerful undertow. Paulo took a vial and emptied it on a blotting paper. He offered a piece of it to Uma.

'I don't use that stuff any longer,' she said. So Paulo swallowed it all.

'Hey, that's too much. What's gotten into you anyway? Come on tell me, what's bothering you?'

'Later, later,' he said, looking down at the waves surging through the opening in the rock face and circling like a yo-yo before emptying deep into the well.

Uma assumed the Buddha position with eyes closed in meditation.

What went through Paulo's mind with so much of dope in his system? Did a strange emptiness take hold of him? Did he see his life crumble like a sandcastle? Did a drug-induced numbness roll over him, sharpening his senses? Could he have heard the sound of the ocean waves disintegrating into multiple frequencies? Did the fluttering of bats sound like machine-gun fire? And the cooing of pigeons on the windowsills of the Retreat House like the cries of big birds—the birds of his nightmares? Was he gripped with fear?

Or did a mysterious strength take hold of him, to leap, to fly out of his body, to disengage from space and time?

Uma was suddenly startled by the sound of a loud splash.

As she opened her eyes, she saw feet being swallowed in the vortex of the whirlpool like in a python's mouth and within an instant he was gone.

She called out frantically: 'Krishna... Krishna... Krishna!'

And 'Krishna, Krishna, Krishna' echoed back, muffled sounds.

She dove in and was taken in by the powerful undertow of the well. She held her breath. She did not struggle. Once she was beyond and beneath the whirlpool, she probed the waters around for the feel of flesh, intermittently swimming to the surface and taking several dives far beyond the ocean well.

There was no sign of him.

By now she was on the Baga side of the hill. It was already pitch dark and a small ragged silvery moon was slowly peering at the water's edge. Uma swam back to Baga. Exhausted, she popped an opium *tola* and fell asleep on the beach.

On the evening of their marriage, Amanda and Winnie had a quiet dinner at Souza Lobo's restaurant. After they arrived home at about nine o'clock that night, she changed into a maroon dress with a low neckline and puffed sleeves. There was a full moon and Amanda was in no hurry to go to bed. She was restless and agitated and suggested to Winnie they go for a stroll on the beach. He readily agreed and added that there was a beauty contest at the Tourist Hotel and that they venture out there. Outwardly, Winnie put up a bright face. Inwardly, he was confused, depressed, not knowing what the future held for the two of them. The cancer was gnawing at his mood, his broken life. Before they left for the beach, Winnie went into the pantry and helped himself to a couple of gulps from a bottle of feni liquor to drown his sorrow.

They stopped at a bar on the roadside where Winnie asked for a peg of whisky-soda and had a refill, while Amanda drank a beer. They sat there for almost an hour among a few hippies smoking pot, Tucaram among them, and then left to go towards the beach away from the main road. Amanda waved at Tucaram on her way out of the bar. Tucaram waved back. He was surprised to see his Amanda with a man at that hour of the night. He quietly followed Amanda and Winnie.

They reached a sand dune by the side of which was a fisherman's hut used to store nets. Winnie pulled Amanda towards him and kissed her. The moon was in full view in a star-studded sky. A single mass of cloud hung suspended in the void as if witnessing what went on below. The ocean waves lapped the shore in their rhythmic monotonous moans that became louder and more ferocious with the rising tide like a constant call from the wild. The silver sheen of the moonlight dazzled on the rising waves and made silver streaks on the sand. Amanda and Winnie sank onto the sand as they continued kissing and caressing each other like rock and river.

Amanda suddenly felt a chill. Winnie motioned to her to enter the fisherman's hut and he led the way. They lay on a bed of fishnets, kissing, caressing and gazing into each other's eyes.

'What went on in the fisherman's hut?' I had asked Tucaram. Initially, he was hesitant to answer my question.

He had told me that while Amanda undressed, Winnie, lay on the sand as if transfixed, drinking in her nakedness. The dress and the petticoat had fallen to the ground in a silken twirl as she had stepped over them and, with one move of her hand, brushed her hair to the side—for a moment it was as if it had burst out in incandescence. It was then that I had told him to stop. I didn't want to hear anymore. I also had sensed that he didn't want to continue. Perhaps they had been carried away on a wave of excitement. It was obvious to me that they made love there. Tucaram had confirmed it in a subtle way. I had once seen a hippie couple make love in the fishnet hut. I had wondered whether my sister looked like a goddess under the moonlight that penetrated through the holes and fissures of the palm-leafed roof—a dark brown cinammon goddess, unlike the white goddess I remembered seeing a long while ago.

Had they been like two wounded statues? Naked. Exposed. Silvery brownness. Silvery blackness.

Perhaps the passion that had been kindled and had burned inside of them, the pain, the suffering, the humiliation of the last few months had finally found its expression in one single act of love.

They had dressed after unfolding the entangled fishnets and walked towards the Tourist Hotel on the edge of the beach where the silvery froth of the waves lapped at their feet. And then she said:

I go with the wind, to sail on the ocean waves,
To a distant shore, where there is no pain.
And if this day is not a fulfillment of our joy,
Then, let it be a promise of eternal love.
In the stillness of the night, you were my dream.
Your breath: the mist on my face, dew drops in
My eyes; your heartbeats like bells, toll in my heart;
Soon, my spirit shall enter your house.
I go with the wind, to sail on the waves....

Before Winnie had time to decipher whose poetry she was reciting or had time to ask her if she had composed it herself, she let go of his hand. And before he knew, she had run playfully into the ocean as if the ocean would sustain her; and before he realised it, a large wave, black as the night, had engulfed her.

He had hesitated at the water's edge for a moment and then jumped after her, but he was no longer as strong a swimmer as he had been before. The surgery had weakened his abdominal muscles and the alcohol had clouded his sharp instincts. Yet, he dived underwater several times and frantically searched for her until he had a severe cramp and found himself sinking.

He managed to stagger back onto the beach. He was desperate; there was no way he could rescue her now. He did not know that there was one other who was frantically looking for her as well. It was the boy Tucaram who had been sitting beside the hulk of a fishing boat, near the fishnet hut, watching over Amanda. He had seen all that went on.

Yes, Amanda, who had untied him from the tamarind tree and given him, pathetic him, sugared bread to eat.

Tucaram had seen her walk into the ocean and Winnie had followed behind. They both disappeared under the waves. He remembered the quarry in the village where Amanda had learned to swim and she wasn't a good swimmer. He was well aware of the treacherous waters of the Calangute beachhead where many had drowned. He ran to the water's edge. There was no sign of Amanda or Winnie. He realised that something was wrong and dived in. He was caught in a powerful current, but he was a good swimmer now. His American hippie friends had instructed him well. He struggled initially, but remained calm.

He felt something touch his arm: A fish? A limb? The hem of a dress!

He grabbed it.

Tucaram had his hands around Amanda's waist. He managed to pull her onto the beach beside the hulk of a beached fishing boat. He shook her hard several times. She did not respond. Frightened and desperate, he ran looking for his hippie friend.

Meanwhile, Winnie managed to find his way to the house of a fisherman he knew. He begged him to wake the others and roll the boat into the water.

'Find her,' he pleaded.

'It's too late,' they said, 'the sea has claimed its bounty: A life. A human sacrifice. And this year and the following year, the sea would in turn provide: Plenty.'

Then it hit him hard like the thud of wood on bone—it was too late now, Amanda must have certainly drowned. As he collapsed, her pieces floated all around him like a capsized and fragmented papier-mâché toy boat.

The fisherman's son took off to the police station to report a drowning and to call Dr Balldesai to attend to Winnie.

It was a tragic day, a sad and cataclysmic day, a day in our lives with catastrophic events I hadn't personally witnessed, but reconstructed what happened after speaking with Uma, Tucaram and Winnie and reading their depositions.

Twenty-four

Miss Goa Contest

At the Tourist Hotel on the Calangute beach, at about nine o'clock that night, the crowds were gathering for the Miss Goa contest. The hotel terrace was festooned with white twinkling lights and balloons; some waved in the ocean breeze, some popped. I stood tall in one corner of the terrace, whisky-soda in hand, in a new, Bombay custom-tailored blue suit and a silvery tie, watching women in saris and gowns and men in suits and shervanis take their seats. I was waiting for Maria to appear.

I had rehearsed all that I would do and all that I would say to her. I had a feeling that it would now all come together. As I was deep in thought, the whisky slowly warming me up, I saw Maria enter with her brother and his troupe and as quickly disappear behind the stage. They were due to perform a duet: *The Rose in Spanish Harlem*. The virtuoso Goan singer Pablo, the upcoming young Romeo and the Portuguese Fado singer, Zico, would also perform, but the main attraction was a Bombay import: The Tony Conception Rock Band.

After Pablo sang a rendition of Jobim's, *O Que Tinha De Ser*, accompanied by the Brazilian chords of El Rei and Maria and her brother performed their duet, twelve Goan girls paraded in silk saris and salwar kameez. Swimsuits were not allowed. Maria, in a red sari, with gold-embroidered borders, a ruby-studded necklace snug around her neck, her hair done up in a cone accentuating her smooth forehead and her long cheekbones, walked slowly and rhythmically on a circular makeshift catwalk, like Nefertiti sailing up the Nile.

'What will you do for Goa if crowned Miss Goa?' they were asked.

'After graduation, I will work for the betterment of Goa,' said Maria. 'I will start an organisation of young men and women and we will storm the villages teaching hygiene, child care and the importance of education.' There was loud applause to Maria's altruistic pronouncement. How noble, how becoming of Miss Goa! I wondered how her ideals would work around mine. All along, my intentions were of migrating to America. I realised that I had a lot of convincing to do. But had Maria really meant what she said? Or was it merely a contest-winning answer?

After much ado and another circular turn on the catwalk, Maria was crowned Miss Goa at about eleven o'clock.

I was happy like never before. Maria's face beamed with joy as she took her place at the table I had reserved. *'Parabens, Maria,'* I said and hugged her. Miss Goa was mine and she danced with me the entire time. She refused every suitor who approached her at the table. After three straight dances: rock-and-roll, the Argentine tango and the slow, cheek-to-cheek, *Noite ao Luar*, which was her kind of music, the boys got the message. What a difference a few years had made. Unlike my clumsiness and awkwardness the last time I danced with her, I was confident now, having learned the dance steps from Paulo and perfected them.

'Wow, Roberto, you dance almost as well as Paulo,' Maria said. The comparison briefly threw me off track, but I let it pass.

For now, for me, it was total victory. I celebrated with whisky-sodas. Maria drank a glass of vermouth and asked for a refill. We munched on chicken and chutney sandwiches. My friend, the bubbly Dr Anil, came to our table to congratulate Maria and tapping me on the back, he whispered in my ear, 'Hey Roberto, what a conquest—what a flower!'

Soon thereafter, I asked Maria to go with me to the beach. We slipped out unnoticed and began walking away from the Tourist Hotel towards Baga, barefooted, with our shoes in our hands.

'I love you, pink rose,' I said.

'I love you too,' she whispered.

The moon was in full view above, suspended like a dance-hall mirror in the centre of our universe. A large thick cloud approached. The wind picked up Maria's wavy hair. With my arm around her, I tucked her close and kissed her. We stood kissing as the waves lapped at our feet and the ocean breeze ruffled our hair. My mouth was on her neck tasting the sweat saltiness of her skin; her body smelled of jasmine. We had walked almost half a mile away from the hotel when we saw the silhouette of a fishing boat keeled to one side on the sand.

'Let's sit there,' said Maria.

'By the side of the love boat?' I asked. 'I once saw a hippy couple make love there,' I added and wondered what passions would unravel if we sat there this time of the night.

As we approached the boat, darkness fell as the moon hid behind a curtain of clouds like a woman hiding behind a veil of innocence. At that very moment, we saw the shadow of a boy running towards the coconut grove. I pulled Maria towards me. We stood there in the darkness, kissing, our bodies clinging to each other in the ocean wind.

As the cloud hurriedly passed, as if it had an errand to perform and gave way to a dash of moonlight, I saw what looked like a body lying by the beached boat.

'Maria, there's the body of a woman,' I shouted as I ran towards it and for a moment stared at the woman's face. 'No, no, it can't be,' I shouted again, turning my face away.

As Maria appeared by my side, I pushed her away. Frightened, she backtracked, running to the other side of the boat. She stumbled over a hard object and fell down.

'Roberto, Roberto, there's another body here! Come here!' she yelled and ran towards me.

'Oh my God, Roberto, oh my God!' She clung to me. I stepped right in front of the boat where I could see on both sides.

I saw two bodies: those of a man and a woman, separated by about a hundred feet. The edge of a dying wave barely touched the rim of the woman's dress while it splashed and pounded the face of the dead man.

As I approached, I saw my sister Amanda and my brother Paulo: both livid, washed onto the shore lying just below and to the side of the dark hulk of the beached fishing boat. I thought I saw some movement in my sister's lips. I ran for help towards the Tourist Hotel. I took a short cut in-between the sand dunes. Thick clouds covered the moon and there was darkness once again as if the end of the world was at hand.

I passed out behind the sand dune.

I don't entirely remember what happened next.

Twenty-five

Shortly Thereafter

It was almost eleven at night. Uma's friend Brandon shook her from her sleep. 'Shit, Uma. Where the hell have you been? I've been searching for you all over Baga.'

'I guess I must have fallen asleep after popping in some opium *tolas*.' Then she remembered. 'Shit man, Krishna must have drowned.'

'Who is Krishna anyway… and where did he drown?'

'The man simply flew over the cuckoo's nest,' she said and then added, 'I must go to the police and report the accident. It is better now than to wait for tomorrow.'

Policeman Bandodkar on duty that night was sitting at his desk eating a masala dosa at the late hour when Uma arrived. 'Come in, Mrs… have seat please… what problem brings you here?' he said, shaking his head.

'I am here to report the drowning of Krishna, well… it's Paulo actually. He is a local guy.' She relayed the events and circumstances of the accident, leaving the dope out.

'It's late Mrs— the hour too late. Tomorrow… we see. You can come back at nine… ten better and file report. No clerk now to take down typing. Good night, Mrs… Much obliged.' Policeman Bandodkar gave a loud belch, tapped his satisfied belly and went back to clean his plate of the dosa tit-bits.

As she was leaving the police station, the fisherman's son arrived all sweaty and panting. He darted into the station past policeman Bandodkar, who became annoyed at the double intrusion this late at night. The boy told him that he had come to report the drowning of a woman; he did not know the name, he said, but she was with Winnie Fernandes. When policeman Bandodkar heard the name Winnie Fernandes, he got off his seat, alarmed. But wait a moment, were the white woman Uma and the fisherman's son reporting one and the same incident? But how could it be? One drowning victim was a man, the other a woman; one was in Calangute, the other in Baga.

'*Arre, bapp*—it is late, *maan!* What to do? Two drownings in one night? Some *jaddu* going on here?'

The boy insisted that he better come. Winnie Fernandes was waiting. He couldn't have Mr Fernandes waiting; his job could be on the line. Finally saying '*ya re, ya re,*' policeman Bandodkar left, his lathi dangling in his right hand and a flashlight in his left.

Meanwhile, Tucaram had located his hippie friend nearby, just beyond the beachhead, who together with another of his friends, ran to Amanda and instantly began cardio-pulmonary resuscitation. Luckily, one of the two hippies was a pro, having been a lifeguard on the Jersey shore and in New York City swimming pools during the summer holidays. After working on her for some time, she began breathing after coughing water from her lungs. But her breathing was shallow and she seemed to have slipped into a coma.

When policeman Bandodkar arrived, the entire dancing crowd was at the scene. They put Amanda in a private van and took her to Goa Medical. Tucaram together with Dr Anil and Dr Flores, a cousin, accompanied her. Paulo's body was hauled in a car and taken to the morgue in Panjim. Nobody had any idea how Paulo and Amanda had turned up there. They had not been seen at the dance in the Tourist Hotel. Some wondered whether it was some underworld drug-related hit. Paulo was of fair complexion and could have been confused for a hippie; besides, it was well known that he kept their company. Amanda's presence was a complete mystery.

Dr Balldesai took Winnie to Goa Medical where, after X-rays and intravenous fluids, he was discharged. It was there that he came to know Amanda was alive, but semi-comatose on a respirator.

I was wandering on the beach like a zombie until Maria's brother found me incoherent and took me to the Tourist Hotel. He told me that Maria was distressed and hysterical when she arrived at the hotel yelling and crying for help and that friends had taken her home to Panjim. She hadn't realised that I had blacked out. She didn't know where I was; there were no lights on the unspoiled virgin beach and she couldn't have seen me in the dark.

When Maria's brother mentioned that Amanda was alive, for a fleeting moment, I felt a sense of overpowering relief. It was then that I came to my senses, shaking off the fog that clouded my mind.

We took a cab to Goa Medical in Panjim. In the predawn silence, the mud roads were empty. I wondered what the day would bring, what slivers of sorrow would enshroud my family, what shame and ridicule would be heaped on us for years to come. I must be strong now, take control of the situation and make some sense of all the chaos around me. Ours was a broken home; its walls collapsed like the shards of a mirror—with grains of sand and salted blood.

It was daybreak when I arrived at the hospital and there I met Tucaram, once an ant-ravaged much-abused boy, now a hero. If he had not been at Calangute on that day, at that time, waiting, Amanda would certainly have drowned.

They also serve who only stand and wait.

I was told that Amanda's condition was serious. After resting for a few hours at a cousin's in Panjim, I went back to the hospital to check on Amanda. Winnie was by her bedside. He told me rather remorsefully that they had been married secretly by Father Loyola the previous evening and all that had transpired. Just then, Father

Loyola appeared on the scene and confirmed Winnie's story. I was surprised at Amanda's plunging into the ocean when she barely knew to swim. I instinctively blamed Winnie for what happened; for not keeping a close eye on Amanda; for letting her walk into the ocean at that time of the night when she barely knew to swim.

Rumours were already flying around like seagulls, their droppings littering the shoreline. Nobody knew how the 'brother-sister' duo had drowned and then washed to the shore so close to each other. The voyeurs of tragedy claimed that it was a suicide pact. Others spread rumours that Amanda was pregnant with Winnie's child. But policeman Bandodkar had tied the pieces together. In this regard, Uma's earlier visit to the police station was a big plus. Anyway, the police aggressively questioned Winnie and Tucaram. Uma was rounded up the following morning. Their stories checked out.

I informed Mama and Papa; Mama began wailing and the entire household followed suit. I held my mother, Tia Rosita and ayah Carmina in an embrace and we all cried together for a long time. Papa sat on his rocking chair totally crushed; he looked into space as if he was in a state of the wakeful dead.

They were in no condition to attend to matters. This double tragedy shattered them like falling glass. Amanda's critical condition hung over the house like a monsoon cloud. The devastation was total. It was left to me to arrange my brother's funeral.

Twenty-six

Last Farewell

When Paulo's body arrived, the only street in the village leading to the house was lined with people wailing and flower petals flying. His body lay in a satin-lined mahogany coffin with shining brass handles. He was dressed up in his black tuxedo that had been tailored in Portugal; it had to be cut in the back to fit him in. A silver crucifix was held in his clasped hands. A transparent veil was spread over his body. Only the outlines were visible. Yet, some dared to open the veil a tiny bit for a last look at the man who was born to be a star. The neighbours Dona Faustina and Dona Cristalina, tough women, the night vigilantes of the dead, sat wide-eyed the entire night, saying the rosary, whispering prayers one on top of another for Paulo and Amanda. Their prayers were expected to reach the heavens and fall back to earth like rain. Most of the village, most of Margão, Panjim and Mapuçá high society, came to pay their respects as the coffin lay instate in the hall for the wake.

The funeral was scheduled for the day after at four o'clock in the evening. Out of respect for my brother and my parents, I sent a message to Winnie and Uma not to come to the house during the wake, for my father and mother would be very upset and there could be a scene. Only I knew that Winnie and Amanda had married secretly on the day that Amanda had almost drowned. I felt that it was inappropriate for Mama and Papa to know about it before the funeral. I also instructed Inspector Andrade and policeman Bandodkar to keep their mouths shut at least until the funeral was over.

An hour before the start of the funeral procession, the family sat in black around the coffin. The servants stood stone-faced like soldiers on guard at the head of the coffin. Tulsi stood at the right side of the coffin, nodding her head repeatedly, calling out in a low staccato voice, *'bab, bab,'* tears streaming from her eyes.

I stood in the balcony to welcome the mourners. Maria, who was still distraught and red-eyed, sat with her mother and brother.

As soon as Tucaram, ayah Carmina and Tia Rosita—who were in the hospital with Amanda arrived—Tucaram handed me a letter from the medical registrar that said Amanda's condition was critical. Her lungs were flooded with water. While I was reading the letter, three middle-aged women dressed in black down to their ankles, with black veils covering their head and forehead, quietly entered the house through the back door. They casually tiptoed into the hall and all of a sudden began screaming: *'Muzzo bab, muzzo putt!'* My baby, my son, they wailed, their upper torso embracing the coffin. One was beating her breasts with clenched fists that by now had turned into chapattis after so many funeral breast-beatings. Their wailing echoed through the house despite the hullabaloo inside. They cried as if they had been programmed to make a statement to the living and the dead of how much this death was felt. It seemed the louder the wailing, the better the dead would hear. I ran into the hall, gently pulled them away from the coffin and asked the servants to take them inside.

A cadre of ten priests arrived, while the pallbearers assembled in the balcony. Pandemonium broke out when Monsignor Lúcio Mendonça, a much respected cousin who was going to preside at the Mass, made his appearance, followed by the Vicar, his assistant and priests from neighbouring and far off parishes. When the vicar swung a censer over and around the coffin, the smell of frankincense drowned the heavy aroma of roses, perfume and sweat. After Monsignor Mendonça blessed Paulo and closed the coffin, Mama, Tia Rosita, ayah Carmina and even my subdued and dazed father rushed to the coffin and held the brass handles.

'*Não levem meu filho*—don't take my son,' Mama ululated.

The family members cried and moaned aloud and the mourners in the house responded in a babble of tongues in Konkani, Portuguese and English. Mama, Tia Rosita, Papa and ayah Carmina would not let go of the coffin. Suddenly, Mama swayed unsteadily and then collapsed with a loud thud that was hardly audible with all the noise and commotion. A group of mourners rushed to Mama's aid and began fanning her. 'Somebody get some smelling salts,' I heard one of the priests utter aloud. I cradled her head in my lap and Maria provided some eau-de-cologne that I held to her nose. She quickly came around and some of the mourners ushered her to her room.

It was the moment of despair and hopelessness to sever the thread that binds a mother to a son… a father to a son… a loved one to a loved one; when flesh doesn't want to part from flesh, when blood wants to keep blood flowing in veins, when life refuses to reconcile with death, when those who are alive wish for the miracle of Lazarus long after it's all over.

Finally, after much effort, the pallbearers disengaged Papa, ayah Carmina's and Tia Rosita's hands and cousins and friends held them in a tight embrace. I went to the balcony waiting for the coffin to arrive.

Two water buffaloes by the roadside watched calmly, intently, as if respectfully, as the funeral passed by.

I was the lead pallbearer. Finally, I couldn't hold it in any longer. I burst into sobs and tears came streaming down my face. Beside me, Maria wiped them away as I carried the coffin for a distance of more than a hundred metres. Suddenly, fogginess appeared in front of my eyes, as I began feeling dizzy. I stumbled and nearly fell. Several mourners rushed to my aid and helped me onto the veranda of a peasant's house on the roadside, where I drank coconut water and rested for a while.

The family sat together in the church. Papa was sitting on the second pew along with Mama and Tia Rosita, who were both veiled. Ayah Carmina and I were huddled together in the first pew. The coffin was opened for the Mass. A fly buzzed above it, the buzzing sound high pitched and irritating. It was left to me to smash the fly with Tia Rosita's fan as it sat on the side of the coffin. The church was full. There wasn't even standing room. The Mass of the Dead was sung.

Monsignor Mendonça began reading the Gospel of St Mark:

'When noon came, darkness fell on the whole countryside and lasted until mid-afternoon. At that time Jesus cried in a loud voice, *"Eloi, Eloi, lama sabachthani?"* My God, my God why have you forsaken me? A few of the bystanders who heard it, remarked, "Listen! He is calling on Elijah!"'

'Yes, my dear faithful,' Monsignor Mendonça said, 'at this time, as always, we call on God, as Jesus did, as he was dying on the cross. *"Eloi, eloi, lama sabachthani?"* And God was there for him and he will be there for Paulo and his family.'

Then he tried to explain the will of God, why God had called Paulo up high. He tried his best and as to usual among the faithful—and everybody there were 'the faithful'—the explanation worked. 'It was the will of God,' he said. 'God had better things in store for Paulo.'

Before they lowered the coffin in the rundown cemetery bchind the church, it was opened one last time for the family's viewing. This time the family was composed. There were no more tears left to shed.

It was the last farewell. We kissed Paulo in turn.

Earth to Earth. Ashes to Ashes. Dust to Dust.

As the coffin was lowered in the grave, the imposing white

bearded figure of Father Loyola appeared. He walked with a cane in his left hand and a single red rose in his right. He had suddenly aged in the last few days. His frame: a bent, solitary old oak tree. He managed to straighten up his stooped image and walked right through the middle of the crowd like Charlton Heston in *Moses* about to perform a miracle. He made the Sign of the Cross, bowed his head towards the family and threw the rose bud on the coffin. I could see Uma and Winnie standing a few feet apart at the far end of the cemetery.

After the burial, Judge Vitorino Monteiro said the eulogy in Portuguese just outside the cemetery gate. He spoke about Paulo's years in the lyceum during the Portuguese days. How a promising young man of such a prominent family had gone to Coimbra, one of the oldest and most prestigious universities of Europe. How he had come down after completing his *Direito*—the law degree—to assume a prosecutor's position in Goa and how the invasion of Goa had changed it all. 'Yes,' he said, 'the ocean had taken him away, claimed him at the very prime of his life. God had called this young man of one of our noble families. It was His will.'

That evening, after I returned from the funeral, I felt empty and profoundly sad. As the night settled in, I was overtaken by a desire to sing for my dead brother and what would I sing if not the *Coimbra Fado*—that melancholy song of the city that he loved so much, whose praises he sang when happy and when sad. And so, I had quietly taken Paulo's guitar and slipped out of the house. I brought a bottle of liquor and sat on the riverbank drinking under a hazy sky and somewhat drunk, I sang the *Coimbra Fado*: '*Coimbra... tem mais encanto... na hora... da despedida.*' By saying farewell to that romantic Portuguese city, I said farewell to my unfortunate brother.

Twenty-seven

Travails of the Living

The day after the funeral and for subsequent days and months, our house had a sullen air of stillness as if time had come to a stop, as often happens after a death.

And Amanda's life was hanging by a thread.

The clock had stopped ticking; nobody had wound it for days. The garden no longer flowered. The chikku fruits and custard apples in the orchard burst open, rotting on the trees. The monkeys roamed all over the place, feasting. The begonias and the roses withered for lack of watering. The Ambassador car idled in the driveway waiting to be sold. Food had lost its taste. Life had lost its meaning. Mama and Papa shut themselves up for days, in the bedroom. Tia Rosita hardly came out of the room; overnight, she seemed shrouded in a cloak of senile dementia. She lay on her bed fingering rosary beads. 'It's the curse—it's the curse,' she would mutter. When I asked her what curse she was referring to, she kept on repeating that it was the curse, over and over. Papa declared a one-year period of mourning, which meant no weddings, no parties and no gaiety whatsoever. Besides, we all had to dress in solid black.

Slowly but surely, after much waxing and waning and many anxious days, Amanda recovered but remained mentally slow and detached. Her recovery was hailed as a miracle. It was as if her love story deserved to be enshrined as a legend. It was left to me to tell my parents that Amanda was already married to Winnie, but neither Mama nor Papa reacted. Whatever their feelings were, they kept them to themselves.

Death had ultimately shattered their ego, their family pride, their heritage and their superiority—death, that reminder of man's fleeting mortality—the ultimate decimation of sky-high temples of pride. Finally, Mama and Papa visited Amanda in the hospital; she remained disengaged with a distant look. After seeing her, Papa was overcome with grief. Soon, he began walking hours on end on the riverbank. Up and down he walked like the tide, hurriedly, hatless in the hot sun and even on moonless nights with a flashlight, as if he was on a day-night-night-day penitential trip. His face grew dark and wrinkled; he lost weight and height. The villagers got used to seeing him on the riverbank. 'Poor Afonso-*bhatcar,* the living river ghost,' they whispered.

The anger towards Winnie and Father Loyola festered in the family like an open sore. Mama certainly wouldn't reconcile with Winnie, at least not now. These things have their own dynamics, take their own bitter time. Besides, what was there to say? There were many to blame and there was much gossip.

But all was not bad. Winnie had finally been to Bombay for a second opinion. There, at the Tata Memorial Hospital, he had a surgical re-exploration. No evidence of a tumour was found. It was only a pancreatic cyst. Obviously, Winnie's cancer was all a mistake. The formalin bottle containing Winnie's lymph nodes was mislabelled. It belonged to a farmer who had cancer of the stomach and was operated at the Ribandar Hospital just after Winnie had his surgery. Obviously the peon made a grave mistake by mislabelling the lymph nodes.

Was it the incurable nature of Winnie's illness that had driven Amanda to the ocean? Or was it the waves that Winnie had said Amanda had spoken about?

I had visited Amanda in Calangute shortly after she came

out of the hospital. She remained diminished, a shadow of her old self; gone were the broad smile, the self-assured speech and the sparkle in her eyes. I had asked her what drove her into the sea. She didn't answer me. I was appalled and saddened at her detachment. She had succumbed to the combined strain of the immense pressures and her own ambiguities that resulted in a sense of despair, a hopeless solitude so elegantly expressed in her poem. She rebelled against the constraints of her society, but was unprepared psychologically to sustain the burden of individuality in her rapidly changing milieu. However, over time and with physiotherapy in Bombay, she recovered.

Amanda and Winnie would ultimately immigrate to Brazil and, before they left, the family reconciled. It was a lukewarm reconciliation, like a bad marriage interview where the prospective bride looks one way and the bridegroom the other. I sporadically corresponded with Amanda and recently, during a lecture trip, I visited them in São Paulo. I was happy to see that they had made a life for themselves with their two children about to graduate from college.

Almost three months after the death of Paulo, I received the results of the American examination: I passed with a high score of eighty-eight. Mama and Papa, together with Tia Rosita and the servants, were utterly disappointed with my decision to leave for America.

'Don't go, Baba,' the servants begged of me. 'What will Mama and Papa do without you? Don't break their already broken hearts,' they said.

Papa appealed to me one last time. 'You are now my one and only remaining son—please, don't go.' Papa's and ayah Carmina's pleas filled me with guilt, but what could I do? I had already accepted an internship position in New York and mailed the signed contract. I requested postponement of my departure for at least a year, but the hospital administrator refused my request. Perhaps, it was the war in Vietnam—there was a shortage of American doctors. I tried to explain to Papa that I would come back after specialisation, but couldn't get through to him. Mama and even Maria, when she came on a visit, supported Papa's views. Maria kept on asking me when I would return to Goa. I told her that I wasn't sure, but if all went well as planned, I would certainly consider returning for good in about five years after specialisation if the opportunities were right. My uncommitted answer unsettled Maria. She wasn't interested in leaving Goa for good and settling in America. And, as if to make a somewhat similar point that my father had made, she said: 'I am the one and only daughter of my Mama and Papa!'

'Besides, Miss Goa, isn't your mission to serve the destitute and the poor?' I said. She thought I was making a joke of it all. She stiffened and walked out. It was the wrong thing to say. I immediately apologised, but she seemingly refused to accept my apology. Subsequently, our relationship soured. It was as if the state of intimacy we had briefly achieved just before we discovered Paulo's and Amanda's body now mysteriously separated and estranged us. Paulo's death and Amanda's condition, had deeply affected all of us, including Maria. We just couldn't bring ourselves to talk about it. We left each other alone, to lick our own wounds.

Was it over between Maria and me? Had death changed us all? Hollowed our bones to the marrow within? For death, when it strikes unexpectedly at a young age, leaves its keloid scars on those who remain: changing, reforming and distorting the landscape of the psyche like a passing hurricane.

To me everything appeared stale, old, oppressive. I badly desired a change of scenery.

My friends gave me a subdued farewell at my cousin's in Panjim. Maria was there in a black skirt and a white blouse, sitting in a corner of the hall, somewhat detached. She had no makeup on. Often, her eyes shifted towards me, as if she was waiting for me to approach her. I had gone to her and held her hand. Her palm was cold and wet; the eyes, those beautiful almond-shaped black eyes were swollen like large black-eyed peas floating in water. Her style of dress had said it all—she was also mourning for my brother. I told her that I cared for her, that I loved her and that I would write to her. She shook her head as if to say, *que sera, sera.*

As custom dictated, my friends sang the Mando of farewell. El Rei accompanied on the guitar and Maria sang countermelody.

'Adeus korcho vellu, paulo. Ai mhojem kalliz re fapsota. Despediru korchea vellar, ho sonvsar naka-so disota....' (When it's time to say good-bye, O' my heart flutters painfully. At the time of farewell, this world turns to dust...)

On the day of my departure, pain and anguish showed on my father's face as we embraced each other and said good-bye. I carried that image like a parting souvenir. In the taxi, I was overwhelmed with guilt and wondered whether we would see each other again. At that very moment it occurred to me that I hardly knew my father, regretting never having a man-to-man talk with him, never knowing what his goals were, his aspirations for himself and whether he felt fulfilled. He was always distant, withdrawn, crowded by my mother. My explanations of my own needs, my dreams, my inner need to explore scientific curiosity, of why I was going to America, did not satisfy him. It was as if he refused to listen; he felt betrayed. After all, I was his favourite son and Paulo, my mother's. However, the distance between father and son was never breached. But that was the norm of the times, ingrained in the culture.

As the taxi left the driveway, the house receded like a ship that pulls from the port and slowly vanishes into the horizon. I was the ship. The house would remain like an overbearing ageing mango tree, a decaying monument to colonial history.

At that moment in time, a cycle of life was coming to an end, the end of the Goa that I had known, steeped in age-old Indo-Portuguese traditions. And, above all, an end to the Albuquerque family, my family; but somehow, I felt it would go on without me, at least for the time being.

As the plane lifted to soar into the tropical sky, the sun inflamed my window with a dash of gold. Below, a ship sailed serenely. Beyond, far away in the distance was a sparkling horizon, a paradisiacal sky: the beginnings of tomorrow.

Twenty-eight

The Shadows of the Past

When in New York, Maria and I corresponded with each other. I had strong feelings for her; however, I was not yet ready to make a commitment at this early stage of my career. Almost a year later, I received a letter with subtle hints of loneliness, news of many marriage proposals and now, her willingness to move to America.

The long-distance pressure on me to marry also continued to build; and finally, after a relentless barrage of subtle letters from Mama and Tia Rosita pointing out the advantages of marrying a Goan, like Maria and Maria's last letter, I faced my marital prospects head on. Unlike in my professional life, there was indecisiveness in my personal choices. Why the hesitation, I asked myself. After all, I had pursued Maria relentlessly when Paulo was alive. I needed to think with my heart and less so with my brain.

Maria's arrival in New York after a little more than a year was anticipated with excitement and a sense of relief; I believed that I was headed in the right direction. Her silver-embroidered green sari-draped self was captivating as she walked down the exit ramp at Kennedy Airport, despite being tired and worn out from the Goa-Bombay-Delhi-Dubai-London-New York flight. This was still the Maria I was in love with. Within three weeks of her arrival, we were happily wedded in both a matchmaking sense and an in-love sense, the best of all combinations. The wedding was a small church affair, with a small reception in a Portuguese restaurant in Newark, New Jersey, not at all like the sumptuous weddings in Goa, with hundreds of guests. I could sense Maria's disappointment. 'We should have married in Goa,' she said. I agreed.

In the beginning, all went well, easily and effortlessly: the short honeymoon in the Algarve in Portugal, the furnishing of the apartment, the visits to Macy's, the selection of drapes and couches and the queen-size bed.

Maria, armed with complex Goan recipes, sang along as she tried to cook, but to her dismay, her dishes lacked the texture and taste of home. We often ended up ordering Chinese; there were no Indian restaurants in Queens in those days. But it was the cold and the dull of the winter that unnerved her the most. When Christmas arrived, the trips to Rockefeller Center, Radio City Music Hall, walks on Fifth Avenue were exciting but highlighted the absence of family and friends. My intense work schedule as a resident in medicine in a New York City hospital—with every-other-day and every-other-weekend on call, when I had to spend the entire day and night in the hospital—unsettled Maria.

One day when I arrived home late, after a gruelling weekend shift, she said to me: 'I can't take it anymore. I'm left at home alone in this dull apartment with no friends, not knowing how to drive, with nothing to do but watch TV for endless hours.'

'Why don't you take driving lessons?' I said.

'And go where?'

Soon thereafter, she suggested going back to Goa for a month and ended up staying the entire winter. I went to Goa to bring her back, assuring her that things would get better after I finish my residency training.

However, following residency training and during my fellowship in infectious diseases, I became totally immersed in medical research, writing and re-writing grants to the National Institutes of Health while Maria felt ignored—a rani stripped of her flowing silks, her many servants in-waiting and her friendly domain. I encouraged her to go back to school, but she showed no interest for reasons that were not entirely clear to me. She showed no enthusiasm for my doctoring or the progress of my medical research either. She had hardly anything to tell me about her uneventful day. We made a few new friends: a Brazilian couple and a few Indian doctors, all bachelors, with whom we went out occasionally for a movie or a dinner on weekends when I was free and not on call.

A new disease, an epidemic: AIDS, was raging and destroying New York City, felling young men in its killing path and absorbing me totally. Maria couldn't entirely fathom my clinical commitments and my passion for unravelling the workings of the AIDS virus. Why bother with all those grants and the recurring deadlines? Why not simply exercise the joy and power in the laying of hands and the dispensing of drugs like my father did?'

'I'm no GP like your father,' I said. 'I'm a clinician-scientist.'

'Then why not specialise in gastroenterology or cardiology, the prime-meat specialties USA-bound Indians preferred?' she kept on insisting like a broken record.

She never took to the New World, always complaining about the dull gray of our one-bedroom apartment building in Queens, the cold winter, the lack of servants, family and friends. She devoured chocolates and put on weight. She became melancholy, sloppy, plump and pale. Her beauty that once overwhelmed me began to fade.

When we made love, she was distant, her eyes looking at the window as if towards the far away enigmatic Arabian Sea, at a drifting boat without oars. Her insouciance, the impenetrability, the change in her personality was unsettling. Was this a sign of depression? I wondered. Thinking about it, a cousin had warned me that depression ran in a distant cousin on her mother's side of the family. But I couldn't convince myself of the latter possibility and summarily cast the thought away. Once, during one of our arguments, she told me that she found me stiff, egotistical, utterly lacking the flamboyance, playfulness and romanticism that was so much the persona of Paulo. Bringing Paulo up in this way opened up old wounds. Since that day, the memory seemed always there: his facial outline in the fogged mirror in the bathroom; a transparent partition in our queen-size bed.

The shadows of the past seemed to accompany us now, playing a destructive role in our lives, as if demanding a share of immortality. The past was not yet over, as if what was dead was still alive. We were young then, never realising that thoughts, deeds, memories—all possess an unrelenting power. Perhaps time, that healer of healers, the eraser of memories, would play its role. Later, the thought of separation, of divorce, had transiently crossed my mind like a sudden unsettling chill breeze, but the meaning of these words, so alien to my Goan family values, were summarily spaded. So I accepted all this and immersed myself more vigorously in my productive scientific life.

A few years later, after my father was found dead on the riverbank, presumably of a heart attack and Mama succumbed to a massive stroke six years later, Maria hoped that I would finally agree to return to Goa, to the opulence of my house in the village and her Panjim city mansion. She hoped I would return as a hotshot MD and take over her aging father's practice. My professorial appointment and chairmanship in a prestigious New York teaching hospital shattered all her hopes. Besides, AIDS research in Goa, and for that matter India, was not advanced enough to accommodate my high-tech laboratory work. A part-time job as a real estate agent kept Maria busy and her attitude gradually improved. However, three sequential miscarriages complicated matters further.

'*Má sorte*—bad luck,' she uttered and blamed her miscarriages on city pollution and the cold winters. Finally, after fertility pills and her mother's novenas, two of my many million sperms wiggled up her slippery slopes to set two of her eggs on fire. She became pregnant.

A son was finally born. The other was stillborn.

After the long-awaited son arrived, the little Goan Maharaja born in America and despite Maria's mother's presence during and following the difficult twin pregnancy, she went into depression and remained depressed for some time. I offered to take her to a psychiatrist but she refused. 'Do you think I am mad?' she snapped. Her mother suggested taking her back to India for a holiday, so baby and wife and mother-in-law bundled up and boarded the wings of *Asoka* to Bombay, then to Goa and perpetual summer. But instead of three months, mother and son stayed for almost a year. Subsequently, holiday trips to Goa were therapeutic like Prozac, resulting in remission of her intermittent phases of depression.

After we bought a house and moved to Westchester, our relationship improved considerably, but when I made love to her, she remained distant. Perhaps lovemaking was an impersonal choice for her, a duty so to speak. Indeed, it seemed we circled around our problems, found different solutions, incongruous coping mechanisms and disembarked at opposite ports of call. While I was laser-focused in the pursuit of science, Maria had very little until our son was born. She doted on him as on a prince. She gained a new lease on life. The baby and gardening changed her disposition for the better; she seemed happy and her mood had a positive effect on our loving. We went on living our lives, occupying the same space, somewhat compartmentalised, accepting each other's ways. And yes, there was a distance between us, a wall that refused to fall. Will this wall crumble now, pulverise into silt and sand? Is it too much to ask of life?

I suddenly feel an urgency to make up for the time we lost.

Twenty-nine

Afterwards

I now get up from the rocking chair in the oratory of my old home, ready to leave. Ayah Carmina places her hand on my shoulder for support, as she attempts to get up from the stool she is sitting on. Her legs barely hold her up without the assistance of a cane.

'Baba,' she says, hesitatingly, sitting back on the stool, 'they both came and wished me good-bye before they left and thanked me for all I had done. It was the waves—Amanda was always attracted to the waves, even as a child.' After a long silence, her eyes half-closed, she continues: 'My poor Paulo—he was devastated with the revelation of his origins. I felt a sense of doom as if something tragic was going to happen to him. I held on to him. He managed to pull himself away and left through the back door. I fell on my knees and prayed.'

'I let him down, Carmina,' I say. 'He had told me about the nightmares, the reason for the drinking and drugs. Perhaps he was asking for help... I never offered any. I didn't know how.'

'It's not your fault. It was the appearance of the captain, the revelation of his origins that finished him. And St Francis Xavier saved Amanda. It was meant to be.'

'And my father—did he know or suspect?' I finally muster the courage to ask.

'No, your Papa did not know. But after Paulo's death, your Mama riddled with guilt and remorse and on the advice of Father

Vicar, had finally told him all. Your Papa apparently listened without a word. He hardly spoke again. It was then that he started walking on the riverbank. It killed him gradually. Don't blame yourself for any of this.'

I'm overwhelmed by a desire to turn back the clock. I wonder what would have happened if on that day in Coimbra, Paulo had reported the incident to the police authorities rather than fleeing from the scene; if Mama had given Paulo the letters from Ana Sofia and had accepted Winnie after Father Loyola had pleaded with her; if the peon hadn't made a mistake in mislabelling Winnie's lymph nodes. These events and decisions and many others were so wrong and shouldn't have happened; at the end, they prevailed and took centre stage. Perhaps it is fate and yet, it's awfully disconcerting that a moment's decision, a wrong turn, a lost opportunity, an unexpected encounter, these incongruous juxtapositions of life can have outcomes of cataclysmic proportions and effect entire lifetimes.

I now go towards Carmina as her face fluidly waxes and wanes from the falling and shifting of the lamp lit at the altar. I pull her from the stool she was sitting on, embracing her aged withering penumbra of a frame.

After I leave the house, the taxi takes me to Maria's home in Panjim. On the way, I think of what Carmina told me: about the white man, Paulo's discovery of his origins just before the end, why mother always protected and favoured Paulo. And now, twenty-one years later, it all comes together.

Gradually, a sense of peace comes over me as the taxi speeds through the tarred road intersecting paddy fields and streams, approaching the city of Panjim. It is as if a great weight is suddenly lifted. Buoyant, my spirit floats like a balloon. Like an eagle, it soars over coconut groves and paddy field.

I run up the stairs of the yellow mansion on the Rua de Ourem, to find Maria, her parents and my son at lunch.

'Where have you been, Roberto? I thought you'd be back in two hours and it's almost four o'clock.' Maria says.

'Dad... Dad, I had a fun time at the beach. The water is warm, nothing like the beaches in New York,' says my son.

'I visited Carmina. I'm sorry I kept you waiting.'

'But I thought...'

'We waited and waited and finally decided to serve lunch,' says my mother-in-law, apologetically. 'You must be tired. Please, sit down and at least try some rice with your favourite fish curry, fried mackerel and beans.'

'Would you like a beer or a whisky-soda?' Father-in-law asks.

'A beer will do.' And then addressing Maria, I say: 'We have to leave, there's a taxi waiting.'

'Where to?'

'I'll tell you later.'

After a quick lunch, we leave for Baga beach. We climb the hill and there, behind the Retreat House, sit on the rock atop the ocean well. I tell Maria everything that Carmina told me. We think of Paulo sitting on the rock, lost, high on dope; of Paulo letting go, flying, gliding in the air like the divers we once saw in Acapulco. What must it have been like to be devoured by the well, spinning in its white foam into its inner depth like in the cavernous bowel of a serpent? And who had he seen there, stretching a hand he could not reach? Uma, Ana Sofia, the son he had never known?

'Or perhaps there was nobody there. How frightful, my God.' Maria says. 'Was there fear at the very last moment?'

A seagull glides into the water and settles on a wave. The sun, a giant persimmon reddens Maria's hair. The wind catches it, blows it across her face and blinds her for an instant. I pick up a flat pebble and throw it into the ocean.

'Did you love him?' I ask. She doesn't answer.

'He was a ladies' man all the way.'

'Yes,' Maria says, as the wind carries the word away like a sigh.

We walk all the way back to Calangute and sit near the spot where we had seen the bodies of Paulo and Amanda on that night. We had never talked about that day for twenty-one years, we never knew why.

Kept it all in. Locked up.

Perhaps it was our Goanness or Indianness, or both. Or perhaps it was a big, deep denial. The seed hibernated within, encapsulated, but now the capsule cracks open and blood gushes in. Will it sprout? Can we let the past pour in, drink it like a bottle of old vintage wine and when the bottle is empty throw it into the ocean, to float on the waves, to be carried to some distant shore or sink to the bottom, crusting for eternity? As these thoughts cross my mind, Maria opens up, perhaps overtaken by the moment. She tells me that before Paulo's death, she was at times confused, unsure whether she loved me. On that night in Calangute as we danced, all that changed. 'You had looked at the moon and said that I, like the rose in *Spanish Harlem*, bloomed in the moonlight,' she says. 'You had shown your romantic self, a self that I thought you never possessed. And then, when I saw his dead body, everything changed. You changed. The Roberto I had experienced for that fleeting moment, I would never savour again.'

'Yes, we all changed,' I say.

As I get up and walk towards the water, sand blows at my face, into my eyes, blinding me for an instant. I wipe my tearing eyes and place my hand in hers. We stand there watching the sunset:

the giant sun, now half a burning ball, as if inflamed, floats on the horizon, oozing blood.

Turning towards me, she says: 'In New York, when I was left alone in the apartment, strange thoughts raced through my mind. I hated that apartment... the grayness in there was morbid. I blamed you for draining away the sunshine, for dulling my life. Did I really love you? I kept on wondering. Had Paulo's death killed something inside of me? I felt his death was a bad omen. His image on the beach haunted me. I saw him in my dreams. I didn't have the courage to tell you. Granted, all this was a delayed reaction and perhaps none of this is your fault. When one is lonely inside, the mind takes on winding, twisting turns.'

I had no desire to challenge her. I was exhausted. The events of the day had drained me emotionally; besides, perhaps she was right.

'I thought I would go on,' she continues. 'I would learn to love. Like so many Indian women do: learn to love. And one day there would be children and all the memories, the resentment over your indifference towards me after Paulo's death, the constant coaxing of my father and mother to get married to you before you find an American, like my cousin did, all that would be forgotten. Somehow it never was. And the miscarriages, the battery of tests did not help either.'

'Did you have doubts about marriage?'

'Yes, I did and the pressure from my parents...'

'Why didn't you tell me?'

'What good would it have done?'

'I'm sorry, Maria, you had to go through all this.'

'I was depressed, Roberto and you... you were too busy with your career and your research. I'm a very sensitive woman—I think you know that. Worse still, I keep it all in,' she says, choking.

'But I offered to take you to a psychiatrist.' She doesn't respond. She looks away.

'It wasn't like that, Maria,' I say, placing my arm around her.

'Anyway, if that is how you felt, I'm so sorry.' After a long silence, perhaps sensing the pain and anguish as I cover my sobbing face with the palm of my hands, or perhaps recognising the stark cruelty in her words, or her own guilt, she says: 'I want you to know that it's not all your fault.'

I hold her in my arms. She embraces me and sobs uncontrollably. We weep together.

I'm overcome with guilt for my presumed insensitivity. I now realise that death seems to have followed me for most of my life, not only in my family, but in so many of my young patients with AIDS, who died in the prime of their lives. This idea of death is impossible even for a doctor to live with, to hold in one's heart like precious possessions, the faces, the lives of young people, of what was, what might have been, until the idea becomes as common as a breath of air or like day and night—a certain repetitiveness. Over time, immunity sets in, an emotional barrier takes shape and a self-created shelf develops, hard and rigid to retract within. While absorbed in these thoughts, a blonde little child with a pail of sand in her hand tugs at my pants. 'Christina, Christina, come here,' her English mother calls out.

On the ride back to Panjim, we promise each other, make a vow to each other, to be open, to discuss our inner feelings, our strengths and weaknesses, without guilt and fear of hurting each other in the process. Perhaps it is time to shed that element of our Goanness. Or perhaps it's too late.

During these past few days, Maria and I had time to reflect on our relationship, to talk about it and to make amends. We also had the opportunity to scout some of the towns and villages of Goa. We were struck and saddened at the decay of my home and other old homes that once reverberated with life. Some stood as empty monuments; others had crumbled into the rubble; and a few palatial ones would soon be opened for tourists. The consolation was that they were still there, though for how long, we would never know, or who would buy them and someday convert them into residential or commercial sprawls.

A few days later we go back to the village, to the house. As the Ambassador taxi makes its way towards the gate, I remember that day when Paulo returned from Portugal. Ayah Carmina was waiting with some peasants from the dismantled estate. She was the embodiment of all the dead ones, like an old urn with ashes of the past, but still fresh, still warm.

My son, in jeans, a red T-shirt and a Yankee hat, feels awkward as the octogenarian Carmina puts her arms around him and the peasants try to touch and embrace him.

'Our baby,' they say.

'Bai, Bai—you have lost weight. You don't eat?' one of the peasants asks, touching Maria's feet. Maria, in a white T-shirt and a blue skirt, smiles, ignoring the remark.

Carmina had been informed in advance that we were coming for a visit and she had taken care that the place was thoroughly cleaned. Yes, Carmina would always be Carmina. She had hired local peasants and what a job they had done. The iron gate was left wide open. The stone lions were restored to their pedestal. The surrounding wall was scraped of weed, the peppercorn vines were trimmed and the bougainvillea were about to flower again. The lights of the Petromaxes illuminate the house, while the weak electric bulbs flicker as the electricity surges and dies as often happens in the village night. Maria is reluctant to spend the night in the house, but António, our son, taken up with the place, insists and we decide to stay. It was as if the house was a memorial of what had been, what had been lost and what, despite everything, survived. I now wonder whether I should rebuild and someday return for good—it would certainly please Maria and Carmina.

As we sit for a dinner of steaming rice and coconut milk

chicken curry, prawn balchão, mango and lime pickle, Carmina approaches with a walking stick and touching my shoulder, she asks: 'Why did you wait for so many years? Why did you abandon the house? I managed to preserve it, fixing the roof after the heavy monsoons, but the monkeys play havoc with the tiles and the termites are destroying the wood.' Shaking her head to and fro, she says, 'I am old now and tired.' As if implying that she cannot go on any longer.

My face contorts in pain. My eyes swell with tears. I motion to Carmina to sit down. António pulls up a chair for her. I take a big swallow of the caju liquor. Yes, I think: we abandon our families, our inheritance and the world we were born in—to live in another world. We cherish our privacy and our independence; we struggle to achieve and to accomplish; at other times we live in anguish in a foreign land not knowing where we belong. And there are times, moments of darkness and chaos when life ebbs and flutters, sometimes to survive, at other times to die. Yet, a moment here, a moment there, life bursts open like a flower that blooms, like rain that showers with everything we have ever wanted or imagined. Is it that moment now?

At that instant, a loud thud and the rattling of the roof tiles and bombastic '*wooh-wooh-wooh-wooh*' startles António and Maria. Before I have a chance to say that they are only harmless monkeys, António runs out of the house. And there they are in the moonlight, perched on the mango tree, their long tails dangling like silver ropes among the leaves.

'Dad, Dad, Mom, I saw monkeys!' He runs back into the dining room. 'Dad, Dad, I love this place, please, Dad, let's stay here.'

That night, Maria, in a pink nightgown from Bloomingdale's, lying on the bed in the dark, turns towards me, while I stare at the canopy of the bed. Touching my face lightly with the palm of her hand, she whispers: 'Roberto, I love you... I love you very much.'

A crescent moon peers through the window and I can see her face—somewhat aged, yet radiant. Her beautiful lips are full and pale pink. I touch her face, letting my finger roam over the outline of her nose, the almond shape of her eyes, the receded forehead, the heart-shape lips. She puts her arms around me and draws me towards her. We lie there amid the quietness and emptiness of the still village night. She tells me that she is overcome by a feeling of belonging; a feeling that comes with age, that life went on no matter what—that we both survived.

She pulls me towards her, holding my unshaven face in her hands, looking deeply in my eyes. Does she see a boat with oars, in a lake, drifting towards her, slowly, then rapidly with a powerful stroke?

I look into her eyes and in them I see the reflection of her, of me, dancing at the Tourist Hotel in Calangute, twenty-one years ago. We lie side by side. Silver canoes moored in a lake under a moonlit sky. 'Pink rose, my rose,' I whisper.

Acknowledgements

I would like to express my gratitude to the team at Amaryllis: my publisher, Vikas Rakheja, my editors Rashmi Menon and Manoj Kulkarni for their unbounding enthusiasm and support for the book; to Pinaki De for the fabulous cover; to my agent Kanishka Gupta for his optimism and verve; to Ms Margaret Mikhno, my most exacting critique; to Tanya Mendonsa for her excellent suggestions, editing, and her faith in this book; to Pankaj Mishra for believing in the work and for his initial support; to Victor Rangel Ribeiro, Grace Schulman and Dr JD Ghosh for their consistent encouragement for my literary endeavours; to the late João da Veiga Coutinho, whose un-bounding enthusiasm after reading the first two chapters drove me to complete the book; to Dr Paul Melo e Castro of Leeds University for his recommendations; to the Two Bridges Writers Workshop, and in particular to Miriam Polli for her creative input; to Frederick Noronha, publisher of Goa 1556, and to my daughter, Tanya Raquel Romero for being there.